A

CUP

OF

LIGHT

Nicole Mones

DELTA TRADE
PAPERBACKS

WITHDRAWN

WITHDRAWN

MASON PUBLIC LIBRARY
HUDSON, COLORADO

D0449984

A CUP OF LIGHT
A Delta Book

PUBLISHING HISTORY
Delacorte Press hardcover edition published April 2002
Delta trade paperback edition / May 2003

Published by
Bantam Dell
A Division of Random House, Inc.
New York, New York

This novel is a work of fiction. Names, characters, places, and
incidents either are the product of the author's imagination or
are used fictitiously. Any resemblance to actual persons,
living or dead, events, or locales is entirely coincidental.

Photo of porcelain cup courtesy of The Metropolitan Museum
of Art, Purchase, Mrs. Richard E. Linburn Gift, 1987. (1987.85)
Photograph by Sheldan Collins. Photograph © 1988
The Metropolitan Museum of Art

All rights reserved.
Copyright © 2002 by Nicole Mones
Cover art by Katie Mitchell

Book design by Lynn Newmark

Library of Congress Catalog Card Number: 2001053782
No part of this book may be reproduced or transmitted in any
form or by any means, electronic or mechanical, including photo-
copying, recording, or by any information storage and retrieval
system, without the written permission of the publisher,
except where permitted by law.

Delta is a registered trademark of Random House, Inc., and the
colophon is a trademark of Random House, Inc.

ISBN 0-385-31945-2

Manufactured in the United States of America
Published simultaneously in Canada

BVG   10   9   8   7   6   5   4   3   2   1

A
CUP
OF
LIGHT

1

FROM HIS BLACK-WINDOWED SEDAN ROAR-
ing to the airport, Gao Yideng looked out on
Beijing. Steel-and-glass skyscrapers, banks, hotels,
international corporations and consulting groups
flashed by. Ads and billboards blinked against
the sky. The future was here. That which was
irrecoverable—the past—had come to seem more
desired, more priceless than ever. And Gao had a
piece of it to sell.

The right buyer would give almost anything
to possess it. The trick was making it happen.

He watched the Jichang Expressway, hands
tight in concentration. Now one of the foreign
porcelain experts had fallen ill on the plane and
the other, the woman, was arriving alone. Perhaps she'd be more malleable by herself than the
two of them would have been together. Not that

Gao would lie to her. But there were many facets of this situation, those that were exposed, those kept from view. The bottom line was the art, and thank the gods, *that* was straight from heaven. It was extraordinary and spoke for itself.

He winced away from the part of his insides that grieved him. It was a dull knife scraping, the same place, familiar, like a well-worn knob of bone. He didn't have enough. He never would. Not the blocks of real estate in Shanghai and Beijing; not the shares of computer companies. Every day of his life was a maw that needed more. He laid his hand across his stomach. And he'd had the dream once more last night.

In the dream he was always back in the famine—1961. He was in the place he grew up, a Yangtze town, in a maze of alleys, with trailing trees and decrepit stone buildings.

And he was with Peng, his best boyhood friend. Out of everyone in his life, all those whom he'd known, Peng was the one person for whom he would have died. What he had with Peng was deeper than friendship. Not love, but something like it.

Peng and Yideng had foraged for food together. Most of their days and nights were devoted to scavenging whatever scraps they could. They were a team. What they found they split scrupulously. Their trust in each other was supreme.

On this day they went along the stone wall that ran behind the slop stream, staying close in, light and fast-moving. There were people back here who still managed to keep a few animals. There was a man named Chu up this way who still had a starving, ornery pig. What every child in the District dreamed of was that on the day old Chu decided to kill that pig, they'd be close enough to get so much as a hair, or a drop of blood, or a whiff of the life-giving skin.

But it was only sometimes, on some days, that this raging pig was fed. And it was fed that day. Destiny smiled on them. As they came close to the rear of the Chu property, the door clattered open. The lugging breaths of old Chu could be heard over the wonderful sound, heaven itself, the wet, nutritious slosh of his bucket.

"I'll go," whispered Peng, and before Yideng could say a word his quicker, smaller friend was gone over the wall.

The pig whuffed and turned around.

"Old bonehead!" Chu called. "Over here!" and he swung the bucket, pulled it back—even Yideng, perched on a ledge now, looking over the wall, could hear the bumpy promise in that soup as it rearranged itself in the bucket—back, further, and then Chu flung it forward and water, offal, bits of food flew in a divine arc across the tiny yard. Peng swung at the same moment, diving out from behind the gardenias and catching, in midair, part of a stale steamed bun. The pig turned on him in a fury, snorting. It stood its ground for only a second before commencing its charge, but that was enough for Peng to gain the foot of the wall. As he scooted up, pulling on vines with one hand and cradling the precious bun in the other, the pig hurled itself the last few feet to the wall and smashed its teeth against the fitted stone, with Peng's bare foot then, just that second, out of reach.

Oh, it had been excellently done. They had run, the two of them, full of youth. They climbed down behind Dongping Lu to a culvert beneath the footbridge. This was a special place of theirs. There was a not-too-fetid stream, trickling through the pipe. No one could see them.

Down below the street, their backs curved to the concrete culvert, they divided the bun in half. No surgery ever received greater attention. Fair was fair between them.

And that moment, at the end of the dream, when Peng handed

him his wet, old piece of bun, an offering as luminous as a handful of diamonds, Gao Yideng felt as close as he ever would again to another person.

Thirty million people died of hunger in the famine. But he and Peng lived.

And now he was in this sleek, faintly humming car, alone, always alone. Yes, he was married and his days and nights were filled with people, but that didn't change anything. He and Peng had long since lost touch. Now all he had was what he acquired, the world he built by adding.

The pain eased a little. He was about to add more, much more, by selling this porcelain. He'd have cash, liquid, against uncertainties. Somehow he felt if this succeeded, he'd never have the dream again.

Strange. Survival, in the famine, had hinged on a ragtag assortment of gifts from heaven like scraps of discarded wheat bun. Now it was the myriad opportunities and fallback plans he conceived and concealed where he needed them. Like this one.

They pulled into the airport. The driver crunched to a halt at a special gate, showed a card to the sentry, and turned down a small side road to a private rear entry.

They stopped behind the terminal. He leapt out, handmade shoes spattering in the puddles left from the afternoon's rain, opened the door into the glaring corridor. He strode between the concrete walls to Systems Management. He checked his watch; she'd be deplaning. *"Ni hao,"* he greeted the computer operator. "If I may trouble you, I need someone flagged."

"Of course," the man said, recognizing him. "Nationality?"

"American."

"Name?"

"Lia Frank."

The clerk tapped a few keys.

"Canada Airlines."

"Eh." The clerk frowned. "That flight's landed. The passenger is not to Customs yet. I'll put it through right now."

"Thank you." Gao Yideng turned and was out the door before the man looked up.

THE PLANE HOWLED down in Beijing with a scream of engines and a clattering roar of overhead bins. It was dark outside, nothing but scattered lights and runways. Five hours had gone by since she'd left David Hong at a Tokyo hospital, safe in the care of their local staff. He'd needed an emergency appendectomy. It was routine as such things went. She was sure he'd be all right.

But now he would not be here with her. And she was taxiing directly toward what looked, from the photos, like some of the finest pots she might ever see in her career.

People like her always went out in pairs. Dr. Zheng would certainly have someone over here in a few days. Still . . . here she was, alone.

Had she remembered everything? With a transient tremor her feet squeezed each side of her brown leather tool case, pushed under the seat in front of her. Lia couldn't work without her objects. She needed her loupe to dial up the texture of a glaze, the heap-and-pile of a cobalt border, the wear marks too faint for the naked eye. The camera was critical with its Micro-Nikkor lens and tripod, and the silver umbrella to absorb the camera's flash. Hard measuring tape, calipers, cloths, contact-lens solution . . . the snuff-bottle light, with its long flexible wire, that let her see deep down inside the longest and narrowest ceramic neck. She sensed the shapes with her ankles, through the thin fabric of her socks; there was one, there another. She wished she could take them out and hold them. Not now. The plane was landing.

If the pictures she had seen in New York told the truth, there were twenty amazing pots waiting for her here. They were imperial pieces from the Ming and Qing. She remembered the blinding, almost physical impact of first seeing the images in New York.

"Are they good?" Dr. Zheng asked her with a grin in his voice.

"Completely *hoi moon*." This was one of the few phrases that people like her always, reflexively, uttered in Cantonese even when speaking Mandarin or English. Maybe it was because the term was Hong Kong porcelain slang; or maybe because the Cantonese just had more sing and sinew. *Hoi moon geen san.* Let the door open on a view of mountains. See beauty. See authenticity. She'd flipped through the photos. One never found twenty imperial pots together. It was rare to find even two. "We have a buyer for this?" she asked, feeling as if every cell in her body were singing.

"We have," he said.

Big spender, she thought, instantly placing the value of these works—assuming, of course, they were authentic—at fifteen, twenty million dollars. "One person?"

"One person."

"Where's the collection?"

"Beijing."

"Beijing!" This stopped her. Fine porcelains almost never came up for sale from the Mainland. No porcelain manufactured before the twentieth year of the Qianlong reign, 1756, and no porcelain of any era from the imperial kilns could leave China. Something like this would have to be arranged or at least sanctioned by the government. Then they issued a special permit. "Is there a visa?"

"Yes. Though I only have the faxed copy." He pulled a page from another file.

She leaned over it. All the chops looked correct, the Ministry of Culture letterhead familiar and imposing.

"Who approached us?"

"A wealthy developer. Gao Yideng. You know the name?"

"No."

"He hasn't been a . . . presence. He might be an intermediary. If it's being sold by a major museum, or the government—well, I'm sure if I were in their position I wouldn't want it known either. How soon can you leave?"

"Tomorrow?"

"All right." His eyes smiled under their hood of brown-splotched skin; his refined hands tapped the desk. He leaned toward her, deepening the hollow drape of his Italian suit. "David?" he said. "Shouldn't David be the one to go?"

"Yes. He's perfect." She liked teaming with David Hong. He was instinctive; she was the mental librarian type. They meshed well. That wasn't going to happen now, though. The plane bounced a few times on the tarmac and hit the runway's wind tunnel. The brakes screamed. It was nine-thirty at night here. Between the flights, the ambulance, and the Tokyo hospital, she'd had it. What she wanted more than anything was to sleep.

But the bright lights crackled on and she moved to the aisle, carry-ons cutting into her shoulder. She could feel the Chinese man behind her looking at her hearing aids, always visible because she wore her hair pulled up. She ignored him. She was used to people's looks.

As soon as she stepped into the open rotunda she punched in Zheng's number. It was morning back in New York, but he'd be up.

"Hello?" he said. "Lia?"

"It's me. How's he doing?"

"Fine. I talked to him in the recovery room." Zheng had spent most of the night on the phone. Now the morning light had turned the dreamlike shadows on his desk into true and luminous objects: a table screen of carved nephrite, a brush washer with a pale celadon glaze. "I think he's sleeping now," he said.

"Good. Well. I won't call him."

"No. Don't. We'll take care of him. He'll be in the hospital for some days, and then it's a five- or six-week recovery. He's not going to be able to help you at all."

"I figured. So who are you going to send?"

He gave a long, thinking pause and then said, "As soon as I send anyone, more people will know."

The implication multiplied inside her with an uneasy mix of feelings. Not send someone? Yet he was right, of course. If word got out, the competition would be all over their seller in an instant.

Because everyone would want pieces like these. This was true even though China was still the poor stepchild in the art world. Western masterworks fetched vastly higher sums than did Eastern ones. A very rare imperial porcelain, like a fine scroll painting or an important religious statue, might be worth three or four million U.S. dollars, while a work by a Western master might fetch ten times as much. But that was what made Chinese art attractive to investors. It was a good buy. And these were treasures, and the true treasures of any tradition were very, very hard to find.

"First look at the pots," Zheng said. "Then we'll talk."

"I'm just the memory person," she joked, but meaning it, wanting to make sure he remembered the kernel of truth in it. She was a data fiend, not a spotter. She wasn't the one with the sure eye who always knew at a glance whether something was real or not. She was the one who backed things up, who could document, reference, and prove.

Doing this job alone was hardly even thinkable. Not that she'd be the first. For a crumb of comfort she looked back through history. Several hundred years ago there was a Hanlin scholar named Zhu, who was sent off alone on a porcelain mission. He had been ordered south by the emperor to oversee the royal kilns at Jingdezhen. He'd written:

Smoke rises day and night.
Who knows about me, alone in the Bingli Pavilion of the Zhao-tiange?

Lia read this in a 1742 *Fouliang Xianzhi,* or *Gazetteer of Fouliang District.* There was a wealth of interesting information in gazetteers. For a moment, she felt okay. She was part of, or at least near to, a tradition. "All right," she said. "I'll look at them."

"Very good, Luo Na," said Dr. Zheng, using the familiar form of her Chinese name.

"My best to David."

"I'll tell him. He's going to be fine."

"Sorry—I've got to go." She had turned the corner and found herself in the Immigration area. The passengers from her flight stood in ragged lines. She waited her turn and then stepped up to the counter with its bank-teller windows.

"Passport," said the Immigration clerk. "Arrival card."

Lia handed these across, watched the man flip through the stamped passport pages. She had a tourist visa. It was the easiest and fastest way to get in.

He checked his computer screen. "Occupation?"

"Scholar of art."

"Purpose of visit?"

"Look at art."

He looked again at the screen.

Lia felt her brow retracting in surprise. This never happened. Entering China was a glance, a stamp, no questions.

The man touched some keys. Then he slid her passport back across the glossy ledge to her. "Step to the left," he said.

"What?" Suddenly her leather tool case felt heavy, like it could drag her to the ground. "What did you say?"

"Step to the left."

She looked. There was nothing there. A wall, unappetizing pale green. A single door. There? That door?

The Immigration officer confirmed it with his eyes.

All right, she thought, and walked to the door. It opened. A Chinese man with high cheekbones, a bald, luminous head, and a fine tropical wool suit smiled and shook his own hands. "Miss Frank," he said in English. "Welcome."

"Thank you," she answered. She removed a business card from her pocket and held it out.

He took it and turned it, checking both languages.

"Please call me Fan Luo Na if you prefer," she said in Chinese. Her spoken Chinese was only fair. She'd had little practice, colloquial Chinese being somewhat removed from the literary forms in which she'd trained for her job.

He was taking out his own card. "Gao Yideng," he said. "My personal welcome."

Gao Yideng himself? She stared. Why would he come, instead of sending someone?

"Your colleague is doing well," he said. "He is out of surgery and all things were successful."

"Yes. Yes, I just called also. Thank you." As she spoke she looked at the card in her hand: the understated corporate logo of his Cloud Development Group and a short, impressive list of his titles. "It's exceptionally kind of you to meet me yourself," she said. "Too kind."

"It's nothing but my pleasure." Amiable wrinkles fanned out from the ends of his eyes and framed the sides of his face. She saw him take her measure, her no-nonsense clothes, her spare, conservative body, and then she saw his eyes rest infinitesimally on her ears. *Didn't expect that, did you?* She held his gaze easily.

"Come," he said. "Your luggage has been seen to. I'm sure you're very tired."

His driver took the expressway to Dongzhimenwai, through an endless forest of white high-rise apartment buildings and office towers, all the same, the repeating pattern left by sudden modernization. When they stopped at a traffic light, Gao saw her rolling down the window, tilting her face to the air from the outdoors. "What is it?" he said.

She let out a small laugh. "The Beijing smell."

He smiled at her. He knew that smell too. It was largely gone now, suffocated by the dust of demolition and construction. Yet the half-fetid aroma still pooled here and there. It smelled neither pleasant nor unpleasant; like garbage, progress, the past. It was seven hundred years of living and dying, all manner of putrid waste finished with a lovely overlay, the delicate *xiang* of each pale flower of culture and learning in its season. One of the city's subtle charms.

The shouts of vendors washed into the car, the roaring and gunning of vehicles, the bursts of recorded music from thrust-open doors. Character signs blinked and glowed in the night, advertising stores, restaurants, businesses; trees and awnings were festooned with light. They turned south on Jiaodaokou and then west into a long hutong, a narrow lane lined with stone walls rising to the old-fashioned curved roof eaves. In through a double gate, then they stopped. Already an attendant was removing Lia's bags and walking them away to a side court.

"The driver will return for you at eight in the morning," Gao Yideng told her from the front seat. He took out another card and wrote on it. "My mobile phone." He handed it to her. "It's always on. Call me anytime, dark or light."

"Thank you."

He looked at her speculatively. She stood under the glow of the streetlamp, not unattractive, odd-looking, prim with intelligence. She also seemed strong. He would enjoy this. "Peaceful night, Miss Fan," he said courteously.

"The same."

She walked away from the car, thinking, why this place? Foreigners usually stayed at big, well-appointed hotels with conference rooms and Internet trunk lines. Secrecy, she guessed. Discretion.

Her courtyard did have charm. Four inward-facing rooms looked out from under wood-arched verandas, intricately painted in ersatz Qing style. At that moment she realized she'd have to draw on her last reserves to even walk the last few steps to the door of her room, where surely there waited at least a bed. A yawn ballooned up in her throat. She liked it well enough. It would do.

WHEN SOME HOURS later she opened her eyes again, in that small room in a side court in Beijing, she did not get up right away but let herself drift. Her hearing aids were out and she was in an ocean of peace. She liked to reach back to this, her silent void.

It was not until she was seventeen months old that she had

been diagnosed and fitted with hearing aids. When they were ready, the audiologist pressed them in and suddenly the sharp, blinding noise of the world exploded in her head. She burst into tears, terrified. Nothing in her life could have prepared her to imagine sound. Later, of course, she came to love being able to hear—for what it was. To her it had its limitations. She also liked not hearing. She liked to lie like this, right now, with her hearing aids out, in the silence. The empty space had a soothing pressure.

She remembered what it was like before. What she did hear was bloated, underwater versions of sounds—especially when people tried to talk at her. It was impossible for her to make any sense of the stretched-out, distorted noises that came from people's mouths. She also heard what she later understood to be the tinnitus commonly associated with her type of sensory neural hearing loss—a roaring, a remote wind, an intermittent wall of interference. She wondered if *this* was a set of signals from the world around her, but it too proved unintelligible.

Luckily the language of objects, with its patterns of form and color and feeling, made sense to her from the start. She started with the things in their apartment. Her mother, Anita, had loved things and constantly acquired them. She shopped, she walked galleries, she cruised flea markets and junk stores. She took Lia. And this in its way was Lia's first tongue, the language of longing and being sated. By the time she started hearing, and others began to "fix" her, certain things in her were already fixed. Objects spoke to her with their form and their finish, their shape, their physical soul. She wanted to know and feel all of them she could.

Yet even to understand the objects in a single room, in a single drawer, took such concentration. One leaf contained a neural branchwork of almost infinite complexity, as well as endless shades of green. External factors such as the play of light and the movement of air multiplied things further. Yet the object itself was constant. It stayed where you put it. You could study it for a lifetime, you could spend years knowing it; it would not change. It would still be there, be the same.

At first she cataloged things by feelings. There was the white-lit joy in the round, perfect forms of her toys; the statuesque upward longing of the legs of a table; the *tristesse* of sun slanting down on her mother's grouping of statues and vases and antique dolls. These became her first memory-markers. They led her, in her mental maze, to the rooms of memory that contained what she knew. This was always her system. It was right for her. Much later she read about how Seneca of Rome had been able to repeat back two thousand names in order, and King Cyrus of Persia had recited the law in twenty-two languages—and then she knew she was not alone. Remembering made sense to her. It was something she was born to do, even if it meant she was born in the wrong time. Some kids played sports, some studied piano; she worked at memory.

She glanced at the clock. Seven-fifty. Driver at eight. She rolled off the bed and stood up and stretched and checked herself in the bathroom mirror. Her eyes were puffy. They were gray and expressive, but they had a sad downcast tilt to them. Swollen, they looked pathetic. She applied a cold-soaked cloth to them, counted to thirty, and pulled it off. Nope. The same. She gave up.

She rummaged in her suitcase. Already things were spilled out over the floor. She pulled out a gray skirt and a long gray tube-shaped top. Had she brought any other colors? She pushed the disorganized pile aside. A flash of red, salmon, chalky white—yes, there were a few other things. Everything was knit, nothing wrinkled. She always traveled like this. She pulled her clothes on in front of the mirror, watching her straight up-and-down body. She looked okay. She always felt she barely got by with dressing and adorn-ment. At least she'd figured out how to put herself together, though it was an act, on a certain level. She leaned over from the waist to fasten her antique-penny-colored hair at the crown of her head, then stood up and braided it all the way down.

Hitching up her leather bag and her computer, she stepped out into the soft morning air. Shiny-leafed camellias crowded up along the covered walkway. Above the arching roofs the sky was blue, faintly tinged with the brown of pollution. Through the old round gate she could see the car waiting. Oh, my pots! she thought. Finally.

The driver took her northwest along Gulou, past the drum tower, and through a maze of hutongs to the shores of Houhai Lake, a long, thin finger of water here in north central Beijing. They drove along the lake and then turned sharply into the walled grounds of a sprawling white house trimmed with red verandas.

A uniformed man in the gatehouse nodded them past. She jumped out and ran in. The garden was gorgeously tended, with light pooling down through trees over rocks and ponds, but she walked quickly through it and up a few slate steps to a stone-paved veranda. At the front door, under the incandescently painted roof overhang, a small man in a brown suit was waiting.

She returned his polite greetings and followed him in over the worn, thin carpeting. It took her eyes a few seconds to adjust to the dark. Then she saw they were crossing a long living room, green walls reaching high up to ornate moldings and European chande-liers, curtains drawn behind square, Chinese-style arrangements of couches and tea tables. The must and smell of decades rose with every soft scuff of their feet. At the end of the living room, they fol-lowed a corridor past a dining room filled with Swiss clocks and a whitewashed, light-filled kitchen. Then the man opened a screen door and they stepped down into an enclosed inner court, across the grass, and up the steps on the other side. He clicked open the glass-paned doors and flung them wide.

"The light should be here, I believe." He reached into the room and brushed the wall. The room choked in an incandescent flood.

She stood staring. It was a vast room filled with wood packing crates. They made four neat rows. She counted. Forty crates. Forty of them. That couldn't be. There were supposed to be twenty pots, which would be one crate. If there were forty crates of pots, there were— She hesitated.

"Mr.—" She turned to look for the man. He was gone.

2

SHE WENT TO THE FIRST CRATE, THE ONE nearest her. It opened easily.

At first all she saw was the nest of packed, tight-spiral wood shavings, flattened by years, springing up as if breathing at last. She sank her fingers in and rustled through. There, the first box. Her fingers traced its cotton-cloth-covered shape.

She unrolled a length of thick felt on the floor and set the indigo-dyed box on it. She eased the ivory bit from its loop and tipped it open.

Resting in the silk was a covered jar in underglaze blue, ornately bordered and inscribed in a faux-Arabic script. She recognized the Zhengde period, 1506 to 1521. The court had been infatuated at that time with the motifs of the Middle East, like this ten-inch jar, almost perfectly potted.

She lifted it and checked the mark and period. Yes. Made in the reign of Zhengde.

She turned on her laptop and brought up her template for measuring, describing, and recording. She entered everything about the Zhengde jar, carefully, quickly, heart going fast. There had to be eight hundred pots in this room. She made digital photos all the way around the piece, recorded all its physical details. At the same time she memorized what she saw and assigned it a place in her memory world. There were already many thousands of pots in there. Pots were the workhorses of her memory, the marching majority of its inhabitants. She loved adding to their number.

To do so she used the age-old method of maintaining an imaginary structure. Through history, mnemonists had done this, stored their memories in temples, palaces, or villas they kept in their minds. Lia had chosen the layout of the old imperial examination halls in Beijing, to which candidates once came from all over China to sit for the three-day exam of their lives. The complex had thousands of cubicles in orderly rows, the door to each marked with a different Chinese character. For her this was ideal. She could continue memorizing all her life and never use it all up. At its simplest level, the memory world was a repository of all she knew, indispensable in documenting the history of pots. But on a deeper level, where knowledge and imagination intersected, this world of brick-paved lanes and cubicles sometimes brought history to life so that she could actually see it unfolding. Whole scenes, events, lives played in front of her eyes. She didn't talk much about this to others. It was hers alone.

But now she needed to make only a surface visit to the memory world, for provenance on this Zhengde jar. She was quite sure it was genuine, *and* old. Therefore it had to have been recorded somewhere. And somewhere she would find it.

She sat down cross-legged on the floor to concentrate, her hands around the jar. She felt it through the pads of her fingers. Once connected to it she walked into memory in her mind's eye. She saw herself passing through the wooden gates into the examination yard, walking down the central avenue where she kept all the reference lists and catalogs. If this underglaze blue-and-white jar was made during the Zhengde reign, chances were it was described, part of the Palace collection or some private inventory.

She found it in the middle section of the avenue, which housed the records of the Palace collection. The jar was listed in "Gems of Porcelain," a catalog of album paintings created for the Qianlong emperor in the eighteenth century. It was there, one of Qianlong's choice pieces, the blue-and-white faux-Islamic jar.

A smile creased her face at that transient sense of completion brought on by a stroke of insight. *Listed in Qianlong's "Gems of Porcelain"*. . . She finished the entry and replaced the jar in its silk-padded box. That was one. She returned it to its crate. Now another.

Standing over the big, old-fashioned wooden packing case, she dug through the shavings with the glee of a child. She could hardly wait for a sufficiently decent hour to call Zheng and tell him.

THE AH CHAN, called Bai, walked in the new morning light through Tian Hua Tang Park in the town of Jingdezhen. The broad-leafed glade cast shadows on the lawn and the crossing cement paths. This was Jiangxi Province, in the rolling mountains of southeast China. Bai's home was here, a small apartment on a gravel street up the hill. In that apartment he studied porcelain. The accumulated virtue of thousands of years of art was not easily known, but Bai believed that every hour of study paid him back tenfold in business success. It took a lot of knowledge to tell the real from the fake. And even in the realm of what was real, one had to have knowledge to successfully offer a small price for a quality article, *jia lian wu mei,* and resell high.

Bai walked the path down through the park, around the tree-shaded lake, and into downtown Jingdezhen, the center of China's porcelain world. For a thousand years this entrepôt of artists, potters, painters, and forgers had been home to the emperor's kilns. Now the place was a mishmash of factories and artisans and backyard producers, a cobweb of ancient streets blaring TV sounds and tinny music and the pneumatic sputter of machinery.

Through the Communist era, the town had been dominated by huge ceramics factories, turning out modestly priced dishware for the world's discount stores. But in the early 1990s the era of privatization took hold and most of the factories closed. Instantly, the artists and small manufacturers sprouted again like mushrooms after rain. Once more, Jingdezhen was what it had always been: a decentralized, polyglot ceramics production center where the greatest Chinese artists lived and worked.

Few of them created modern pieces. Most strove to reproduce the great works of the past. Some of these were great works in themselves, every bit as demanding as their originals. Yet Jingdezhen was also the place where the real thing could be found—rare, magnificent antiques—because here the traffic in pots was brisk and continuous.

And this trade in antiquities had spawned another world in Jingdezhen—the world of smugglers, ah chans, people like Bai. Without them the old masterworks would never make it out of China and into Hong Kong. And until such pots crossed that magic border they would never fetch more than a fraction of their potential price. Never mind that it was a terrible crime to take them out, punishable by death. A bullet in the back of the head. Banish bad destiny. There was unthinkable money in it.

There were men all over China in this game—some smuggling out ancient religious statuary, others classical bronzes—but in Jingdezhen it was porcelain, and men like Bai were the traveling businessmen in the middle. In Hong Kong in particular, where they avoided names as much as possible, people called them ah chans. The generic form of address suited everybody. The buyers and sellers wanted to know as little as possible about the illegalities, while the ah chans themselves wanted to be known by no one.

It was just past ten in the morning, early for Bai. Generally he slept late. Today his mind was a buzzing jumble of plans.

Already the air around him was humid and raucous with birds. The hillside was a deep-green jumble of banana trees, bamboo, and miniature palms. He slid his hands into his pockets and his mind went to the thing he'd been thinking about, considering back and forth, all through the night. He had the opportunity now to take a really big job. Profitable—and dangerous. He didn't like to risk so much. But for half a million *ren min bi* . . . Bai squeezed his eyes shut. He could do anything with that amount of money. He could take Lili, his third wife, and launch a business in Hong Kong. That was the real porcelain world. That was the place. He could become a dealer. A man of knowledge. His heart raced with the rightness of it.

And if he failed, if he got caught . . . but this was a thought from which Bai had to willfully turn away. He could not get caught.

Just leap, he thought. The jobs he was used to were smaller jobs, the modest shipments to Hong Kong, the few brocade boxes tied in plastic string, held so delicately between his knees on airplanes and in the cabs of rented trucks or cars. And there was always a celestial moment when the money changed hands in those fine Hong Kong ateliers. Then he was briefly not an ah chan at all but a real businessman, legitimate. A learned man in porcelain. A dealer and a scholar. Destiny favor me, he thought.

He looked down the hill at the spreading smokestacks of Jingdezhen, where life was still grittily real. Where on the lawn below him, middle-aged people in soft clothes moved through tai chi in wobbly lines. Where in front of him, egrets, tall, swaying, lifted and planted their long legs. The light ran warm and mottled down the path.

He thought about what he had said to Gao Yideng, the man from Beijing who had called him. "Three days, then," he said, agreeing. "We'll meet in Shanghai. We'll discuss it."

He had written down the address of the meeting place, a teahouse on Huashan Lu. And as soon as he hung up he started thinking. So many pieces to move. How? A ferry? Trucks? For this amount of money I can do it. Curse danger out of my path. I can.

And he blinked the morning sun away from him as he moved down the street, into the busy center of the town, and closer and closer to the longed-for, cigarette-stained darkness of the Perfect Garden Teahouse, just a few blocks ahead.

LIA SAT ON her heels before a pair of *doucai* Yongzheng bowls, decorated in brilliant enamel with the Eight Daoist Immortals among swirling clouds. She picked up one and cradled it. She understood the glaze through the glassy resistance it gave her fingers. To her, the clarity of this finish was what the word *refinement* meant. Just holding the pot, she was lighter and higher, a little more evolved.

She put down the bowls and typed. Now again she came to the

need for a linkup, some suggestive proof of origins, a tie-in to the web of art history. This time she didn't need to go into her memory world. She knew already. There was a similar pair of bowls, executed and ornamented like these, in the collection of the National Palace Museum in Beijing.

She picked up the next one. It was a blue-and-white dragon dish from the Xuande period. So fantastic. Waves of disbelief churned through her as she looked at it. How could an assortment this big, with this much cream, just materialize? Where had it been?

The blue-and-white dish was fine, gorgeous in fact, of the quality that might have been owned by the aristocratic classes as well as the emperor. She had seen a lot of these in this first crate. Yet she had seen a few undeniable masterpieces too. Imperial pieces. This was the thing experts like her most dreamed of finding, pots commissioned by the emperor.

Because these pots were the most perfect, the most truly priceless. They literally could not be improved upon. During the thousand years of imperial production in Jingdezhen, overseers had judged all the creations of the artists at the emperor's kilns. Works deemed utterly perfect were sent to the capital for the Son of Heaven. Others, whether imperfect, overruns, or simply too experimental, were destroyed, some achingly beautiful but still destroyed, and always in the same ritual fashion—with a metal rod rammed down on them and the shards thrown in the pit.

The artist had to go back, each time, and try again. Because if the next pot crossed the invisible line and was perfect, it would be borne as exquisite treasure to the Son of Heaven. And it would become immortal.

By modern times, the emperor's holdings had become, if not the largest, arguably the greatest art collection in selective terms the world had ever known. Continuously built for eleven centuries, it stayed in the Palace as dynasties came and went. Each new emperor inherited the art; many added to it. Despite losses, much remained intact. Jades, scroll paintings, bronzes, porcelains, calligraphy . . . more than a million masterpieces had accumulated by the dawn of the twentieth century. This treasure was not moved out of the Forbidden City until 1931, and then only when the Japanese occupation of Manchuria extended to within a few hundred kilometers of the capital.

Could this group have come from the Palace holdings? She sat back and scanned the rows of crates. It was outrageous, unthinkable. She had to be rational. Yet one thing was sure: Wherever they came from, the pots were stunningly valuable. They were worth—she saw the numbers take dizzy shape in her head—more than one hundred million dollars. That was more than she could even imagine someone paying, so she pushed it aside and went on working.

"YOU HEARD WHAT I said," she repeated to Dr. Zheng. "There are eight hundred of them. Roughly. More or less."

"That's not possible," he said for the third time.

She could feel herself smiling. "Look, I've checked two of the crates. Twenty pots each. Twenty drop-dead pots. And there are forty crates total, same size." She understood; it *was* too much to believe. In a world in which it was a major event to find two, first they had twenty. Now eight hundred. And so far, they were breathtaking. "How's David?" she said, nudging her well-loved director off his closed loop of amazement.

"Oh! He's fine! David's fine. He's just where he's supposed to be today. Lia, don't worry. Hospitals in Japan are first-rate. He's being showered with attention. Half the Tokyo office is there!" Dr. Zheng grumbled affectionately over this loss of productivity, proud of the network of relationships that held together the working world around him.

"But of course I worry. The last time I saw him he was being wheeled into the O.R."

"He's doing fine."

"I'll call him when we get off."

"No," Zheng said quickly. "David doesn't need to know what you've just told me. It would serve nothing. It would gain us nothing. Think what it could cost. Eight hundred pots! *No one* can find out."

"I see what you mean. Then I'll call him but I won't tell him."

Zheng laughed, his characteristic little staccato bounce. "Impossible! You? You're a terrible liar."

She laughed. "You're right! That's true."

"Don't call him."

"Not at all?"

"I'll tell him you are asking after him."

"All right," she said. She put her reluctance away because she trusted Zheng. He had taught her and guided her and he had never, ever tried to fix her. "So who will you send?"

"I have to think. If anyone, it should be Phillip, don't you think?"

"Definitely. In fact he's the only one."

"But I'm not sure it's the best thing."

"I was afraid you'd say that again."

"For every additional person who finds out about this, a thousand points of danger arise."

"But I need someone with me."

"We'll see. At least we should avoid the word getting out as long as possible. In any case, Phillip's in England. I can get him back and ship him out again if we need to."

She calculated. "If I did it alone I could finish in ten days. Well, twelve. I'm still not sure that's a good idea." A job like this needed more than one pair of eyes. They both knew it.

"I'll call Phillip. I'll at least see what it would take to have him close down what he's doing and come back."

"I'll work as fast as I can in the meantime."

"Good. My God! Eight hundred pieces!"

"If it's what it looks like," she said.

"If it's what it looks like," he repeated, and they both smiled and hung up.

She checked herself in the mirror. Now she was ready to go out and look for food, look for entertainment, or even just walk. For this she would turn her hearing aids up. She loved walking on the streets of China. She loved controlling the volume on her world, and this was one of the times she liked it up high. Walking through a Mandarin-speaking crowd, hearing the evanescent bubbles of their lives as she passed their pockets of conversation—their jokes, their gossip, their talk about what they were going to eat and whom they were going to see—this was always soothing to her. She liked to feel the ways in which other people were connected with one another. Here she could eavesdrop almost invisibly. She was tall, white, female; people never thought she was listening to them. She could walk with her hands in her pockets and be part of things.

Glancing back at the mirror, she touched her cheek. Her face was too long, her eyes too sad. She had tried makeup, every imaginable way, but it never seemed to really make her look any different. She was getting older too. Lines were showing in the corners of her eyes. She was becoming faintly severe. Sad and severe, bad combination. She smoothed up her hair. Maybe she should stop wearing it in a braid. But it was truly most flattering to her head to have everything come to a point on top. Really, she said to herself, look. She tilted her face. You're all right. You can't complain.

IN JINGDEZHEN, THE ah chan Bai walked the first of three sets of broad, shallow steps up to the Long Zu Temple. This was a temple to the local god. Towns and villages in China often worshiped gods of local repute. Sometimes these were heroic historical personages who had morphed into legend; sometimes they were spirits who were thought to control the region's prosperity. The god of wind and fire who inhabited the Long Zu Temple was the latter sort, overseeing the art of porcelain in Jingdezhen and the fortunes of all men who had their hands in it. He was the god of the kilns.

Bai's European shoes made a satisfying patter up the worn-down stone steps. Large statues of temple dogs guarded each level. At the top, a stone walk divided a grassy terrace where a caretaker raked in a pleasingly ineffective rhythm.

Walking into the temple, Bai's mind flew back through the hush of spirituality to thoughts of his home. He saw the land his family had occupied since the reign of Jiaqing, given up under Communism, and then reclaimed again. The mountains were fragrant and dense with leaves. It was a place of brushworked beauty. But he was a modern man, a Chinese of the global era, and so he had gone to the city. There was nothing for him back in Hunan.

He stepped into the cavernous main hall. It was dark. The ornate, timbered ceilings were lost above in the shadows.

For hundreds of years this main hall had held the principal altar to the porcelain god. Now it was a museum, open to the public. He strolled past a dusty exhibit, with a fake altar and some token signage; the real altar, for those who still worshiped, was kept quietly in the back. At the end of a short hall he stepped around a sign forbidding passage in both English and Chinese.

Others were forbidden. Not people like him. He entered the small room from the side and stood before the little shrine, eyes lowered before the bronze altar-figure. Electric candles with glowing red bulbs framed the statue, along with bowls of fruit in twin pyramids and incense smoke curling upward. He took three sticks and left a coin in their place.

The first two he lit on the small oil lamp burning next to the incense, chanting under his breath for his two friends, Hu and Sun. He worried for them. The two men were leaving tonight, carrying their futures on their backs. They were transporting a pair of magnificent Yongzheng period famille-rose vases, each four and a half feet high. Neither had ever moved anything of unusual size. They'd been reluctant to bring in partners. Destiny, thought Bai. Safe passage. He rocked the two burning sticks between his hands and stuck them in the bowl of sand. There was so much smuggling in China. Most of it, though—most of the volume and the value— was goods smuggled *into* China. It was an unstoppable flood, everything from cars to cell phones to tankers full of oil pouring into the country. Billions of dollars' worth of goods, staggering levels of lost revenues in Customs. Bai always hoped, in his prayers, that this incoming flood would continue to displace governmental attention from the activities of men like him.

Now the third incense stick. This one was for him. He suspended it in the lamp flame until it caught. The glowing tip was his success, the sure burn his safety. If he made it through he could take Lili to Hong Kong. Just take her and go. His own glow started deep inside him, in the pit of his middle, and spread upward.

Bai perched the stick in the sand by the others and brought his offering out, unwrapped it from its layers of cloth. It was a pot, of course, a Wanli blue-and-white stem cup. It was not real. It was *fang gu,* a copy. This one, of course, was primitive, crude, quite inexpensive. Such a piece was perfectly adequate when dealing with spirits. Spirits were vain, easily fooled, known to be satisfied with even remote facsimiles.

He stared at the rising ropes of fragrance, the glass eyes of the god. Maybe he was going to taste success. If he did, he'd get a new name. That was how it was among the ah chans. A man got his midlife name when he made his big win. Now they just called him Bai, or sometimes Long Neck Bai on account of the birdlike way his head sat on his shoulders. No more of that. Just Emperor. Emperor Bai. *Call me Huangdi.* Elated, filled with the sweep of blessing, sure all he desired was coming his way, he bowed low to the god and left.

JACK YUAN TOOK the call on the deck of his cliffside house in Cannon Beach, Oregon. The wet wind ruffled the plastic tied over a stack of logs and shivered the salt-air-stunted pines that grew up along the sides. The deck was cantilevered out over five hundred sheer feet of rain-wet rock. "This is Jack," he said into the phone.

He walked to the rail, listening. It was Dr. Zheng. He leaned over the roiling Pacific. Gleaming piles of black rock materialized, rose, then sank and vanished in the pulse of waves and foam.

"I have some news," said the age-darkened voice from New York.

"I'm listening." Jack curled his hand to shield the phone from the roar of the sea. Jack had never met Zheng in person, though he thought he knew him, knew him well, by his voice, by its range of shadings and its manifold moods. Jack had bought through him for several years now. He liked Dr. Zheng. He felt he could rely on the gentleman's discretion.

Discretion was important to Jack. He bought secretly. He wanted everything anonymous. He had an uneasy relationship with the advent of major money in his life, and he didn't like people knowing what he had.

In any case it was easy, collecting anonymously. He used proxies. He planted people at the auctions, speaking urgently in multiple languages into their cell phones, knowing that as the bidding went into the stratosphere the art people would be studying them, guessing, trying to connect them to buyers, dealers, and agents they knew. Meanwhile he would place the winning bid through the one person he knew no one would have been watching—the obvious person off on the side, speaking English. It was so easy to predict where people would look and what they would think. He felt a familiar dash of pity. Human society was so much less mysterious than he had once thought, than he'd hoped. It was sad.

He hadn't always been interested in Chinese antiquities; he'd bought other *objets* first. But there came a point when he had stared into the mirror at himself every day for too long, at his glossy black flat-combed hair, his cashmere golf shirts, his overengineered athletic shoes. He was neither white nor truly Chinese. Then he bought a few porcelains through Dr. Zheng. They were ancient and exquisite. They made him feel more himself, even though he was a lifelong baseball-cap wearer from Alhambra, California. "Has Miss Frank seen the porcelains?"

"Yes. She's seen them."

"And they're good?"

"Oh yes," Dr. Zheng said in a voice oddly tickled with laughter. "More than that. Wonderful! But that's not the thing."

And the thing is? Jack thought, waiting.

"There are more than you think."

"What?" A wave crashed down below and poured spray up against the rock face. Jack was straining into the phone. "How many more?"

"Eight hundred."

"What!"

"Eight hundred," Dr. Zheng said again, slowly.

I did hear that, Jack told himself wonderingly, staring out at the strip of red molten sun spread under the lowering clouds, fading its last into the ocean. "How is this possible?"

"I don't know," Dr. Zheng said.

"Where did they come from?"

"I don't know that either. Not yet."

"Eight hundred," Jack repeated slowly. He had been knocked back for a second. Now his mind cracked open to the sudden and fundamental upshift of possibility. Everything notched forward.

Eight hundred fine porcelains. It would be unthinkably expensive. His wife, Anna, would never permit it.

"You'll have first right, of course." Dr. Zheng's voice jumped straight into his brain. "But you need only take what you like. We have many other buyers." There was a smile in his voice. "Believe me, we do."

"Let me think about it," Jack said. He'd been knocked off balance. He didn't want to rush. Still, he saw a possibility as he stared out at the churning gray Pacific. He saw a lens dial in, and everything grew clearer, brighter, higher in the air. Gulls flapped and cried. Exaltation surged. He knew this feeling. When he'd been a young man, single, he'd had it every time he fell in love. He was married, he didn't fall in love anymore, and now this feeling came to him through acquisition. Like this, he thought, fine porcelain:

He'd be with friends. They'd have tea. Some of mankind's most radiant works would be passed from hand to hand. "What would you say is the total worth?" he asked Dr. Zheng.

"Oh. Quite impossible."

"Ballpark."

"Really. Lia just got there. She's alone. It will take days just for her to open all the boxes—"

"Roughly," Jack said, patient.

"You mean if they're all authentic. Because there's that too."

"Yes." Jack waited, enjoying it. He could almost feel the old gentleman readying his pencil. He stood on an edge in his life. And this particular precipice, on this deck a tenth of a mile above the waves, would never come again.

Zheng coughed. It was as if he couldn't bring himself to say it.

"Yes?" Jack said.

"Well over a hundred million dollars. Over a hundred fifty million. I really can't be more specific."

Jack took this in. "How long will it take her to do an inventory?"

"Some time. Some days."

"Let me think, then."

"Please," said Dr. Zheng, "be at your ease. We'll send you selected photos, piece descriptions. These will give you an idea."

"Great," said Jack.

He was going to talk to Anna. Already he was thinking strategy. Art made money. It could be an asset to a portfolio. Still. He knew his Wharton MBA wife would not take kindly to so much money being put into delicate, breakable objects. After they hung up, Jack stood a long time staring at the surf boiling in the last gray wash of light.

"IT'S AMAZING," DR. Zheng said to her. "I have the feeling he's considering taking all of it."

"That would be nice."

"And quiet."

They could feel each other smiling. "Is he a big collector?"

"New. Young. He's been working up to this. He buys silently. Chinese-American, software money."

"And our seller?"

"I checked. Never bought or sold at auction," Zheng said.

This sounded right to Lia, though it made this deal even stranger. She was used to seeing the major collectors from the Mainland at the big auctions now in Hong Kong, London, and New York. They were stepping into the vacuum sucked out by the decline of other countries.

But she'd never seen Gao among them. He'd never been to the previews, the cocktail parties. He was never one of the ones they would mention when a delicious new piece turned up for sale. "Fung would pay half a million for this." And: "What about Toller? Oh no, he's getting a divorce." And: "Pity Martinson died! He would have loved this."

"Is everything real so far?" Dr. Zheng asked her.

"So far," she said. "I'm pretty sure—no, I'm quite sure. What I've seen so far is real." She made her voice firm to rule out the fear.

Fakes slipped through all the time, and art insiders knew it. She had heard museum people say, late at night after the restaurant had emptied out and the glasses were in disarray upon the tables, that if only ninety percent of their holdings were authentic they'd be happy. That meant a lot of fakes—oh, but they were excellent fakes, fakes that had dazzled everyone. And then they would always fall into the same unanswerable argument: What exactly made a fake a fake, when everyone who saw it was sure it was real? What lay deeper in it to recognize?

The fakes in Chinese art, of course, were different. In Western art, fakes intended to deceive. In China, quite often, they aimed to pay tribute. Reproductions had long been a serious, respected artistic practice. Great works were born from this. They were copies, yes, but made by real artists, out of love. Some changed hands, were lied about, and turned into forgeries—this was inevitable. And some of these in turn were so good that they fooled everybody: buyers, auction houses, experts, people like Lia. This was the thing she most feared.

"I have to believe there'll be fakes," she said to him. "So far, though, I haven't seen one."

"Are you sure?"

"No," she admitted. "That's why I don't want to do this alone. How's David?"

"Fine. Getting better every day. He'll be a few more days in the hospital, then he'll be flown home. Don't worry about him. You have enough to think about."

"Are you going to send Phillip?"

"I'm still thinking about it. Let's hold off. Day by day, eh?"

"Day by day," she agreed, and they hung up.

3

LIA CAME TO THE BOTTOM OF A CRATE THE
next midday. Checking it, checking it again, waving her hands through the wood shavings, she
found a box she'd almost missed. She brushed it
off, unhooked it, tilted up the lid, and then
stopped.

Could this really be? She blinked at the small,
delicate porcelain for a long, wheeling moment.

Tilted on its side, surrounded by white silk, it
seemed to be one of the Chenghua chicken cups.
But that would be impossible. Those delicate little
Ming masterworks, made in the late 1400s for the
Chenghua emperor, were some of porcelain's
highest stars. Whole careers were devoted to
them.

She ticked through the whereabouts of the
eighteen chicken cups known to still exist. The last

one to sell at open auction had fetched almost four million U.S. dollars. There were eight in the National Palace Museum in Taipei. Two in Beijing. Five of the cups were in museums in the West: three in London, one at the Met, and one in Geneva at the Collections Bauer. The last three cups were in private holdings. None of these could change hands without her knowing it. So what was this? A nineteenth?

That's beyond imagining, she thought, but then she looked at it again, so impossibly, radiantly beautiful.

Up from her world of memory came something the seventeenth-century scholar Shen Defu had written of these cups: *The five colors are the crown of the past and the present*. True, she thought. The absolute centerline hues of the *doucai* palette.

She picked it up. A featherweight. It felt perfectly balanced. She was going to have to take it outside in the natural light. She had to really see it.

Her heart was pounding as she packed the cup back in its nest and latched it, carried it outside with her square of felt. It was three steps down to the grassy court. Wind frilled the acacia trees along the side.

She unrolled the felt and lifted the cup out again. She held it to eye level. Fantastic. The proportion, the shape and balance were just what they ought to be. It was a feeling more than anything else, but it was sure and deep and it ran like a stream of light all through her: The cup was right. The porcelain had that vanilla-toned, off-white warmth that came from the clay used during the Chenghua reign, never dead white, always soft, alive. It was an effect almost impossible to reproduce, and this cup had it right. A very good sign.

I'm not going to turn it over yet, she thought. Everything was moving at half speed. She was aware of a ringing in her ears. Was it the nineteenth cup, or something else?

She looked at it critically. None of the obvious signs of forgery was present. First of all, it was not a copy of any single other cup. *Fang gu* artists were usually faithful to one prototype. They rarely thought to combine aspects of different cups. Because many gorgeous full-color photographs of the well-known Dreyfus cup had been published when it changed hands at auction a few years before, this cup had been the recent favorite. If she were to see a fake chicken cup, she'd expect it to copy the Dreyfus. Yet this one didn't. Another thing: The painting was sweet, easy—not overdefined as most modern copies were.

She turned the cup over. For a lurching instant her whole consciousness was a digital player on skip. The characters were perfect. *Da ming cheng hua nian zi.* Made in the great Ming Dynasty, reign of Chenghua.

Or was it a replica from a subsequent reign? The Chenghua chicken cups were so exquisite that they began to be copied almost immediately. She canceled each possibility in her mind. It was not a *fang gu* made in the Kangxi reign, because the clay in use then was a purer, clearer white. And it was not a copy from the Yongzheng reign, because copies produced then always seemed to reflect the harder Qing palette. The colors on this cup were soft and blurry-edged, following the Ming sensibility.

Chenghua. But how could it be Chenghua?

She half closed her eyes now. She lifted the cup and ran her fingers along the rim to feel how it bloomed out to the lip—yes, there, it was right. Then she did the same thing around the base rim. Though unglazed, it would have an inimitable smoothness if it was almost six hundred years old. My God, she thought, touching it. It had the exact worn quality, the softness of centuries.

Now she needed the loupe. She went all the way around the circular painting, the chickens and rocks and rosebushes. She played with the instrument to get just the right tilt. Then she went in deeper, below the luminous glaze, under the softened fields of color. Here she found the infinitesimal kiln faults, the bubbles and pocks, the singular DNA of every work in porcelain. And then higher up, on the surface tension of the glaze, the near-microscopic wear marks. These were little stilettos of touch, of abrasion, of the movement of air itself. They accumulated. It took centuries. They should appear natural and completely random. She squinted. Unbelievable. They did.

Then she put the loupe in her pocket and held it away from her eyes and looked at it.

Oh no, oh no. Something was nagging at her.

It was the blue wash of color on the rocks. Too forced.

She turned the cup in the light, looking at it again. It *was* too good to be true. The painting was masterful, the hens and chicks and fronds of grass glowing, effortless . . . and yet the blue on the rocks was too hard. She had to admit it.

She looked again at the mark and period on the bottom. This also was a little too perfect. Most of the true Chenghua cups had fainter reign marks. On the underside of the Dreyfus cup, as a matter of fact, one corner of the mark had washed out almost completely during firing. This one was so clean. Why hadn't she seen that before?

She hit bottom with a crash.

My beautiful Chenghua cup, she wanted to wail. She held it up to the light. Real? Fake. Fake. But it was absolutely fantastic, so graceful, so fine. She held the piece out again, fifteen or twenty inches from her eyes. It might be the best fake she'd ever seen.

She packed it up again, feeling a scraping little fishhook of fear. One fake was enough to start rending the fabric of a deal like this.

Through the tear would slip other fakes, and others behind them. It was impossible to have this many great pots. There must be fakes. Lots of them. More of them.

Ones she had already missed.

She went back to the first crate and started again. A Song celadon crackleware bowl. Then a Xuande stem cup, a Yongzheng incense burner, a Wanli plate. She was going too fast. She couldn't stop herself.

"*Xiaojie*," she heard from the door. Miss. She half turned. It was the driver.

"Oh yes," she said. "Sorry." She looked at her watch. It was past time. "*Deng yixia*," she said, Wait a moment, and quickly packed up the pots to make them safe for the night.

BACK IN HER room she opened her laptop and dialed up the photos of the little cup, merged the images to move the three-dimensional model around. The emperor himself had commanded this design, drawing his inspiration from the twelfth-century Song painting of a chicken. She turned the image, looked at it from each side. If she could see the emperor with his cups, if she could feel his desire, she'd understand this fake better. She would know this near-perfect thing more fully.

To see the Chenghua emperor, she had to go into the deeper level of her memory world, the one that was accessed by completely letting go of the present. This was the realm of memory in which pieces of the past showed themselves. Whether it was imagination or erudition or some mix of the two she didn't like to ask. It just happened.

To do it, she went back to her silence. She picked out her

hearing aids and felt the instant blooming of an empty space. She was alone again. She cleared her mind. She willed herself through the gates and into her imaginary examination yard. She walked down the central avenue, then into the east quadrant. The streets of her world were empty. There were no people. There were sounds—leaves and wind and skating pebbles—but never a human voice.

It was a bad idea to crowd the memory structure with people. In Rome, twenty-one hundred years ago, the anonymous author of the *Ad Herennium*—still one of the greatest standing works on memory—had written: . . . *the crowding and passing to and fro of people confuse and weaken the impress of the images while solitude keeps their outlines sharp.* So Lia saw the clean-swept lanes between her testing cubicles as wide, bare stones, always lit with changing shadows under the leaves of the trees, but empty of people. Though she did let Albert in. He was one of the few. Albert had been her stepfather for a few happy years; he had introduced her to porcelain. She had loved him, and in her memory world he was welcome.

But she had passed him back near the entrance, his image, never speaking, radiating kindness. She walked the silent avenues lined with all the rooms of her life, all the worlds of porcelain: the purist aesthetic of the Song; the *mi-se,* or secret color olive-green porcelain of the Tang; the ornate virtuosity of the Qing.

She came to the Ming Dynasty: hundreds of examination cells stuffed with data and pots and poems and remembrances. Here she was at the reign of Chenghua, ninth emperor of the Ming Dynasty. Marked on his cubicle door was the character *hai,* or child. She had chosen this character for his cubicle because when he was a man, a child was the thing he most wanted. All Lia had to do was open the door in her mind's eye, and she saw him at the annual ritual at the

Temple of Heaven, Peking; 1474 by the Western calendar. His personal name was Xuantong.

He was brought here once a year. Before the tallow candles and the brass figure of the god, he prayed on his knees through the night. This was the first phase of the ritual.

He'd had his eyes on the statue for hours. It glimmered under the leaping candlelight. The metal eyes were flat and dead, but he knew the god's spirit shone within. The emperor believed in divine providence. Maybe once he hadn't, but now he did, for he himself had finally been given a son. Moreover, this son had lived—the first of his sons to live— and was safely growing up.

He had loved only one woman. She was the wet nurse who'd fed him as a baby. When he came of age he made her his concubine. She liked to dress alternately as a man and a woman. He adored her. She bore him a son but the infant died.

After that, the sons he had by every woman also died mysteriously. Whenever the empress or another concubine managed to bear the emperor a son, the baby died. Soon everyone, even the emperor, knew it was his concubine who was killing them. And now his line would die with him.

Until he learned in one breath, in seemingly a single heartbeat, that he had a son after all.

From outside the door Xuantong heard the murmured breathing, the stone-shuffle of men's feet. The Officials of the Sacrificial Court had arrived. Finally. It must be near dawn.

He stretched his aching legs and slipped the ritual satin cap on his head, the satin boots on his feet. These were never worn except on this day, at this moment. Like all the other sacred objects, the plum silk robes, the Tablet of Heaven, the blue jewel called Symbol of Heaven, they were hidden away through the rest of the year. Their power was in their concealment. Like the survival of his boy.

He paced slowly outside the Palace of Abstinence, down a few marble steps into the walled courtyard. The officials swept low and touched their foreheads to the earth.

As he stepped past them he heard the first boom from the Taihezhong, the Bell of Supreme Harmony. It could be heard miles away. He glanced up at the stone tower. Inside, two men were dragging a suspended log back, pulling it as far as it would go before releasing it again and again. The log crashed into the bell with a bone-ringing reverberation.

Ahead of him, through the ancient cypress trees, he saw the Temple of Heaven against the lightening sky. The shape so pleased him. The way its circular inner wall exerted itself against an outer square. The way the four Ling Shing Men, *Starry Wicket Gates*, stood in white marble at the cardinal points.

The day he had learned of his son's existence also was the day he reached the bottom of his sadness. Childlessness was bad for any man, but he was the emperor, and his shame soared in all four directions.

His chief eunuch, Geng Tie, noticed. "Is it headache?" he asked kindly.

"It's not headache," Xuantong snapped. "It's that which Uncle well knows."

Geng Tie felt his frail heart tugged as he looked at this unfortunate, weak-spined, art-minded man he had served for many years. He was ineffective as emperor. He had been born to patronize art. And he needed a son. He had to have a son.

Was this the time to tell him? They had waited five years. The child lived, the child thrived. And no one knew of his existence beyond a sworn secret handful in the palace. "But your majesty," Geng said.

"What?" Xuantong was irritated.

"But your majesty has a son."

Xuantong stared. "Bie shuo," he said, Don't talk like that.

Geng Tie stood trembling. "Your majesty has a son," he said again. "We have kept him hidden in the Court of Quiet Virtue. Forgive us, your loyal slaves. We sought only to preserve him. He is healthy, ready for schooling. His milk name is Huobu."

And so Xuantong had flown, his silk-encrusted robes flapping. He leapt over stones and potted plants, the eunuchs fluttering in a line behind him. He raced from his living quarters to the far northwestern corner of the palace, to the remote court shaded with a lace-leafed elm. Over the sill, around the spirit wall. There was a boy, right in front of him, eyes wide and face as round and tight-skinned as a plum. The nursemaids around him fell to the ground in reverence.

"Who was it?" he gasped to Geng Tie, now lurching up behind him.

Geng Tie understood. He meant the woman. "It was a little slave from Guizhou," he answered. "Right after Spring Festival six years ago. We hid her in this court until she delivered."

Vaguely, Xuantong recalled the encounter. He had been walking back to his quarters from an audience with his ministers. His retainers walked a short distance behind. He surprised a girl with a covered bowl stepping out of an arched gateway. Their eyes met and there was an insouciant smile to her, a careless light of laughter, until she realized who he was and froze. He found this diverting. She set the bowl on the sill and made to lower herself to koutou, but he stepped close to her and stopped her. He didn't want a reverence from her. Instead, he parted her skirts and slid one hand between her legs. He could feel her trembling. After a minute he pulled her skirts all the way up. He lifted her a few inches to sit on the edge of the stone wall, and he favored her, without thinking about it, opening her jacket to play with her at the same time. It only took a few minutes. The eunuchs stood back on the stone path, watching.

A quick pleasure with a slave. He had forgotten it. "Does she still live?"

The eunuch nodded.

"Elevate her rank. And the child . . ." Xuantong *considered. Continue to keep him a secret, or name him crown prince right away? He had a son!*

Now, approaching the Temple of Heaven, he felt connected to all the earth for the first time. He watched the pale iridescence come alive on the marble under the rising sun. Flawless, he thought. As perfect as the sacred porcelains waiting on the altars within: the red, yellow, blue, and white, colors of the sun, the earth, heaven, and the moon. Perfect as his paintings, his jades and bronzes, but most especially his porcelains. Porcelain lived forever. And the potters at Jingdezhen were doing magnificent work, the best since the reign of Xuande. He was about to commission them to make a set of wine cups, in honor of his son. The prince.

Xuantong saw a hen-and-chicks motif, after the Song painter Huang Chuan. It was a supreme paternal symbol. And it echoed the design of a much more ancient ritual cup pictured in the Book of Rites. The cups, the chickens scratching in the dirt with their little babies all around, would invoke the love of a parent for his children, of an emperor for his subjects. They would be truly celestial.

At last the deep tolling bell ceased. He glanced across the great expanse of trees to the tiled roofs of the capital. He knew that throughout the city, men, women, and children had heard the bell and emerged from their homes. They would be standing in their lanes now, facing the Temple of Heaven, facing him, the Son of Heaven. He smiled. His face was lit with an easy benevolence. In his mind's eye he saw the chicken cups.

"I found a fake," she blurted out the instant Zheng picked up the phone. She'd been beside herself waiting to call him. She knew exactly when he got to his office, when he clicked the lid off his steaming mug of tea. She knew just when he'd be ready to pick up his private line.

"A fake what?"

"A Chenghua chicken cup! Can you believe it?"

"Hmm," he said with a smile in his voice. "Audacious."

"Oh, it's good too," she assured him, "it's beautiful. The clay color is fantastic."

"How did you know?"

"The painting—the painting is awfully good. But it's too intentional. You know."

"Oh yes."

"And the reign mark is too clear. Too nice. You know, the artist thought of everything. Even the wear marks are random. But to paint with that Chenghua subtlety—this was done by a master! I have to admit." She swallowed. "It had me going for a while. I had to look at it a long time."

"A chicken cup!" Dr. Zheng was still taken with the boldness of it. "Doesn't he realize how much it would take to convince us there is a nineteenth cup in the world?"

"Who? Gao? Maybe he doesn't know it's a fake," she said. "We don't know who put the cup in there. Or when. But I'll tell you, it's good. Amazingly good."

"A chicken cup!"

"I know. And who knows what else? This could be just the start."

"Oh," he said. "Expect more. You'll find more." He said it matter-of-factly, with the half-charmed rue of someone who knows. "Marvelous, isn't it?" She heard the popping skitter of his laugh. "That the first one should be a Chenghua chicken cup. It's so impertinent! When was it made?"

"Recently, I think."

"How I'd love to know the artist."

"And I," she said. Because whoever had created this cup understood what *hoi moon* meant. Yes, she wanted to meet the maker of this cup, very much. "I'll try to find out," she promised him.

"Luo Na," Dr. Zheng said. "If anyone can do it, it will be you."

IN SHANGHAI, IN Sophia's Teahouse on Huashan Lu, Gao Yideng waited for the ah chan. He was an executive and a master at delegation, but this was his extremely personal matter and he would handle it himself. If he succeeded in selling this collection, he could take payment anywhere in the world, and almost no one would know. It was a private lifeline into which he had put a great deal of thought.

He watched the door. While he waited he drank the delicate tea called *bai xue yu,* snowy buds of jasmine. From speakers behind the creamy walls a saxophone rippled quietly. The square, border-inlaid table in front of him was set with clean, contemporary tea ware and, for the ever present and soothing reminder of the past, an ancient wooden caddy filled with antique tea implements: wood tongs, a paddle with a twirled handle. This place was both safe and quiet. No one knew him.

The bell jingled above the door, and a string-bodied southerner came in. They knew each other at once. Gao took in his puffed-up hairstyle, his weak chin and insufferable sunglasses.

"Bai Xing," the ah chan said, touching his hand briefly to his chest in introduction as he slipped into the sage-green leather chair opposite. "Bai Xing" was as close to a real name as he ever gave out. It was not his original name given by his family either, but his long-standing, most-favored sobriquet.

"Thanks for coming," Gao said.

"You too."

Then the waitress was there in khakis and a black T-shirt, silver drops in her ears, pretty. Bai quickly scanned the menu. *"Gong ju hua cha,"* he said, Paying tribute to the emperor chrysanthemum. This tea choice was a luck charm for the ah chan, since Emperor was the name he wanted to earn when this was over. Emperor Bai.

Gao Yideng was watching the waitress. She was one of the young cognoscenti, with her hair cut straight across at chin length and her eyes well-honed and world-weary. Quite a contrast to this ah chan, who was still too fresh and unschooled to realize he was risking everything, his life, which was of inconceivable value, for half a million *ren min bi,* which was nothing, only money. Yet the man from the provinces wanted this risk. He was keening for it. That showed in the attentive angle of his face and the glitter in his eyes.

Gao looked briefly away from the ah chan and out the window. Facing them was an apartment building called White Pearl, the characters still carved in its lintel stone. It happened to be the first building Gao Yideng had ever bought. It was five stories, fifteen apartments. He had strung together a barely tenable web of bank loans, investors, and money from overseas relatives to do it. In the end all of them had profited hugely, but at first it was terrifying. He had the unbearable, pounding press of other people's money riding on him. He had to look at the drab shell that was still Shanghai back then and say, yes, in ten years it will be transformed. And he'd been right. It had sprouted a gleaming, futuristic skyline. Land prices soared, though as in Beijing, building went too far and vacancy rates had been frightening. But Gao's positions had been good, well timed and well chosen.

And he had chosen well with this art collection too. He had acquired it at the right time and now he'd release it at the best moment. He knew a veiled government sale was perfectly plausible to the Americans, as long as the visa was in order—which it was. The visa to Hong Kong was the main thing. And the visa had cost him dearly.

It was in Hong Kong that the Americans would take delivery of the art. And once in Hong Kong, the porcelains would be untouchable. That was what Hong Kong had always been, a free port, no questions asked. It had been so under the British and now, back under Chinese rule, it still was. Once art or antiquities were in Hong Kong it ceased to matter who had owned them, or how they had gotten there. They were legal.

Caches of such past glory turned up all the time in China. To find art, to buy it as Gao had done and resell it in China—this was perfectly legal. It was getting it out of China that was hard. "Mr. Bai," he said to the ah chan. "This contract will be quite demanding."

"I'm ready," Bai said. "If you get me the right vehicle I can do it."

And Gao smiled his thin smile.

LIA DREW OUT a white Yongle vase, high and round-shouldered in the *meiping* style, incised with a design of delicate mimosa leaves. A pot like this was called sweet-white. The dulcet glow came from advances in clay and glazing made during the Yongle reign. She had once sorted through fragments of sweet-white discovered in a Ming stratum of an ancient kiln off Zhongshan Road in Jingdezhen. She saw through and through why sweet-white lent itself so perfectly to the subtly traced, incised style the Chinese called *an-hua*. And here it was in its fullness and perfection, right in front of her. The *mei-ping* vase was six hundred years old, and as nuanced and lovely as the day it was made. Similar to another one mentioned in an inventory of ceramic monochromes from the Palace Museum in Taiwan.

She put her hands on the vase, wrapped her fingers in a loving net around it, closed her eyes to take it in. It was her fingers that finally understood a pot. It was through her tracing skin that she truly knew the softness of a sweet-white glaze.

The more she had learned to touch pots, the less she had wanted to touch other things. It was too much. And her touch sense had too many memories of men in there too, men who had held her and had their hands on her and now were gone from her life. Each had left his imprint behind, snowflake-specific. Every man had had his own way of showing love, and not-love—removal, disdain, distractedness, impermeability, all the things that hurt—through the touch or the stroke or the supportive cupping of his hands. It was not easy to live with touch memory. So she reserved her hands and fingers. She wore clothes with pockets and used them.

She'd been selective with men; at least there was that. She was glad now, but when she was younger she'd felt diminished by the fact that she hadn't had so many lovers. She often waited a long time before meeting someone. She had learned not to look, not to wait, to focus on her work. Then she met a man she came within an inch of marrying.

Evan was an heir to a newspaper family, fifteen years older and more confident. He had left the Midwest and come to New York to prove himself—he wanted to make money, lots of it, enough to show his family theirs didn't matter. So he developed real estate. By the time she met him he was forty, and wealthy in his own right. Now he was ready for a new challenge—he confided this in her as soon as they became lovers—he wanted to collect art. He was like so many men who collect after earning their fortunes: impatient, omnivorous, wanting all the knowledge right away; wanting exactly what money cannot buy—taste, connoisseurship.

Only much, much later was Lia able to understand how good she must have looked to him at first; how perfect an opening she represented. He saw how she would be, standing next to him, and this he loved, but the essential Lia, the heart still waiting, went unseen. He loved what she brought and not what she was.

She always remembered a certain moment after they were engaged. He was on the phone and she in the next room, on the other side of a glass window. He held up his palm in greeting to her, his tan, comfortably lined face split in a grin of affectionate embarrassment that let her know he was talking about her. She smiled back, but tuned in. He never remembered her proficiency in reading lips. He never edited himself. And with the insecure curiosity of the younger woman, she wanted to know everything he said, especially about her.

That's right, that's exactly what I'm going to do.

Evan was grinning into the phone. Lia knew he was talking about buying art. She watched as he spoke again.

Of course she's going to help me! She's going to make me a pile of money.

He listened, and laughed.

Naturally. Why do you think I'm marrying her?

He laughed and raised his hand to her again from the other side of the glass, smiling, that sly, contrite look. She turned away, churning, until he got off the phone. When she confronted him he said: Oh, Lia, grow up. Of course that's one of the reasons I'm marrying you. It's not the *only* reason. I can't believe you're complaining about this! He treated the whole thing as if it were silly.

But it was not silly to her, not at all, and that was the true problem beneath the false problem—that even her honest admission of this did not move him. This was the beginning of her backing away. It hurt, breaking it off. But she'd never regretted it.

And now she was past thirty, more realistic. Somewhere there would be someone with whom she could feel at ease. Someone she could help, who could help her. It shouldn't be so impossible. As for that jolt of what she used to think was love, that seemingly perfect mirror that puts the inner self up in ecstasy, for judgment by another human soul—at least she knew by now that that was not love at all but a forgery of the most insidious kind. She didn't believe it anymore, she didn't want it, and she didn't wait for it.

Now, the Yongle vase in front of her, she finished typing and pressed a button that would send the vase to her own private computer archive at the same time it went into the inventory. Everything in her memory world was in computerized files too. Naturally she wouldn't take a chance on losing things. But it was a point of honor with her not to retrieve information from the computer, only to store it there. She made herself rely on memory.

She took the sweet-white vase back in her fingers, wrapped the whole surface of her palm around the swelling glazed body, the magic, mathematically perfect swirls of the design against her skin. She cradled it back into its soft little white manger and closed it up.

4

THAT NIGHT, WALKING ACROSS THE LAMP-
lit entry court, she noticed a far gate opening into
another set of courtyards. It was arrestingly irregular. Up close, she saw it was built of jagged
ornamental rocks. She ducked her head and
slipped through it. A court cut by rose-lined paths
opened out in front of her. Thin steles of rock,
shaped by nature, stood up punctuating the grass.
Four rooms looked inward. Three of them had
windows that were jammed: blue-and-white porcelain, severed stone Buddha heads, cups with
fanned arrangements of brushes, knockoff ceramic *san-cai* camels and horses after the manner
of the Tang Dynasty.

She saw at once that foreigners lived here,
long-term residents. They used arty fakes to evince
their personas, to specify and declare themselves.

She did the same; she knew she did. She liked to think she did it with greater deliberation.

At home, in New York, the rooms of her apartment overflowed. In this she was like her mother, who had similarly packed the little Virginia place in which she'd grown up. She remembered easily the ripe tang of humidity on a day twenty-five years before, as they stood in the summer flea market together, rifling a bin of old buttons. Those were the times she remembered her mother happy, walking home, laden with finds, eyes alight with new things; she remembered herself basking in this reflection.

Though Lia's apartment was full, her objects were fakes—great fakes. She had phony Russian icons and da Vinci drawings, a heaped-up altar of Buddhist statuary, and a Fabergé egg. And she had her pots, of course, the few copies she'd found that were good enough to live with. She was very demanding when it came to the pots in her home. And then her books; she kept her best, most transporting porcelain books stacked in squat columns, around the floor. She knew where everything was. The place mirrored her mind. She could put her hands on a book, on an image, in an instant. Now, *her* apartment was interesting, she thought with a vain thrill as she cast an appraising eye around the lit-up windows.

She saw a movement on the path and stopped. A thin cat with butterscotch stripes and high, skulking hindquarters walked in front of her.

She called to it. It froze.

She sank close to the ground, called it again. The animal lifted its amber eyes and looked at her, tail straight up and cocking steadily.

"Be that way," she said to it. Then she stood and looked at the room at the end of the court. Vermilion support columns framed the door; its glass panel was etched in a repeating wood-scroll pattern. But the windows were empty. They were hung with plain white cloth at half-height, for privacy. Nothing else.

Just then a light flipped on in the room. She stepped out of the pool of brightness. A fair-haired man with a boxy chest walked across. He was carrying something. A CD player. He was changing the disc, and he spun the new one as he dropped it in; it caught the light. She held her breath. But he wore headphones. He couldn't hear her.

He could hear music, though; she could tell by the rhythm in his step as he passed out of view. American, she thought. Though she couldn't say why. It might have been carriage, or maybe attitude, or a way of wearing clothes. But she could tell.

She backed up. Then she was in the shadows and she slipped back out under the irregular rock gate, into the circle of lamplight, past the geysering fountain and the driveway, through the main gate, to the street.

LIA MADE HER way to one of the theme restaurants currently popular in Beijing. She liked them. Some were based on gimmicks. There was a place called Fatty's, for instance, with a big triple-beam scale right inside the door. Anybody who weighed over one hundred kilos got thirty percent off for their whole table.

Other places were based on historical eras. Those were Lia's favorites. There were the Maoist places, the Cultural Revolution places, the imperial places. The restaurant she walked into now was a faux-world of 1920s Beijing. The staff sported frog-button tunics, while old-fashioned acrobats, singers, and storytellers entertained from the stage. The food ran to pickled radishes and cabbage in mustard seed dressing and earthy braised soybeans mixed with the chopped leaves of the Chinese toon tree. Her chopsticks roved around the table, and she thought about her eight hundred pots.

She was an experienced appraiser. For nine years she had worked at Hastings. She remembered the job interview. She was given the on-the-spot test. It was the way Hastings always evaluated new hires.

"Don't be nervous," Dr. Zheng had said as he laid objects out in front of her. "Just tell me what you think."

She knew to him she must have looked all wrong. She was tall. Her hair was pulled up in a tight braid, defiantly strict. And her clothes didn't make sense.

No, as Dr. Zheng often said to her in the years that followed, laughing about it: She didn't look anything like most of the women he hired. They wore pearls and suits and had pert Anglo-Saxon hair. But that didn't matter, as he always reminded her. What mattered was the test. "Just tell me what you think," he had urged her that day. She remembered how he extended his dry fingers to the first pot on the left, a blue-and-white bottle-formed vase, *meiping* style. They were all blue-and-whites. But not all the same. Not at all.

She remembered how she looked from one to another, comparing them. Then she lit on the first one. "It has a high-shouldered form in good proportion," she said quietly. "Porcelain smooth, a good clear white—may I?" She moved to pick it up.

"Of course."

She lifted the vase and rotated it. "No mark and period," she said, and tilted the base, which was empty, in his direction.

She returned it to the table. She came closer to study the painting, hibiscus blooms framed by ornate medallions of scrolling leaves. "Beautifully rendered, spacing just right. But the blue—the intensity of it—there is something about the heap-and-piling." She moved right up next to it now, studying the infinitesimal mounding of cobalt grains that fooled the eye into seeing a field of blue.

Yes, he thought. Keep going.

Now she put her hands on it again. She closed her eyes and brushed her fingers over the little mounds of cobalt. She looked like a person reading braille. "It's just too deliberate," she said. "It feels contrived. It's in the right style for the Ming prototype, but it's troweled on too much. I'd say it was made in the Qing, maybe in the Qianlong reign. Though it wants you to think it's a vase from the Yongle reign in the middle Ming. That's what it wants you to think." She shot him a glance, half questioning.

He would only answer with an encouraging smile, and she turned to the second one, a Ming blue-and-white fruit bowl. "Sturdily made," she began. "A little thick. The design is *lingzhi* fungus." She turned it over and read the six characters, *da ming xuan de nian zi*. "Made in the Xuande reign, great Ming Dynasty," she translated. "And this heap-and-piling . . ." She lifted it to the window, where the natural light was most revealing. "This one is deep, but free. It's naturalistic."

"So . . . ?"

"It has that artlessness." She looked at him. "It might really be from the Ming." The bowl had a faint filmy coating all over it. She angled her index finger to set the slightest ridge of nail against it and scraped a patch clean.

She held the bowl up to the light. "I have seen more vivid blues," she admitted. "It's not quite the best of its type, is it?" She glanced at him for confirmation. "But I think it is from the Ming."

"Do you think it is real, then?" he said, pushing her. "Made in the Xuande reign?"

She turned the bowl each way in her hands one more time, then replaced it on the table. "I believe so. Though as I said it is not so very fine. Still, I cannot prove its age. I have never seen it anywhere, in any catalog or any listing, no, I am sure of that."

"As far as you recall."

"Well, actually, I do recall. I make it a point to retain all such things."

He raised his brows in a look that said, elaborate.

"It's just my hobby, memory."

"Memory," he said after her.

"Mnemonics. Cultivation of memory. I've been working at it since I was small. And, you can see, I happen to be interested in porcelain."

He looked at her, surprise and calculation twining in his face. He pointed to the third piece. "What about this one?"

Of course, she knew and he knew that memory was only half of what made a great pots expert. Half was the database. The other half was feeling and instinct. Only then could one distill. *That* was what made a great eye.

She studied the third pot. It was a blue-and-white moon flask with the same kind of overt, studied heap-and-piling she had seen on the bottleneck vase. The Ming style had been much admired in the Qing, but when artisans of that later era had attempted to replicate it, they'd been inclined to go too far. Not that that made the piece a fake, exactly. Fine works from the best Qing reigns had enormous value, whether after a Ming prototype or not. The painting, of a young scholar being carried over the waves on the back of a dragon after a triumph in the imperial examinations, was finely wrought, if a touch mechanical, in the way Qing wares often were. She needed more details.

She turned the flask over and looked at its base. *Da qing qian long nian zi.* Made in the reign of Qianlong, great Qing Dynasty. Plausible. But then she looked more closely at the character *qing.*

Two parts of the left-hand radical were connected by a diagonal stroke, which was technically incorrect.

That character's wrong, she thought.

And then in the next instant, blooming over the first thought before her heart even beat again, she knew she had seen it before. This fluke—or signature, whatever it was—was stored in her memory.

So she went inside in her mind, to the examination yards. She visualized a quiet night, a stone walk lined with cubicle doors. On each door was a character, a concept she had chosen out of love: similitude and grace and impersonation. Finally she stood in front of the door marked *peng*, to flatter, to shower with compliments. Here she kept memories of minor imitative works, the lesser *fang gu* pieces, the merely decorative. Not here. To the next pair of doors, marked *zi* and *da*, which together mean vanity; here were memories of the forgers who could not resist leaving telltale signs on their *fang gu* . . . and here—she looked again—here was the man who had written *qing* this way. He worked in Jingdezhen in the 1840s, in the reign of Daoguang. He'd operated outside the imperial workshop system, a freelancer. He didn't last. Foolish of him to have always left his signs on the mark and period. What was his name? Ask again. Wait. Wei Yufen. Yes. Wei Yufen.

"Wei Yufen," she said to Dr. Zheng.

His eyes looked like they were going to drop off his face. He opened his mouth and closed it again as if he thought he must have heard her wrong. "Say it again," he said.

"Wei Yufen. This was made by Wei Yufen."

"I am amazed!"

Oh good, she thought, with her usual crashing dissonance of triumph and terror. That meant she was right.

"So it is a fake?" he prompted.

She turned back to the piece. It was actually quite wondrously made. "Real or fake, it was made by Wei Yufen in the reign of Daoguang, but after the Ming prototype."

"Miss Frank."

"Yes?"

"Would you like a job?"

"Yes!"

How awkward she must have seemed then, Lia thought; how young. She was better now. She had experience. No one had to fix her; she was right already. And she could do this. Yes. She finished eating and got up to leave.

IN ANOTHER RESTAURANT, in the Beijing Club across town, Gao Yideng met his friend Pan, a Vice Minister of Culture. They sat in the high-ceilinged bar, its walls filled with shelves and lined with books. Gao had exactly twenty-five minutes to allocate but appeared relaxed and companionable behind his brandy. "Heard any news?" he asked his friend.

Pan drank deeply. He understood the question. For years now Gao had been a major donor to several of the museums under Pan's purview, and Pan had clearly noted a passion for porcelain. Gao loved to know what was being bought and what was being sold within China. He also loved the gossip about things being spirited out of the country. They both knew that as fast as privatization was bringing China's heirlooms out of the shadows and onto the market, at the same rate they were draining away. It may have been a trickle next to the flood of goods being smuggled *in* to China, but it was a bad loss all the same. Pan wiped a sheen of sweat off his brow. "There was a shipment of gold-leafed Buddhist statues, Han

Dynasty, intercepted in Shenzhen last week. And they caught a fairly sizable cache of porcelain leaving through Yunnan."

"What's going to happen to it?" Gao's eyes were bright with interest.

"It will be a choice of several museums. We have to hold more discussions." When antique masterpieces were seized, they went to the government for allocation—if they made it past corrupt and avaricious local officials.

Gao listened attentively. Of course, he was not being real with Pan. His questions were atmospheric. What he really wanted to know was what came through between the words. So far, very good. Pan had still not heard anything about his own pots.

And of course Gao would not be the one to tell him. "My dear friend," he said with a crinkling of sunny warmth, and raised his glass to touch it against that of the other man. They clicked, raised them to their mouths, and drank, Gao taking his first sip and Pan draining the last drops of his. Gao smiled over the top of his glass, in the dim light from the egg-shaped lamps all around them. "Always a pleasure to see you."

MICHAEL DOYLE, THE wide-chested man from the back court, rolled his bike out to the hutong. The rapid, high-pitched clicking of the wheels followed him out of the main gate, where life and noise rose around him. He swung onto the seat in a single movement and pedaled into the brown miasma, weaving through the people, their talking and laughter, the carts and the bicycles down Houyuan'ensi Hutong. The lane all but disappeared ahead of him in the dirty mist.

It was unwise to exercise outdoors in Beijing, even now, even after they'd improved the air some, but Doyle didn't care. He'd been ill already. It might come back but this was no longer a thing he feared. Not that he wanted it. But he was prepared.

He rode west through the flat, interweaving labyrinth of walled lanes, the mass of his body balanced easily on the thin wheels of the bike. Through the open doors set in stone blocks, worn down by centuries, he peered into the bricked-up tunnels where people lived. There were only a few neighborhoods like this left around the city, this infill of tightly built rooms that had used up every square meter of the old courtyard homes decades ago, as the population swelled and people needed more space.

He remembered the house he'd had in L.A., the flat-angled roof and the little white room next to the kitchen where they ate. But he was here to forget that. He put his mind on sounds. There was the creak of wheels coming up behind him, punched through with the vendor's three-syllable cry. Wind made a shushing ruffle in the overhanging branches. He pedaled under the trees.

Wooden gates passed him with old brass joins, geometric patterns of rivet; tiny shops with sliding aluminum windows selling soda, gum, cigarettes, and local phone service, one *yuan* a call. He thought about all the things that had brought him here, the white wall and the IV drip of his own hospital room; his wife's suitcases, ready. She'd been a saint to him through his illness. Nothing but love. Didn't leave until he got better.

So he'd taken this fellowship. He wanted to cycle for hours in the smoggy hutongs. He wanted to pound the extreme border. He wanted to leave life behind. China forced him awake with its strangeness, despite the dark-gray, head-in-the-yoke heaviness of its quotidian life. He had thought it would be a good place to let go. So far it had been.

Finally his mind felt empty and good as he hurtled west through the leaf-spotted light, legs going, fingers loose on the handles. He breathed deep, as deep as he could, almost feeling the particulates, welcoming them, inviting them in to sear and settle on his lungs. World, he thought, come in.

5

AFTER SHE'D FOUND THE CHICKEN CUP she'd called Gao's *shouji*, or handphone, using the number he had written on his card that first night. She left a message that she would like to talk to him. He left her one in return asking her to meet him for dinner, apologizing with precise courtesy for not having invited her to dinner already, he was at fault, he'd been away from Beijing. So she took a taxi that evening to the address he gave her.

The car passed rows of stores selling Mongolian cashmere, Italian shoes, designer watches, and the newest flat-screen televisions. She saw an old man on a wooden stool selling candied crab apples on skewers, the sticks radiating in a sticky red starburst from his pole. Next to him stood another man, leaning on a Mercedes, talking on a cell phone. Just past this they turned into an alley, bouncing on potholes and uneven pavement, past the office blocks and the white-tile apartment buildings. These high-rise palaces were where most Beijingers seemed to be living now. They were full of the things that promised to make life right: rushing elevators, reliable plumbing, and high-floor windows revealing a stationary army of near-identical buildings receding across the city's smoggy plain. But down here the alley twisted between smaller, older buildings, and the car finally stopped in front of one of them with a simple wood-framed entrance in Japanese style.

Inside, Gao Yideng was waiting for her on the floor of a tatami-matted room, shoes off. He rose to greet her. He probably had multiple wireless devices in his pockets connecting him with associates all over China, but here in this little restaurant room he appeared solitary and relaxed. "How do you find the pots?" he asked.

"They are magnificent. As you must know." They settled in across from each other.

He poured green tea. "I hope you understand why at first we failed to mention the full . . . extent of things."

"I think I do," she said. And in fact, despite the shock of arriving here and seeing hundreds of pieces, that aspect of the situation now seemed favorable. Only she and Dr. Zheng knew, and their position was undeniably better for it.

Food he had selected began arriving at the table. They talked about Beijing, the modernization, the rate at which everything was being wiped away. Sake was served. They both leaned back slightly from their cushions to allow the kimonoed Chinese waitress to pour. Neither touched the alcohol. "There is one piece that fascinates me," she said finally.

"Which?"

"The chicken cup. Do you know it?"

"From the reign of Chenghua, that one?"

"That one."

"Yes," he said. "I know it."

She took her time eating a small piece of eel off the tips of her chopsticks. Interesting, she thought; he knew the piece and he said so, straight out. Moreover, he knew it was Chenghua. She wondered what else he knew. Obviously he had an affinity for pots. Which type was he, the tycoon or the connoisseur?

In her experience, those who collected pots, who owned them, fell often into two types. There were the corporate heads, tycoons, self-made men who had achieved wealth and now wanted discernment. They wanted the best, all at once. It was not necessary for them to love what they bought.

Then there was another kind of buyer—the person like her, but with money, who loved pots. Sometimes these clients had art-history knowledge rivaling that of well-known scholars. Sometimes they were obsessive and crazy. From Gao's knowledge, and his clear avidity, she would take him to be the porcelain-lover type. On the other hand, he fit the life-profile of the tycoon. "The Chenghua cup is lovely," she said. "A wonderful piece."

"Thank you."

"But if it is real"—she spoke casually—"if it is real its discovery is rather important. Forgive me if you already know. I have no wish to waste your time outlining the obvious. But only eighteen of these cups are known to have survived in the world. That would make this the nineteenth cup. If it's real."

He took an edamame pod from the plate and easily, using only the tips of his chopsticks, split the pod and extracted the shiny little bean. She watched with admiration. She couldn't control chopsticks like that. He placed the bean inside his mouth. "If it is real," he repeated.

"*If* it is real, its discovery is of importance," she said succinctly, still keeping her voice light, playing out his line.

He looked at her. "Is it not the case that of the eighteen cups, two are here in China? Among the holdings of the Palace Museum?"

"That's so," she said.

"Most are in Taipei."

"Yes," she answered. "Eight. Mr. Gao. Are you saying that this is one of the two cups from Beijing?"

"No," he said in quick retreat. "I don't know that."

"I see." She put down her chopsticks and smiled at him across the table. Her braid had come over her shoulder and she reached up and flipped it back. She could feel him looking at her ears again. Take a good look and wonder about me, she thought. You probably want to know why I use these old-fashioned things instead of implants. You'll never find out.

Of course Lia could have had cochlear implants if she'd wanted them. She didn't. She didn't want a plate surgically implanted in her head. Moreover, she'd be trading one electronic universe of sound for another, neither being the full, natural spectrum experienced by those who could truly hear. She'd gotten used to her set of speakers. They didn't catch the high frequencies—the jingle of keys, the microwave buzzer—as well as implants did, but she really didn't care. She didn't want to change. She liked the ease with which hearing aids could be plucked out. No plate inside you. Your head was yours, your world your own.

"Mr. Gao. I must compliment you. Whether the cup is real or not, it's an exquisite piece. Beautifully made. Very *hoi moon*," she said, and then repeated in Mandarin: "Very *kai men jian shan*," Open the door on a view of mountains. "Truly it is one of the nicest works I've ever seen." She looked at him steadily. "So perhaps on reflection you will decide not to sell it."

"Perhaps," he agreed. "Suppose the cup is not real." He looked back up at her. "Who do you say it is who made it?"

"I don't know the answer to that. Not yet." She picked up her mottled stoneware cup of green tea and drank from it, left her sake cup alone. Interesting little lagniappe of a power play. Neither touched the alcohol. "But you could help me also, Mr. Gao, if you would be so kind. I can better sell your pots with a full story. Do you mind? A few questions?"

"Of course I do not mind." He leaned his bare gleaming head forward, the spirit of cooperation.

"If I may—how did the pots come into your hands?" She let the question hang, and waited. She was prepared, of course, for him to lie; that was her departure point, her ground-zero assumption. If he was standing in for a government sale he would have any number of reasons for not wanting to tell her so. The decision-makers behind the transaction would not want it publicly known. In any case he had the visa. That said certain things.

He settled his chopsticks down on their porcelain rest before answering her. "Originally, the collection was bought from a family in southern China. That was some time ago. It has been in storage."

She wrinkled her brow. Must have been some pretty deep storage, she thought. Things this big were very hard to keep quiet. "Before that," she said. "Where was it before that?"

"Buried on this family's land."

"How?"

"No one knew. Everyone who lived there was killed in the war. Another branch of the clan moved to the land later. Many years after *that,* they found all these crates while they were digging a garden."

Gao and Lia smiled at each other. The smile acknowledged that the tale he'd just told her was a very, very common story in the

Chinese art world—a cliché, really. It was a patently predictable story to pass off. It could be false. It could also be the truth. "It is true," he said as if following her thought.

She felt oddly inclined to believe him—maybe. "Just your own guess," she said. "How do you feel the pots came to be there?"

He gave her a long look filled with speculation. Finally he shook his head. "No one knows."

No, she thought, that's wrong. Someone knows. Stories, flares of lightning, surprising events: These were like wafts of smoke or fragrance over a town or a rural district. Many people sensed them. People whispered to each other. And they remembered. It was there.

She waited and watched.

"I'll tell you one thing," he said at length. "It's possible these pots were separated from the Palace in 1913."

"1913?" She was surprised. This date seemed to come from nowhere. The war years, when the collection was in flight, were what she would have expected.

He saw her surprise. "It was because of your countryman! Your American! Mr. J. P. Morgan! It was he who in 1913 tried to buy the contents of the Forbidden City for twenty million dollars." Gao pronounced the words with pinpoint pleasure.

"Ah yes! You are right. I know that one. A great story. And what if he had succeeded!" And he almost had. Morgan dispatched an American man to Peking to make the deal, and the whole thing came shockingly close to consummation. But then Morgan died—with no warning. The deal stopped in its tracks.

"It has been said that some works were moved out of the Palace for inventory during those talks," Gao told her. "In such cases there are always things that are never moved back."

Okay, she thought . . . interesting. "And the sources of these suppositions are reliable to you?"

He nodded.

"Then I will check into it. I will certainly be able to let you know later."

"Really," he said, impressed.

"Really. But one condition. You have to find out more about where these pots have been. At least try. *Shuo hao-le ma?*" she finished, Are we agreed? And to make sure he understood her touch of levity she raised her sake cup to him.

"*Shuo hao-le,*" he said, We're agreed. He picked up his cup; they touched and drank.

WHEN SHE GOT back to her room she was still thinking about whether her pots could in fact have been removed from the Palace in 1913. It was distant but conceivable.

Somewhere she had this inside. Once at the Morgan Library she had read through all the files on the failed transaction. All the players had been there, their cables with their crossed-out drafts, all the details of the deal that had almost moved the world's greatest art collection to the other side of the Pacific.

She turned off the lights and changed into the minimal, clingy things in which she slept. She felt like going to the bottom end of the memory world, to the place where the past played out in her mind. It was tiring to animate memory, but some things were worth seeing. This was one.

She took her hearing aids out and felt the safe, filling swell of silence. She sat on the bed with her knees up to her chest, wide awake, the gates to her personal world open.

The cubicle she sought was down a side lane, in the early twentieth century, before the wars, when a crushingly wealthy American set about acquiring, madly, and built a magnificent collection. When he trained his sights on China, J. P. Morgan sent a young American, a man named F. H. McKnight, to do his bidding.

It was March 21, 1913. The air was filled with clacking Pekingese voices, the roaring hiss of gaslight, and the creak of wheels on the dirt-packed street between the warehouses and the godowns. It was night in the port. Wooden sidewalks bumped and clattered with the streaming passengers. They were dazed to be on land, dazed by the new sounds, the fervid smells, and the terrifyingly strange stalls for food and drink.

Frederick McKnight stood at the end of this street. In front of him swarmed men pulling carts, hauling rickshas, shouldering burdens several times their own size. Light popped and flickered from burning lanterns. The Western women's faces glowed in the light as they held their bags close to their bodies. Men, high collars, mustaches, eyes down, also picked their way along the slat-boards. Up at the other end waited horses, mules, and drivers.

Not an automobile in sight, Frederick realized. Peking was some miles inland. Travel by cart would take hours.

He realized he would have to apply himself to his arrangements, and did so. For two silver dollars he secured a man with an open, horse-drawn cart to collect his trunks and carry him to the city. Four hours, the man made him understand in pidgin. Frightful, Frederick thought, but what else was there to do? At least the night was fair.

A gentleman, he had naturally offered to make arrangements for Mrs. Grosbeck, the woman he had befriended aboard the Constantinople. She'd informed him she could make her own. She did this with a lilt in her voice, not in the least standoffish. She also said, with an appropriate lightness, that she did hope she'd see him later.

Frederick replayed her words in his mind. He was aware of his arms and shoulders moving under the blue serge of his suit, the perfect posture required by his stiffly starched collar—he was a fool to have worn it. No one cared. Not in this place. He reached behind and unhooked it, slipped it off. Instantly he felt better. He slipped it into his bag.

Mrs. Grosbeck wouldn't care about his collar.

They both happened to be booked into the Wagon-Lits. He was twenty-nine, unmarried. She was recently divorced. At first her extra-marital state had struck ambivalence into him, but as she had quite briefly and without emotion told him her story, he had come to see that, in her shoes, he might have done quite the same thing. Yes. Quite the same.

And here they were in China.

Frederick climbed into the cart after his luggage. Somehow he had imagined something grander, a regal stride down a gangway into a for-eign land, him strong and imperturbable. Not this gloomy dark, the jumping shadows against the mud-walled buildings, the squawking cries and the straw-slapping shoes of the coolies. Amazing. He settled down under a heavy pile of blankets, head propped where he could watch the stars. It was so good to be off the boat.

He slept. When he awoke he saw gliding above him the walls of the city proper. They were rolling down a dark boulevard. On one side were buildings in pagoda shapes, on the other an endless wall, massive and silent.

The driver heard him and looked back. "All gate close," he called over the hoof-clomping. "Go north side, Xizhimen. Open late."

Frederick waved a hand and lay back down. Now he could see the curving tiled roofs and trees, so thick, their branches and leaves meeting overhead. After a time they came to the Xizhimen gate and flowed through it with the tide of late-night traffic—carts and rickshas and pedicabs and a bobbing sea of men on foot. He stared. Men in gowns, some very fine, flapping lightly over trousers tight to the ankle.

Inside the city walls they navigated a network of streets lined with low buildings. Stone walls enclosed round gates and turned to follow narrow lanes leading off. Overhanging balconies glowed with colored lanterns. By the time he was unloaded in the Legation quarter, at the Wagon-Lits, the feeling of being in some strange dream was complete.

In the hotel lobby, under the glittering chandeliers, he saw more Chinese men of consequence, in gowns of silk. Mandarins, he thought; look closely. It's with them you'll have to make a deal. But he could not think, he could not penetrate, he was dizzy with strangeness. He stumbled to his room, fell on his bed, and slept until the next afternoon.

And now it was ten days later. Now on this night he adjusted his cravat by the fluttering lamplight. He studied himself in the carved rosewood mirror, his hair shining and flat from its center part, his eyes lucid with excitement. He was a gentleman. No one could say any different.

It had been easy here. The world of foreigners was small, interconnected. He'd only had to call on the few people recommended by Mr. Morgan's office. At once he'd been introduced to Fleisher, a European of vague nationality who published two English-language papers here in the capital. Fleisher in turn brought in White, who did something at the American Charge D'Affaires Office.

This White had a Chinese partner named Shi Shu, who acted as agent for the Chinese imperial family. The Qing Dynasty had fallen two years before, and the emperor's family continued to live in the rear quarters of the Forbidden City. They were surrounded by art. Priceless, unimaginable art. Paintings, jades, bronzes, calligraphy, porcelains, textiles, jewels. They had palaces in Mukden and Jehol too—same thing, according to Mr. White; art stacked to the ceilings in closed rooms. "My good man," White had said. "You cannot imagine it.

"And," White had said, leaning toward him as they strolled the temple grounds of the Shrine of the Star of the Foremost Scholar in the Land, "it is for sale. All for sale."

Ah, then Frederick had been brilliant. Every cell in his body had screamed with the excitement of acquisition, but he'd kept himself casual. "What did you say to be the purpose of this temple?" he asked. He feigned disinterest in everything, even the little hilltop pavilion in front of them, even, especially, the deal White was preparing to put on the table.

"Ah. This is the deity who gives success in the imperial examinations. Success or failure!" Despite Frederick's careful aloofness, White was relaxed and charming in his gray striped suit. "The examination candidates flocked here to worship. They came from every province in China. Before going to the examination yards to sit for the jinshi, they came here and begged the god for success. With success came riches and position, guaranteed for life. With failure—well, loss of face was the least of it."

"As to the collection you mentioned," Frederick said at length, after many quiet minutes of studying the statues of the god within. "How might one inquire further?"

"Let me talk to my Chinese associate," White had said, and gone on to point out the other nearby temples, the Temple of the Evening Sun and the Hall of Ten Thousand Willows. He chatted politely, filled with zest and knowledge, ultimately surpassing Frederick with a show of bright, courteous apathy.

But he had inquired. The discussion had begun. And that was many days ago and now they were moving toward agreement.

Frederick smiled at himself in the mirror. Welcome to Peking, Frederick Henry McKnight, he thought. His face, his eyes, everything was ablaze with possibility. His heart too.

"Ready?" he said to Eileen—needlessly, for Mrs. Grosbeck had been dressed twenty minutes or more, sitting by the window in the brocaded chair, watching the pulse of life in the street below. The men in their dark garments, the ricksha carriers loping with their musical cries, the robed gentlewomen, walking wide-legged on their bound feet, everyone talking,

laughing. *A soft roar seemed to rise from the street in China, only it was like nothing he'd ever heard before, no machine sounds, no traffic; instead a tide of human voices.*

"I'm ready," she said to Frederick.

He felt a surge of gladness. He hadn't sorted out his clear feelings for her, but he liked her. She made few demands. She seemed to want to spend time with him. His abdomen tightened. She'd been married, he knew. She was not untried. She walked and sat and stretched and crossed a room with her whole body.

And she had intelligence. She had helped him compose the cables back to Davison, who worked for Mr. Morgan. The financier's wishes came through Davison. They had talked about removing some items from the Palace for inventorying—this had been the suggestion of Shi Shu—but Mr. Morgan had said no, leave everything intact. They had traded descriptions of the scope of the collection, and many many prices.

How much to say in these cables seemed extraordinarily delicate to him. Even though they were composed and sent in code, one never knew. And they must read just right to Davison and Morgan. Still, he had stiffened at first when she took a pencil to his first draft of block capitals and sketched in edits.

"Doesn't that sound better?" she asked, pushing it toward him. He looked at it. She was right. It was ambivalent in all the right places, toned, diplomatic.

"I stand in your debt," he said. To which she wrinkled her nose. No dry mentalist, Eileen.

And so tonight he was taking her along for the meeting with Shi Shu—a critical meeting, the most important one yet. Shi Shu had been high in the Manchu bureaucracy, and still went to work every day, for the family, inside the Forbidden City. In the matter of the art collection he was their direct and sole representative.

A week ago, Frederick never would have brought her. In America, he wouldn't have dreamed of it. But now he knew he wanted her there. She helped him. She saw what lay behind words and gestures. Later, when they were alone, she would sit with him and help him sort it out.

Not that he'd tell the others they were friends, a man and a woman. Nothing really improper had happened. Nevertheless, that would not do.

He had already introduced her to White and Fleisher as his cousin. It had been believable. It made it easier for them to go about together. And she'd absorbed it in the best of humor, seeing its utility instantly. They were relatives. This was their protective cover.

Davison had cabled them Mr. Morgan's final line on price. Tonight, if he could bring Shi Shu into that range, they would have a deal. And a new door would open and his new life would start.

He lifted the glass cover of the gaslight and snuffed it out. He turned to her and extended his arm. She rose, brushed imaginary lint from the cream-colored lace overlaying her high-cut, rustling dress. It struck him that most foreign women looked strange in this world. After seeing the layered silk garments of wealthy Chinese women, he found the cinched, fussy dresses and the great hats of the Western ladies overstated. It was never true for Eileen. Her clothes were straight-lined, tailored from fine cloth, simple. She claimed to dislike hats. Stay with me, he thought impulsively, feeling a warm flood inside himself of wanting her.

"I'm ready." She rose and walked toward him. Before she could reach him they were both caught by the sibilant whoosh of an envelope being pushed under the door.

He walked to it and picked it up. "It's a cable," he said, tearing it open. He read.

"What is it?" she said, for she saw his face sagging in disbelief.

"Mr. Morgan is dead."

"What? Was he ill?"

"No. It was unexpected."

They looked at each other.

"It happened in Italy." He read the rest of it. "All negotiations canceled." He looked up at her. "It's finished," he said. His future had been directly in front of him. Now in a heartbeat it had evaporated.

"I'm so sorry," she said.

He nodded.

They stood facing each other in silence.

"Let's go tell them," he said.

"All right."

He held out his arm. She took it and they walked out.

Lia slipped under the sheet and blanket and stretched out; sleep would reward her now. She felt at ease. She was sure the pots hadn't been moved out in 1913. They were still there when Morgan died.

Before turning out the light, she slipped one hearing aid back in, picked up her cell, and called Gao's voice mail. "I wanted to let you know the pots could not have been removed from the Forbidden City in 1913. I checked. So please keep looking. And," she added, "thank you for a most pleasant dinner."

6

THERE WAS A CURATOR NAMED LI, AT THE
First Beijing Antiquities Museum, who sometimes felt he was the only person on earth who
cared about the volume of cultural treasure being sneaked out of China. He came to work
every day, seeing the steel net of the new, modern, globally denominated world settle over his
city and transform it. There was the promise
of order and progress. He didn't know if he believed it. It was still China and still a chaotic world
underneath.

Illegalities were no secret. The tides of smuggling; the black market; corruption and graft—
these were so ubiquitous as to have been taken for
granted by most people.

But Curator Li hated seeing his civilization

dismantled in front of him. He hated the apathy of the people he saw around him. He hated the art leaving.

When he went to Hong Kong he always visited Hollywood Road. The galleries there were packed with pieces from China. He would stand in front of the windows and feel the pressure rise inside him. None of it could have been legally brought in. There had to be an army of smugglers, a world, a universe.

In porcelain, Li had picked up a little bit about how they worked. There was a loosely knit constellation of cliques and factions, jealous, competing, radiating out from Jingdezhen over a net of Chinese towns. Once in a while Li was able to forge a link with someone in one of these places and soak up gossip about what was going on, what was being moved out, and where it was heading. The connections never lasted, for the ah chans were shadow men. They might talk to him once or twice, then disappear again. All he could do was listen and wait.

This week he'd heard a man say there was a rumor in the south. Something about pots. It made his mouth clench and his slim fingers drum on top of the desk not to know.

Li's *danwei* was a small, well-endowed museum established by the People's Liberation Army. In the late nineties the PLA had been required to divest itself of all its for-profit businesses, which were many, some hugely successful. They then found themselves in possession of an enormous fund of cash. Part of that money went to establish this museum. Everyone knew that, at this time in history, most of China's greatest art treasures, at least those that were movable, were already outside the Mainland. The imperial collection had ended up in Taiwan at the end of the war and, absent reunification, was never coming back. Yet that still left a huge tide of masterpieces in flux around the globe: works owned by museums, by collectors.

They came on the market at times. And they could be bought, by the PLA's museum as well as anybody, and brought back to China.

Not that Li and those in the hierarchy overhead were above a little posturing to see if things could be gotten back for free once in a while. A few years back a pair of Qianlong *falang cai* vases, fantastic imperial pieces, had come up for auction at Armstrong's. They were openly advertised as having been looted from the Summer Palace during the opium wars. They had been in European collections in the one hundred and fifty years since.

Somewhat brazenly, the Ministry, at the behest of the army, had publicly demanded that Armstrong's return the vases as war loot, unrightfully stolen. Hadn't similar allowances been made with art taken from Jews during the Holocaust? This was only one hundred years further back. Oh, Li remembered with glee how the art world had held its breath for several tense days. As it should have. The vases were stolen! But Armstrong's had held firm and said no, we are going to sell them, and Li had been forced to attend the auction in Hong Kong and bid, keep bidding, keep upping the offer of the PLA's cash, all under the blessing of his superiors, until in the end he had to pay out more than two million U.S. dollars for the pair. But he got them. He did bring them back.

And while he scraped and budgeted to make such purchases, the smugglers were moving porcelains out of China as fast as they could travel.

Maybe what he'd heard was true. Maybe something big was happening, something about pots. He touched a button on his computer and let his eyes play down the names on his call list, looking for the one, the right one, who might possibly know.

THE DRIVER WAS carrying Lia that morning along the shores of Houhai Lake, the bending trees half obscuring the long finger of water. She remembered that this was the body of water to which candidates who failed the imperial examinations came to drown themselves. There were always those who chose to hurl themselves in the water rather than return home to face their parents. Now their ghosts were here forever, mourning by the banks of the lake.

The idea that anyone could feel so tied to their family interested her. She herself, in her tiny family web, had always seemed to be someone's project, and this was a thing to be escaped as much as a thing to which to cleave. There was only so much that she could endure of being repaired by others. Albert had never done it. Dr. Zheng had never done it. That was one reason she respected them, loved them.

Her real father had never tried to fix her, not that she respected him or loved him. She felt a bitter chuckle weave up her throat. She had only met him once. She had tracked him down; the encounter had been so dispiriting that she had often wished she was able to forget it. In her world she kept the door on him closed.

She'd found him living in a single room, subsisting on four or five minor patents. He was her and her mother to the tenth power: junk, piles, effluvia. There were subscriptions to professional journals, indexed, spanning decades. There were years of canceled book-request slips from the public library, alphabetized. He was a prisoner of proliferation. Like her apartment, his was crowded— but it was squalid, not artful. And the last insult: He looked like her. Same columnar frame, same drooping eyes. Although she was beautiful, in her way, she knew: She had long, abundant hair and eyes that may have been a bit sad but also radiated humor and intelligence and warmth. And she knew she had a high-wattage grin.

She could always crack the ice with a smile. No, she wasn't so like him.

Forget him, she thought.

Just then the driver turned away from the lake and into the gate of the villa. Her heart lifted at the thought of today's pots, just ahead, waiting. She didn't need to think about her father. He could stay in his memory room. He didn't have to come out.

IN HONG KONG Stanley Pao sat back on a leather couch and talked to Gao Yideng on the phone. "And for what percentage? Mmm, I don't know. Five more tenths of a point. Yes." Stanley smiled faintly. He was in his seventies, a sleekly plump, patrician man who wore his white hair pomaded straight back, just long enough to disappear neatly under his collar. He liked to sit with one hand on his rounded stomach. He spoke in slow, measured tones and never dropped his refinement of manner. He lived alone here in this magnificent old apartment in Happy Valley, which looked over the racecourse. He had always lived alone, except for his prized Pekingese dogs. He had never married. He was the sort of man after whose personal life people did not ask and whose partners, whoever they were, did not appear with him in public.

Not that he didn't let some of his vices show. One of them was horse racing. Not only could he see the track from his windows, he could see the giant screen over the track for simultaneous video close-ups. At dawn he watched the horses exercise as he took his tea. But mostly, he followed horse racing on his computer, which was always kept running on a side table in his porcelain room. A keyboard always lay beside him on the couch. Results from races around the world appeared regularly, and in between, charts of thoroughbred bloodlines and streaming reams of racing data ran endlessly down the screen. Offtrack betting, in some form or another, was available in most cities of the world. Horses raced every day. Stanley played right here, placing bets, paying out or collecting through the keyboard on the sofa beside him. It was one of the games he loved in life. Though business was fun too. He listened to Mr. Gao. Ah, now the commission sounded right. Now he was getting close to feeling satisfied. "I think this will be possible," he said. Nothing jolted Stanley off his phlegmatic calm. "Of course," he said, "the porcelain must be fully inside Hong Kong."

Both men, several thousand miles apart, smiled into their phones. This was the beauty of Hong Kong's law, as they knew.

"So I transfer it to the American representatives. They'll contract their own packing and crating?" Stanley knew the details of a job like this well. He had been a private porcelain dealer for many years, receiving selected clients in this room. He only served those lucky enough or powerful enough to be invited here to his home, where his beloved prizewinning dogs ran free in the outer rooms; where here, in his climatically controlled inner chamber with the racetrack view, millions of dollars' worth of rare porcelain was on casual display, cluttered, grouped on tables and floor and shelves and every available space. Fine pots from the Ming and Qing and the Tang and the Song. Piles of art books with relevant cross-references to museum collections around the world. Yet there were many fake pots in the room too. There were fakes even an amateur could spot, and also fakes that would fool anyone—even him, the *éminence*, if he didn't know better. The interplay between doubt and faith, between the eye believing and the eye distrusting—this was the real surge for Stanley Pao. This was what kept his soul afloat.

He listened carefully to Gao Yideng, but at the same time he also made a decision about betting on a race at Saratoga. One hundred U.S. dollars on number three in the fifth. An amusement, an intriguing moment he would set up for himself, later when the results of the race came in. "And the Americans and I will arrange air shipment."

"Yes."

"And none of the pieces will be sold in Hong Kong?"

"No."

The elder man allowed himself a long and thoughtful sigh of disappointment. "Regrettable," he said. Pots of truly celestial quality were so impossible to find.

He himself swept Hong Kong for imperial pots constantly. Daily. He spent a lot of time on Hollywood Road, that narrow looping curve on the hill above Central where the dealers in art and antiquities strung along in constant competition with one another.

When Stanley walked down Hollywood Road, his first clue that a shipment had come through was the sight of Unloader Ma— a big, beefy Chinese who wore balloon-shaped shorts and a billowing T-shirt the year round. He was the man who took the crates off the trucks. He went up and down the street freelancing.

When Unloader Ma had things down and stacked on the sidewalk, Uncrater Leung would take over. Leung was the opposite of Ma. He was a wiry, well-muscled man, older, gray-headed, with attentive, long-fingered hands. In his trademark cargo vest with innumerable pockets, he'd go through the mountains of rough-textured pink paper in the packing crates, removing the pieces in their bubble wrap but also checking every inch, never missing any separated handles or lids or loose pieces. While he worked, the pink paper would twist and wave in the wind down the street. Often this would be the first sign Stanley Pao would see—a skinny, wind-skipping banner of pink paper. And then Pao would walk faster, because he would know Uncrater Leung was working up ahead. And that meant something new was in town.

And with any luck, it might be something good.

There was one other way to find out if something choice had come into Hong Kong, and that was to go down and eat at the Luk Yu. Not at dawn, when the venerable four-story teahouse was packed with Chinese stockbrokers. Not at eight or nine, when the people who kept birds came in. Not at ten or eleven, when the art dealers showed up. The best way to find out was to go at noon, when the ah chans came for breakfast. They always ate at the Luk Yu. They hated for their rivals to see them and know whether they were in town or not, but at the same time they couldn't resist seeing which of *their* rivals was there. So they all went to the Luk Yu.

And when they celebrated, it was special.

They always did it the same way. There'd be abalone spilling over platters, big steaks, *baat-tow* or eight-head, eight to a catty, smothered in oyster gravy. And then there'd be the pig's lung soup with soaked almonds and stewed pomelo skin. Roast squab with Yunnan ham. Then shark's fin. The victorious ah chan, the one who had scored, would treat all his friends. And two thousand Hong Kong dollars would be stuffed in his favorite waiter's pocket on the way out.

"All right," Stanley said to Gao Yideng. "Until our next meeting." As soon as he clicked off, he dialed his chauffeur. He had an itch to go to Central and sniff his luck on the humid air, see how his destiny hung around him, open his senses to the bracing aromas of portent. "Ah Yip," he said in his customary drawl when the second ring clicked over to his driver's voice. "Bring up the car." He looked at his watch. It was quarter to twelve. "I am of a mind to lunch at the Luk Yu."

"I'LL TAKE THIS one," Lia said to the woman behind the counter, and pointed to a tabletop box of fake Peking enamel, topped with a large brass knob shaped like two mandarin ducks. Her mother would love it. She might even give it a spot on the sideboard in her little dining room, where the cream of her animal canisters from around the world was displayed. This was by no means Anita's only collection but one of her longest-running, and it gave Lia real pleasure to unearth something that would make an addition to it. Her mother had spent years acquiring animal canisters, figurines of Depression glass, geometric trivets, and antique photographs of men in military uniform, to name only a few of her obsessions. Anita had been buying these, scheming over them, placing them and rearranging them for years.

It was always a great moment when she presented a new find to Anita. She could feel the glow between herself and her mother, the light of pleasure that could not be faked. Lia sensed at those moments that she was fulfilling her mother's truest desire, for Anita lived through the lines of her collections and wanted Lia to live there too.

Lia smiled to herself, watching the clerk in the Beijing shop wrap up the faux-enamel box. She loved her mother, even though the constant half-giddy improvisation that was Anita's parenting had included some terrible mistakes.

As a small child Lia had only one annual link with her father, a Christmas card. These cards were among her first treasures. She had whole myth systems around them. He existed; these were his relics. One day she'd find him.

And then when she was nine she learned that all the cards had been written and mailed by her mother. Every year her mother had sat down and invented a message to her daughter, faked another person's handwriting, and gone out and mailed it to her. Anita so needed everything to be right—at least, on the surface, to *look* right—that this for her was a nurturing act. Years later Lia understood. But then, on that day, she felt only rage.

She locked herself in her room. To her waves of tears and her kicking of the wall, Anita kept coming back with her sweet, half-reasonable protests. She'd lost track of him, she'd *wanted* to lose track of him, it had been best, she hadn't wanted Lia to be hurt. Anything to keep her from being hurt. Yet Lia felt at that moment as if she were being more than hurt, worse than hurt, maimed actually, killed by love. "But it's because I love you!" Anita kept calling to her through the door.

Lia threw all the cards, one for each year of her life, into her metal wastebasket. Fakes. They were fakes. She lit a match to them. She knew she would pay for this later, but for once in her life she did not care. They went up in a quick whuff of flames. Only then would she open her door and stand defiantly in front of the little fire, the backs of her legs smarting and tingling from the jumping heat.

Now she was a mature woman and she saw that her mother had done the best she could. Of course she could not remake the world for her daughter. Why would she even try? And yet Lia herself tried, she knew she did; she tried all the time. Her system was just a little different. Better too. She fit the package into her purse and stepped out of the shop into the roaring street.

AT THE SAME time in the south, in Jingdezhen, the ah chan answered his phone. "*Wei.*"

"Old Bai." It was Zhou.

"*Ei,*" Bai answered companionably. In all the loose-knit society of ah chans, there were many who called themselves Bai's friends, but Zhou was one he really trusted. It was Zhou's help he had asked with this job.

"The others are worried," Zhou said.

"About Hu and Sun?" Bai had a bad feeling himself about the two of them trying to move that pair of huge famille-rose vases.

"They've not arrived."

"Oh," Bai said. Not good. Very not good. This was their third day out. Hu and Sun should be in Hong Kong by now.

"They're not there. I've talked to Pak and Ling."

Gentle knots formed in Bai's midsection. "Call Old Lu," he advised. "As soon as there's word in Hong Kong, he'll know."

"All right," Zhou said. "Keep your handphone."

"It's on," Bai assured him. He was walking down the street, taking his wife out to an evening meal.

"I'll call you later."

Bai slipped the phone in his pocket and went on walking with Lili along the putting, honking, cement-and-asphalt streets with their open-mawed retail stores and stalls. Bins spilling out into the street were piled with baskets, metal goods, hardware, but most of all porcelain, because porcelain was the heart and bones of Jingdezhen. Bai bought his wife a length of plum velvet and he saw with satisfaction how the package made an acquiescent weight against her legs, and how she smiled at the feeling of it against her.

He felt good in his fine cotton shirt, open two buttons down, his woven leather shoes. Bai liked to dress as if he were a wealthy Italian stepping off a yacht. An art dealer, a learned man.

It had rained the night before, leaving the low concrete town in a state of fresh-washed June optimism. Bai and Lili turned off Jingyu and walked down a repeating, narrowing pattern of side streets, their road surfaces cracked and potted, sidewalks heaved up around the swelling, pulsing roots of trees. Here in the south, life multiplied almost before one's eyes. It was one of the things that gave Jiangxi Province its red-soiled beauty. They stepped over the erupted, corrugated sidewalk and into the Hui Min, a tiny open-air restaurant.

Lili was the third wife he had taken. Each of the women knew, sketchily, about the others, but they preferred not to know much and also to forget what they did know, as it suited. Each of his wives was from someplace else, as he originally was, undocumented, part of China's floating population. He kept each of them in simple comfort if not in style. They all knew he had more than one place to lay his head, and with all things considered they accepted this. He was like a lot of other ah chans this way. They added wives. It was a tacit return to an old pattern of concubinage, although this was the modern world and one had to keep up appearances. The wives had to be in different places. They couldn't all live under one roof as was done in the past. The ah chans liked to joke to each other that their wives, of radically descending ages, would all meet only once—at the man's funeral.

Neither of Bai's other two wives lived in Jingdezhen. One lived in Houtai Township, a village in the hills forty kilometers north-east. The other—the original girl he had married near home, in his youth, under the naive impression he would remain tied to her forever—still lived outside of Changsha. He visited both of them when he could. He enjoyed seeing them. But Lili was his favorite. She was the love match. She was the newest and the youngest.

Still, here in Jingdezhen, he didn't stay with Lili all the time. He spent many nights in his own simple cement-walled apartment, a place he had bought and with it finally obtained his *hukou,* his residency permit, in Jingdezhen. It had been an important thing to have at the time he bought it and still today had value in the largely privatized economy, for it still got a person certain medical care and benefits and an acknowledged geographic notch in society.

In his own place, Bai liked to stay alone. This was where he kept his books, his collections of auction catalogs, his museum publications, his files of photocopied articles from art magazines and academic journals. If he wanted to be a great dealer one day, he had to learn. He knew it was so.

And as long as he could afford it, as long as he could continue to prevail over his risks, he'd keep Lili in her tidy little room down in the warren of quickie dwellings below Jixing Street. She didn't mind. It was better than the dirt village in which she grew up.

Lili was a good girl, round-faced and red-cheeked. She was completely open to him and he felt safe with her. She loved him without any adult reserve. It made him want to do anything for her. They had married quickly and informally at the county registry office. With her he had begun to think, for the first time, that he might be ready to have a son. Here in Jingdezhen, or—if he really got half a million *ren min bi*—maybe in Hong Kong.

When they married he had brought her to his apartment, just for a few days until he secured her a room down below the lake. The first night he had taken her on the bed. She had lain still with her arms and legs spread, as if nailed to the earth, but she had smiled up at him when he lay over her, her eyes round with surprise and pleasure, and he'd seen how she would learn. Late that night he awoke to see one light burning, on his desk, and to see her elegantly naked back to him, cut down the middle by her black braid, her face bent in wonder over the turned pages of an art book, porcelains, celestial perfections such as she, a village girl, had never seen. He lay perfectly still, watching her. For a moment he just wanted to watch her, her response to beauty, the glow of her pleasure over the rustling pages, while he let his imagination play over what he might do with her next.

And now they entered the restaurant by sidling past its two giant burners out on the root-buckled sidewalk, the powerful flames chuffing up around the woks. The owner let out a hoarse cry of greeting and they called back, loud and good-natured.

They sat in one of the two tables inside the stall, round, covered with white plastic. A tiny electric fan mounted on the wall rotated over them. "Have the eggplant with chiles and onions," he told Lili solicitously. "Have the pork belly with potatoes." Then he beckoned the owner in her sauce-splashed white apron. "Two Pepsis!"

Lili smiled at this unexpected pleasure, her polyester red-checkered sleeve touching his, her arm against him discreetly. He felt the warmth from her. The Pepsi came in big, cold plastic bottles. To him it was a slosh of too-sweet yin, it made his teeth hurt, but was it not what international people drank? And was that not what he was now?

His handphone rang. He fumbled and snapped it open.

"*Ei*," said Zhou.

"You talk to Old Lu?"

"I did."

"And?"

"Nothing."

Bai pushed away the clenching feeling. There was still time. "We have to wait for them to surface," he said to Zhou.

"Aren't you going to Hong Kong?"

"Yes, soon," Bai answered. Nothing explicit needed saying. "I am trusting Hu and Sun will have arrived by the time I get there."

"As am I," answered Zhou.

They hung up and Bai looked back at his wife, her arm still next to his, her face tilted up to him; "Lili," he told her gently. He poured Pepsi into her glass. "I'm going to be away for a while."

JACK YUAN STOOD at the honed limestone counter in his kitchen, watching his wife make coffee. She had a small mouth. When she was concentrating, as she was now, measuring the beans, it hung slightly open to form an O.

"I got a few photos and descriptions in an e-mail this morning," he said. "They're incredible."

He saw the corners of that plum-colored mouth lift: recognition. The opponent was back in the ring. She straightened and poured the water. "You know what I think."

Yes, he knew. She had made herself very clear. Anna Sing, self-confident, daughter of a prominent cardiac surgeon, Jack's match on all fronts, the original material girl. Anna did not want him to buy the porcelain. "Art should not be that much of our portfolio."

He shrugged. She was right. But this was also the kind of opportunity that would never come again.

He looked at her; thirty this year. She glowed with beauty: her skin, her graceful limbs, the life in her eyes. It was impossible to believe she was not healthy in every way. Life should be all but bursting within her. Yet so far, nothing. They should buy the porcelain. Couldn't she see that? "We'll talk about the art later," he said.

She gave him a look that said: You bet we will, Jack. And I'll end up on top. But then she returned the gentleness in his eyes with a softness of her own, slid the pot into place, pressed the ON button, and moved over to where he stood by the counter.

7

LIA WORKED THROUGH EIGHTY POTS THAT day. By now she had found a table and pushed it over to the window under natural light and covered it with extra felt. She had her lights set up, her camera on its stand. She had everything she needed to appraise treasure from heaven.

Only she was alone. There was no one she could whisper to, no one she could call, no one with whom she could exult.

If she could tell anyone she would tell her friend Aline. She looked at her watch. In L.A. it was three in the morning now. Aline would finally be asleep in her secluded place in Coldwater Canyon. She would have drunk too much, smoked too much, and stayed out with her friends too late, then driven home to her true friends, her Ming jars and her Song plates and her Qing jardinieres, not to mention her collection of masterfully faux Etrus-can statuary. Aline had a wonderful eye for fakes. Her prize was a knockoff Stradivarius, which she liked to leave out, on the side-board, its bow carelessly across it as if its owner had just left off playing for a moment. Oh yes. The very thought made Lia shiver with pleasure. Aline would have the breath knocked right out of her if she heard about this. She would get on a plane and fly to Beijing instantly. Lia would be unable to stop her. What fun it would be to call her, to dial her number and wake her up and tell her how many drop-dead pots were in this room, in Beijing, right now, right in front of her.

But she couldn't call Aline. She couldn't call David. "David is doing well," Zheng had told her. "The Tokyo staff is with him. You concentrate." Okay, she thought. And took a deep breath and lifted the lid on the twenty-third crate.

BAI MADE IT out of bed at noon. The damp heat of his studio de-cided for him in the end. The sheets were twisted around his legs when he finally climbed out of them, his face puffy and creased. He dressed and walked in a gravel-crunching rhythm down the hill to town. It was cool, where he was going. It was dark.

He pushed open the door of the Perfect Garden Teahouse. "*Ei,*" he said to the proprietor, and passed through the next set of doors, to the tearoom.

His friends, his circle of smoking, serpentine men, were al-ready there, talking in a mix of Mandarin and local dialect. He crossed to them. Bai loved to wake up at the Perfect Garden. He liked to be in this dimness when it was past noon and the hot sun was shimmering the sidewalks. To drink tea here, to smoke. To talk about the pots coming in and going out. To lounge on the leather-seated chairs around the tables, to smell the dank, sour note of beer from the night before.

They also liked to be here at night. Often they'd be waiting for the shipment of one man or another to arrive. There was always an agreeable gamble in it. One never knew exactly what the piece would be—how fine its condition, how rare its pedigree. Each time was like the first, a new chance, starting over.

They would drink and smoke through the waiting and the wagering and the laughing banter, then like a clap from heaven it would be time and they would roam outside, milling together. Cars would be waiting. They'd go to the river dock, or the back of the train depot, or to any one of the many warehouses down bumpy dirt-track roads out of town where they waited late at night to meet trucks.

Pots came from all over China. Some had been bought from families who had saved them as heirlooms, or *zu chuan*. Others had been robbed from graves, especially the more ancient pieces—but never by the ah chans themselves. Plundering tombs was low work. Men like Bai would never do it. It was with reluctant distaste that they even did business with the men who did. Whatever the source, when the goods came into Jingdezhen they would ride out that dusty track at night to meet them, bumping down between the red loam fields, the rice paddies, and the muddy river.

The truck might be small and the load light. Sometimes those cargoes were the most precious. The lid would come up, and then one of them, say Qing-Enamel Kan, would lift out the wares for which he was known: a snuff bottle in the shape of a gourd, painted in overglaze enamel in a curling design of leaves and vines and smaller gourds.

"*Hoi moon,*" someone would breathe.

Someone else: "Mark and period?"

And Kan would turn it over. A four-character Qianlong mark in seal script.

Who would know, who would be able to connect it? It might be Old Zhang, the most erudite among them. Zhang might say: "See the form of it—the double gourd, covered with a design of smaller double gourds. See the color, the midpoint between tea and gilded gold. Both these aspects are like to a much larger piece, much older, a bronze double gourd inset with jade. It was in the collection of the Shenyang Palace. And in the reign of Qianlong this sort of tribute to it was made."

"*Jiu shi,*" they would say, admiring, Just so.

But on this day in the teahouse, they all sat in a circle, slouched low with their feet spread out. All the phones were on the table. Bai ordered tea, five-spice eggs, and preserved cucumber. Old Zhang shook a cigarette from his pack and extended it, along with a relaxed monosyllable of welcome. Bai took it and uttered the briefest, most implicit thanks. They were friends. Most things had already been understood between them.

He took a drink of tea, lit his cigarette, drew in from it. "Any news?" he said.

Old Zhang shook his head. He knew Bai was talking about Hu and Sun. "They aren't there yet."

"No one has heard from them?"

"No one."

"Maybe by the end of the day," Bai said.

Old Zhang tightened his mouth. He knew, they both knew, it was really too late already. Their two friends should have been in Hong Kong by now, celebrating, having passed their pair of four-foot famille-rose vases down the line to the next owner and pocketed the substantial difference.

But they hadn't. No one had heard from them. The men around the table passed silent prayers up.

Two younger men from Ningbo went back to paging through a catalog from an art auction house in Shanghai. "See this fine ox-blood plate, Xuande reign—"

"That! You call that fine? That's only the midrange of fine."

"Blow gas."

"It's so!"

"He's right," put in Han Fengyi from across the table. "I've seen that plate! I had the chance to buy it five years ago. I turned it down!"

"Suck pustules! You did not!"

They all laughed.

"I did! It was too expensive!"

"Yes, and in Sichuan dogs bark at the sun," Bai retorted, which was a way of accusing Han of being afraid of his own shadow. They were merciless with Han. He was one of the few among them who attached himself slavishly to one dealer, supplying him as faithfully as a dog. The rest of them freelanced. Their business was fluid. They carried greater risks but their wins were fine, sometimes superb.

"Listen now," Bai said quietly to his friend Zhou, seated next to him. The others were talking. No one else was listening. Zhou put down his polished wooden chopsticks.

"I have a big job coming up," Bai said. "Transportation." He turned his teacup to swirl the last few drops. "I'm going to need help."

Zhou refilled Bai's cup.

"I'm going to Hong Kong tomorrow," Bai said. "Carrying a few things and picking up some cash. Then when I come back—"

"Call me," said Zhou. "Let me know when you're ready."

"I will," said Bai. He would pay Zhou a few thousand *ren min bi* to do the overnight driving so Bai could save himself for the ordeal of crossing the border. That final gauntlet he would run alone. Zhou knew this. It didn't need to be said.

Bai smiled. This deal was brilliant, bright as the sun, that bright. He saw the avidity on Zhou's face. The plan had that streaking, powerful feeling, the unmistakable scent of luck.

"Good," he said after a minute. He liked the way it was growing around him.

THERE WAS ONE other person Lia was longing to tell about these pots, and that was her former stepfather, Albert. He loved porcelain. He didn't have much money, but he knew to buy wonderful things in less than perfect condition. During the years he'd lived with Lia and Anita, two pieces stood in the dining room: a globular water pot with a mottled tea-green glaze, Kangxi period, and a chrysanthemum-shaped bowl in celadon from the reign of Qianlong. They were miraculous. They shone with their own light. And Albert made her feel that it was all right to sense a connection to objects, because objects in their perfection resembled love. And when they were imperfect, you loved them for their flaws too. As it was in life. She remembered holding the pale chrysanthemum-shaped bowl, with its curving ribs, to her cheek and feeling its diamond-clean glaze on her skin.

She'd looked him up again as an adult. He lived overseas most of the time now, but they'd managed to meet in New York six or seven years before.

Typical for Albert, he'd wanted to meet at the Met. There was an exhibit of Chinese scholar-objects he thought they ought to see. As she ran up the stairs she saw him standing at the top, his suit as shapeless as ever and he more corpulent within it. His face was ruddier and his eyes more pouched with age. But his brushy mustache was the same, as was the kind smile in his eye.

"Lia!" he said happily. "Look at you." He took her in, her rangy height, her same long hair, only now she was a woman, grown-up and graceful.

She raised her brows ironically and made some joke of it. Now, looking back, it was clear she'd been younger and more attractive then, though at the time she hadn't thought so at all. Then she never thought she looked good enough. Always it seemed she could only appreciate herself in arrears. She was never happy to be exactly what she was at any present moment.

They walked together into the exhibit, past brush rests and water pots and scholars' rocks, calligraphy and table screens and vases, paperweights, boxes for seal vermilion, and inkstones. Walking beside Albert, talking, sharing memories of Anita and her things, Lia felt a sense of family love completed. It was only for a minute, and it was only a wisp, but she felt it. Why couldn't you have been my father? she thought, the way she often had as a child.

"Tell me about your work at Hastings," he said.

She could see the pride in his eyes. "Best job in the world! I don't know how it happened. I get to look at pots all the time. I mean, that's actually what I get paid to do."

"And who could deserve it more?" he said. They had paused in front of a brush holder made of *zitan* wood, burled and rolled like rushing water. Seeing it brought the past to life: the smell of charcoal in the brazier, the propulsive movement of the scholar's brush on silk. It was just one facet, only an instant, but it was a world. And now it was in her memory.

"Are you married yet?" Albert was asking. She saw him looking at her hand, which bore no ring.

"No."

"No one?"

She made a rueful twist of her mouth. "I'm waiting. You know."

"You have time," he said kindly.

"I know."

"You're unique, Lia. The right person will come."

He meant it nicely, but she felt a sad thud at the well of perceptions she knew was behind it. She was not beautiful in the traditional way, though she had her own grace, a sort of serene allure that was the meeting point of intelligence and physicality. Still, she had no glamour. And so many men, even smart men, wanted beautiful women above all. Not women like her, not obsessive, hyper-internal women with thoughtful eyes and tightly pulled-up hair who lived in alternate mental worlds.

She couldn't think about this now. She had been pushing feverishly all day and she had to keep going. She put her hands into the crate, sank them into the pliant little wood spirals, and felt for the next box.

SHE TRIED TO change her clothes before going out to eat in the evening, but it degenerated into another joust of self-doubt. Lia wasn't much good at her appearance. Even the hipper, more attenuated look practiced by worldly women of her generation didn't work for her. Most things she tried just looked wrong.

So she'd settled into layering knits to reasonably flatter the straight line of her body and carry her through all situations. It worked, even if it was only an accessory or two away from a uniform.

Tonight, though, she didn't like anything she had brought. She should be creative. She rooted through the drawer. She should buy something else. She stood in front of the mirror in her underwear, plain cotton, because when she was alone she wore only the most comfortable things, and undid her hair. It fell past her waist. She generally hated going out with it down; there was too much of it, it was too loose in the world, it attracted attention. Sometimes she clipped it at the back of her neck. She did that now.

For the rest, she would compromise. She settled on a close-fitting knit vest and a narrow bias-cut skirt. It almost didn't matter what she wore or what she did, she thought as she darkened her mouth with lipstick. She was still going to look dry and old-fashioned. Or maybe not. Her eyes were big and gray, not bad at all. She smiled and saw how it transformed her. And she picked up her purse and went out.

CURATOR LI WAS on the Internet, scrolling through museum sites and reading newsletters. He was searching for some mention of this thing about which he was still hearing whispers, this movement of a large number of pots. Nothing stayed hidden forever. If it existed he'd find it. Maybe here, in the electronically webbed art world.

Li jumped from a London-based art magazine to a Hong Kong auction house and watched the screen fill up with images. Nothing. Frustration hooked into him and gave a sharp, cynical pull. Was the story real or false?

He quit the server and turned away from the screen to a newspaper article. Their museum seemed to draw mixed public reaction no matter how much good it did. Last week they had bid on and failed to win an important piece of Tang ceramic statuary, more than a thousand years old. In the eyes of the public, they had failed to bring the piece home. What could they do! They had bid to the limit of their budget this time.

But there might be these pieces, on the move. Maybe he could stop them, though he wasn't sure how. All he could do was keep looking. And keep asking.

MICHAEL DOYLE WALKED out into the hutong the next morning to go to work and saw an American woman with a satchel and computer bag waiting at the gate. She had a long braid. Her back was turned to him. "Are you staying here?" he asked her.

She jumped. She hadn't heard him. He was used to this; people were startled by him. They said he moved like a cat, big as he was. But then he also saw she wore hearing aids. "I didn't mean to walk up on you," he said.

"It's okay."

And he saw her wary expression relax into one of bright-eyed humor. He liked her smile. She was nearly as tall as he was, though slighter. He smiled back.

"Yes, I'm staying here," she said.

"I haven't seen you."

She had seen him. "I haven't been here long."

He looked her over, all her bags, her quirky work clothes. "What're you doing in Beijing?"

"I'm here to look at art." This was her standard answer; it was truthful but limited. "I do pots." She took out a card and handed it to him. The card was the quickest way to convey everything, her credentials, her affiliation. Most people didn't know anything about porcelain, or what it meant to "do pots," but Hastings was a well-known name. People's faces always notched with understanding when they glanced at her card.

"Lia Frank," he read. He slipped a card out of his back pocket and held it out to her. He was broad but she saw his hands were fine, and the hair down to his wrist soft and sand-colored. She took the card. *Michael Doyle, Biochemist, Chongwen Children's Hospital.* On the other side the same thing in Chinese. "Are you a doctor, or a researcher?"

"Researcher. On a fellowship. I'm studying children's lead levels in Beijing."

"Oh! That's important. Good for you."

"Thanks," he said.

"Sounds depressing, though."

"It is, if I let it be. At the end of each day I try to forget. You know?"

"I do know," she said in a soft voice, thinking: Remembering? Forgetting? You have no idea.

"What's in your duffel?" he said.

"Tools. Everything for looking at pots." She touched the leather in a note of protection.

"And with all your tools, what is it you look for?"

She looked at him, her big eyes brimming with amusement, long quick fingers twined through her shoulder strap. Her hair was pulled up tight away from her face, and she could feel the faint pleasing weight of her silver hoops in her ears. "Fakes," she said.

"Ah. You mean forgeries?"

"Exactly what I mean."

"So forgery must interest you greatly."

"It does."

"I have a friend you should meet."

"Really?" She could feel herself rising out of her long legs, chest against her shirt.

"He's into fakes."

"Is he a dealer?"

"No! But he does make money from fakes."

"You mean that's his job?"

"No. He works with me. This is a thing he does on the side."

Her mouth was half open now, interest pulling it up at the corners. "What? Tell me."

"I could. Or," he said. He wore the bemused look of someone talking on his feet, half surprising himself. "Or you could come with me and find out." He moved his weight lightly from foot to foot. "Come look at fakes with me and An. We're going anyway. Day after tomorrow."

She gave him a half smile. "How can I resist, if it has to do with fakes?"

"I'll leave you a note, when and where. What room are you in?"

"Seventeen," she said.

"Ah. Side court?"

"Side court."

"I've got to go," he said.

"And believe it or not"—she pointed down the lane to a far-off car whining toward them—"there's my ride too. It was nice to meet you. Michael, right?"

"Doyle," he said. "Call me Doyle."

"Oh?" She turned her gaze on him. "Really?"

"That's what people call me. See you," he said, and still smiling, he turned and walked away. He could hear the car grinding to a stop behind him, door opening and slamming, the engine roaring up and then evaporating away down the hutong.

His mind went to the hearing aids. So she had hearing loss. But as soon as they'd started talking he'd forgotten about it. They had just clicked into conversation.

And he made a plan to see her again. That was odd, for him.

Especially because he could tell she was smart and offbeat. She was interesting, and thus at the beginning the bar was already bumped up. She was also pretty, in a way. And serious. He saw this from her reserved, intelligent mien and the controlled light in her eyes, and her business card, even. The serious type. Probably looking for a good man. He couldn't be anybody's good man. Not in the foreseeable future, anyway.

Since his marriage ended he'd had his liaisons. He still needed to make love; that at least was intact in him. He still had to hold women, please them, and explode in vulnerability with them as much as he ever had. But caring was not something he could reawaken. So he limited himself to women who wanted lighter attachments. That was what he looked for now.

He touched the card in his pocket. There was no point in misleading her. He'd take her to meet his friend An Xing; they would look at fakes, the three of them, together. It would be fun and diverting and then it would be over. How lovely. Lovely to meet you. Good-bye.

He slipped his headphones out of his shoulder bag as he walked and turned on Cheb Khaled. He loved *rai* music. The Algerian singers were so brave, so irresistible to the part of him that just cockily believed he could do it, walk out on the gangplank and keep living. *Rai* was vital, secular, sexy, and just for singing it some of the musicians had been shot by Muslim fanatics. The rest of them kept singing.

Especially he loved listening to *rai* in China. Here he was already out of place. He was thick-bodied and pale in the sea of Chinese, arms swinging loose, the opposite of all the people around him. Yet when he was out in the hutong, if he had that sinuous, wavering voice in Arabic filling his head, everything seemed right. The world was foreign, he was foreign. It fit. He walked lightly over the stones, happy for a few minutes in his music and his otherness and the quality of the north China light.

THE AH CHAN Bai leaned his head against the train window, rattling south on the rail line from Nanchang to Hong Kong. The red dirt walked away from the tracks in neat squares, dividing the rice paddies that terraced down to the river. From the froth of greenery on the other side rose the single tower of Fo Liang Temple, its roofs graduating one atop the other toward the sky.

With his ankles Bai squeezed the tied-together boxes of the few pots he had just procured in Yanjing. None were imperial wares but all were fine heirloom pieces. He had paid well for them—well for inside China, anyway. That sum was nothing compared with what they would fetch for him in Hong Kong.

His eyes followed the slow brown river as the rails clacked and the future spun out in his head. Down by the water, cattails waved in feathery golden clumps and morning glories, brilliant purple, twined up the red-dirt banks. It would take nine hours to reach the border. There would be a heart-pounding moment through Customs, but he had receipts showing that these were reproductions made by manufacturers in Jingdezhen. It was believable. The receipts looked right. The pots were good, though not breathtaking.

He carried the boxes exposed, wrapped in plastic twine. Sometimes the best way to do it was openly, brazenly, with some paperwork to make it look right and a crowd all around him to swirl him through. Stopping at the counter, handing over his passport, holding his breath. Undistinguished. One of the crowd. A stamp, a wave. Then he'd be through, with money, enough for a while.

It was enough cash to get himself a truly superb fake too. He knew exactly what he wanted. When he came back home to Jingdezhen he was going to see the man he considered one of the earth's greatest living porcelain artists. And he was going to commission a replica of the Chenghua chicken cup.

8

THE NEXT DAY SHE OPENED THE TWENTY-eighth crate and took the first pot from it. She drew a sharp breath of joy. It was a Ming moon flask, blue and white, depicting a dragon swimming among scrolled lotus blossoms. She could see it was from the reign of Yongle, the early 1400s.

She lifted it. Ratio of weight to mass was very important. It was invisible to the eye alone, and sometimes overlooked by those who fashioned replicas. The composition and density of clay, the exact mode of firing . . . everything had to fit. Lia could sense how much a thing should weigh. When she surrounded a piece with her fingers and lifted it, she knew a little more about whether it was real or false.

Though she herself went by feeling, she had

the computer take the weight too. She activated the scale feature and clicked down the top of her laptop, which in this position took readings to a hundredth of an ounce. Weight and dimensions were transferred by the computer into the appraisal report. She took the flask up again and turned it every way. So *hoi moon*. So ideally shaped. And such a sedate, noble hue to the Yongle cobalt design.

Yet there was something else that had caught her eye about it: its box. Glued along the bottom, on one edge, ran a thin strip of crumbly yellow silk. Some kind of mark, most likely, from an inventory or catalog. She centered the flask on her felt tray and took up the box and turned it over.

After the last royal family moved out, several attempts had been made to list and assess what was in the Forbidden City. Mostly they were sporadic, partial stabs at a job so huge it was almost impossible to complete. And of course, everything had ended on the night in 1931 when Japan had occupied Manchuria and the art had to be carried out of the Palace.

But each time Palace officials had tried to sort through what they had, they'd hired people, made plans—they'd kept records, which were left behind. And they also left all manner of histories and lists and schedules. Lia had seen quite a few of these. They were in her memory.

She sat on the floor against a rolled-up rug that braced her back. She needed a minute of quiet to go down to the bottom. She was looking for this particular cataloging effort—the one that had marked its boxes with strips of yellow silk. She wanted to fix it in time. Then there'd be one more point in the chronology, one more moment when she knew these pots were still inside the Palace walls.

She took her hearing aids out. The emptiness inflated in her and she felt the familiar wash of pleasure and acceptance. There were the gates to the memory world; there was the way inside. She walked the brick lanes, reviewing what she knew. She found discrete nuggets; records, photos, newspaper accounts, Palace documents, and memorials. After a while they came together to form the picture in her mind.

In March, 1924, a young man awoke in Peking.

It was the tapping of his Ayi on the rice-paper-and-wood-lattice window that awakened him, her melodious voice saying his name. He pulled the quilts closer about himself. Not yet.

Then he remembered. Last night his father had spoken to him of a new post, with the Committee for the Disposition of the Qing Imperial Household Possessions. It was perfect for him. His education had been classical, aiming him, as thirty-eight generations before him had been aimed, at success in the imperial examinations. Yet he would be the first of his line not to sit for them. They had been abolished. The old examination yards had been knocked down.

He dressed quickly in the frigid room, lighting only the small oil lamp, leaving the brazier cold. He secured his trousers at the ankles and then fitted a gown shaped like a close sleeveless jacket over his shirt. Out of the room he hurried, across the flagstones and through the open gate to the Chrysanthemum Court. It was not time for chrysanthemums. It was Third Month. The air was wet and spiked with cold. The Gobi dust had not yet blown in to cover everything with its fine silt.

Breakfast was hand-cut noodles in a soup of young chicken, mantou, pickled vegetable, and green tea. The Wens ate lightly in the morning.

Guangyu took his place at the table opposite his white-haired father, in a low wooden chair inset with natural marble that falsely appeared to be an ink painting of mountains among clouds.

"Second Director Tian of the Committee sent his valet here this morning," said Guangyu's father.

Guangyu inclined his head.

"You are to go there today and talk to him." The older man knew this work would suit his son. Guangyu did better with art than anything else. And it was an official post too—of a sort.

So Guangyu went downtown to an office near the rear gate of the Forbidden City and met Second Director Tian.

The young man found the Second Director preoccupied behind stacks of aging, crumbling inventories, their spidery archaic characters organized according to forgotten systems and principles.

So many back courts in the Palace had been closed off, dust-covered, unused for many decades, and yet were filled, stacked, with boxes from floor to ceiling. Guangyu knew this; it was a thing about which art lovers whispered. There were scrolls, rare books, textiles, porcelains, paintings, bronzes, enamels, calligraphies, diamonds, jade, treasures from all the corners of the empire and from beyond all seven oceans. All of it jumbled together, piled up, half forgotten.

Guangyu stood in the Second Director's office, nervous in his well-made gown. He was educated. He could recite the Five Classics and develop an elegant eight-legged essay on any Confucian citation. None of that mattered anymore.

"Mr. Wen. How fast can you write?"

"How fast?" Guangyu thought he might have heard wrong. *"I suppose . . . forty characters a minute."*

"Oh! Very good." Second Director smiled. *"The job is yours."*

Guangyu stared. Did the man really not care for his academic rank? His knowledge of art?

Tian pulled out a sheet of paper and swirled his brush. *"What objects would you like to list?"* He looked up when Guangyu did not answer. *"Come!"* he said. *"Paintings, jade, bronzes, porcelains—"*

"Porcelains," Guangyu said.

"Porcelains." Tian wrote directions on a piece of paper and handed it to Guangyu with a smudgily printed map. *"Go to number twenty-four,*

the Pavilion for Listening to Cicadas. Rear court, southeast room. Begin there."

Guangyu looked at the map.

"And here," said Tian. He handed the young man a roll of yellow silk tape. "Every box you list should have a strip of this glued to the bottom." Tian held up two fingers to show Guangyu how long the strip was to be. "Otherwise you will lose your way. There are too many works." He smiled again. "You will see."

Guangyu made a reverence, offered his thanks, and went away down the hutong, past the gangs of children shouting rhymes, the old men airing caged birds, the women carrying home food. He crossed the street, darting in a youthful pulse of excitement between the rickshas and carts and sputtering motorcars. Men on foot formed a soft, dark-moving tide of gowns and fedoras. Itinerant vendors offered fruit and hot teas. Ruddy-faced market women rearranged their vegetables.

He passed a few girls of his own class too, well-bred girls, avoiding his eyes as they were trained to avoid the eyes of all men, hidden behind robes, nothing of them visible except dark eyes and the slim fluttering ends of fingers. He walked past them, clutching his map and his roll of yellow silk tape, to the rear entrance of the Forbidden City.

A guard examined his paper and waved him through. Guangyu had never imagined he would enter this part of the Palace. Until just recently the last Qing emperor, Pu Yi, had lived here.

Now in front of him lay the imperial garden. He turned away from the artistic arrangement of rocks and twisted trees, the famous viewing pavilion. The marble balustrades, the paving stones of mosaics and fossils, the aged and massive Joined-Together Cypress, all of these he saw, awestruck, but kept walking. Here were the pavilions that had once housed the minor females, the passed-over concubines, their handmaids and eunuchs. Past the Palace of Pure Affection and the Palace of Southern View, then an opening, a turn to the right, and he found himself on a narrow street running north–south, which was flanked by high, tile-roofed walls. Everything was empty and silent. He stepped through a gate in the east wall that took him away from the larger ceremonial buildings—the Hall of Worshiping Ancestors and the Palace in Honor of Talent, in which, if Guangyu remembered correctly, congratulations were traditionally offered on the birth of a son. Away from these he entered a dusty labyrinth of smaller courts, barred by massive ceramic-tile spirit screens and topped by roofline arrangements of guardian animal figures. Between the broken, abandoned paving stones, tufts of grass pushed up. There were acres of this. He still had not seen another person.

Here. He stepped over a half-rotted wooden sill, into the Pavilion for Listening to Cicadas. He stepped up on the porch of the southeast room and peered through the dirt-streaked glass. It was impossible to see anything. Were those piles of boxes? He tried the door. It opened.

It was dark. Dust powdered up in his mouth and nose. He lit a small military-style oil lamp. The yellow glow jumped on the cluttered objects that filled the room and threw strange shadows against the high walls. It was cold. The ash on the little charcoal brazier had gone greasy with time.

Guangyu clapped his hands together for warmth. Boxes were stacked up of every size, from the smallest, to hold a miniature carving or an exquisite little inkstone, up to boxes half a meter high that might hold bronzes or urns. Some of the boxes were covered in brocade, but most were the indigo cloth favored by antiquarians, museums, and merchants. The whole heap was dusted with Peking's yellow silt.

He turned to the pile nearest him, positioned the oil lamp, and opened the first one. He looked in. Time stopped. On its side, in a custom-crafted nest of snowy white, lay a moon flask in underglaze blue. Around its globe-swollen base a dragon swam, its yellow eyes blazing amid the lotuses. From the reign of Yongle, he thought. Or maybe Xuande. He tipped it over to look. Yongle.

He put the flask in its box and laid out his writing things. His best boat-shaped ink stick. It had a poem by Du Fu stamped on it and a most graceful swirl of clouds. It dissolved into water to make wonderful ink, with a pigment that made his characters flow like yifan fengxu, a boat in good wind. He wetted it and ground it in his inkstone.

He pressed back his journal book and began to write: Inventory of the Pavilion for Listening to Cicadas, southeast room. A blue-and-white moon flask, the dragon swimming through the lotus. Made in the reign of Yongle. *Then he stopped, and cut a narrow strip of yellow silk ribbon, and glued it on a bottom corner of the box. Done, recorded, marked.*

Lia sat in the big room at the villa, amid the crates, holding the Yongle moon flask in underglaze blue on white. The dragon was so delicately delineated. The jar a perfect sphere in her hands, closing to an impossibly narrow and elegant neck. It was a full moon of articulate form, lovely and lovely forever.

Now she knew it had been in the Palace as of 1924. It had been in the inventory done during that year. She was closer. A little closer, anyway. Here in the modern world, the real world, she held the same box marked with a faded strip of yellow silk in her hands.

DOYLE WAS ON his way to the Haidian District of Beijing with his friend and colleague An Xing to pick up a child's baby tooth. The mother had called this morning. Her daughter's tooth had come out the night before.

They always went out to the homes together. An did the talking in Chinese, and Doyle provided the conservative, calming presence. With his thin, straight, almost colorless hair falling forward in his eyes and his burly, benign physicality, he looked more respectable than An, who kept his long graying hair in a ponytail and on this day wore an African National Congress T-shirt.

All the children in the study had been measured at birth by their cord blood. All of them were worse than that baseline now, according to their shed teeth, every one; this was clear even though the measures for lead in blood and in the solid tissue of a tooth were not directly compatible. A few years before, Beijing had stopped the worst of the air pollution by changing to unleaded gas and closing down some coal power plants, all to win the Olympics. Whatever it took, was Doyle's opinion. He and An hoped that soon they were going to see the rates of lead toxicity level off.

"Dr. Yang, thank you, thank you," Michael said politely, and An translated to the woman, dressed and faintly impatient to leave for work. She handed him the tooth wrapped in a bit of paper. She was a university professor, he had noted from the file. Doctorate in meteorology. Seeing the families, meeting them, was a thing that remained hard for him. Sometimes it threw him off track all day. "Tell her we'll send her a letter in three weeks with the child's current levels," he told An.

An translated, and even Michael understood her response.

"Fine," she said.

The two men briefly locked eyes and bit back other things that might have been discussed, for the mother didn't want to hear. This was the part Michael Doyle couldn't really get. If it were his child he would be all over the researcher wanting to know what it meant and what he could do. But it was not his world. Not his child.

Yet there were a few children in the study he had come to care for. Gong Ping, the daughter of another hospital co-worker, and Little Chen, who had developed leukemia and been back to the hospital often. He kept them in a special spot in his mind. But with the others he couldn't care, he had to release them to their fates—like Xiaoli, the little girl who lived here. He could follow them. He could document. Someone else had to do the rest.

Outside the apartment he pressed his bulky body lightly against the edge of the hall window frame and watched through the glass as Dr. Yang stepped out of the building down below and walked away up the street, her steps snapping against the sidewalk. She was small, compact, professionally dressed. Then An came out with the tiny tooth in a glassine envelope, labeled, in its box. *"Zou-ba,"* he said, sliding it into his pocket, Let's go.

DOYLE WOKE UP the next morning on his back, not sure where he was for a second, in his old low-slung fifties house in Mar Vista maybe, where the light had poured in through the glass walls over the banana plants, the birds of paradise, the spreading ficus. He had lived there with Daphne, his wife, small and round-shouldered and curly-headed, the opposite of this American woman he'd just met.

Daphne was a lawyer. They'd been satisfied by each other, by who they were and their positions in the world—that was part of their magic. They had the gratification of the well-placed partner. Their love brought that kind of happiness.

But her feeling for him was burned out by the long storm of loving him through his illness. She crawled with him all the way to the wet edge of dying. It was beyond intimacy and fear. He felt she'd give anything to make him live. At times that was what kept him breathing. Much later he realized she was saying good-bye. Maybe both were true. He did survive. And she left, because things never worked between them again.

But now he was a world away, in China. He had a different life.

He knew its boundaries. And he knew every inch of himself now too. He put his hands on his abdomen, pressing it, circling the mysterious float of forms and functions inside him, feeling for the grain, the pea, the tiny pebble that did not belong. The tumors could easily come back. The chance of it happening again was high. And so he checked, he felt, he knew his body as well and as far down inside as a man possibly could using his own hands against his skin. He did this to comfort himself. Each time he did it he felt as if he had bought himself another day. He could go forward. And forget what he would never have. Just forget it.

He stretched, letting go of it. He looked at the clock. Time to get going.

ON HOLLYWOOD ROAD in Hong Kong, Bai watched as Unloader Ma took the crate out of the back of the truck and walked it gently up to the edge of the sidewalk, under the awning of the building. When it was snug against the wall, out of the sidewalk's bobbing stream of people, he stepped back and sent a formal nod to Uncrater Leung, who stood off to the side under the awning, relaxed, smoking a cigarette. Leung dropped his cigarette, stepped on it, and walked to the crate. He eyed it a moment, then began taking out delicate little prying tools, producing from his many-pocketed vest everything he needed to tap the crate open and prize out its securing tacks and nails. Everything—every nail, every ounce of packing material, every scrap of wastepaper, every spiral of wood shaving—would be thoughtfully packed away by him for reuse. Now he had the crate open and the pink tissue was flying.

Much as he wanted to stay and see the treasures about to emerge, at that moment Dealer Ng opened the door and beckoned him inside. Bai followed him. "You have something nice for me?" Dealer Ng said over his shoulder.

"Very nice." Bai smiled because he carried the famille-verte plate, famille-rose vase, and the Qianlong bowl in *falang cai*. He knew the dealer was going to like them.

Ng took Bai into his back room and poured tea, then set the plate, the bowl, and the vase out on the rimmed, felt-covered table. He turned up the lights, a specially installed spectrum. And only after a careful, harrowing examination did he erupt with admiration and pronounce them, with great pleasure, very *hoi moon*. They discussed price, at some length, and enjoyed it, and leavened the process further through the prolonged viewing of additional pots. They consumed tea and reached agreement.

And then came the information exchange.

"What's going on in Jingdezhen?" Dealer Ng asked. His voice was light but he was listening hard. He knew the ah chan understood: Who was making what. What copies were coming down the pipe.

Bai dropped to a low tone. "There is a potter named Yang Shu making a substantial series of monochromes, borrowing from the Song. Also, someone at the Institute is making a set of twelve-month cups." Bai would never trade his most prized artist contacts, like his highly esteemed friend Potter Yu, on this modest bargain. "Now if I may have the benefit of *your* opinion." Bai brought out a photograph of a Qianlong overglaze enamel vase.

Ng looked at it, tipped down his glasses. "Lovely. It is very like one that has been written up in the Idemitsu collection." He went to his side wall and pulled an exhibition catalog from a long, tight-packed shelf. "See," he said, opening the book.

Bai saw. The style of decoration, the range of hues from the famille-verte palette, the particular mustard and brick and green, the pattern along the rim. "Trouble you to copy this page?" he asked.

"Of course." Dealer Ng processed a few pages through a machine and handed them over, to the ah chan's ornate thanks.

They settled in cash. As soon as the Mainland man was paid, Ng felt impatient for him to leave. The dealer wanted to be alone with his new acquisitions, to call his most treasured friends. He would close the shop, they'd come over, he'd bring out his best tea. Ah, if others knew the delight of holding objects of divine beauty for a time, having them to show your friends—if others knew, everyone would want them. And everyone would become an art dealer.

Bai sensed the dismissal. He offered a concise string of formal thanks and good-byes. But even as the ah chan turned to the door, his cell phone was ringing and he was digging it out to answer it. "*Ei!*" he said when he heard his friend's voice. "Now? Yes? All right. The Luk Yu. I'll be right there." He turned back again, inclined his head once more, and was gone.

Ng Fan watched him through the glass until he vanished beyond the edge of the gallery's windows. The dealer went to the front door and locked it. He dialed down the store lights. Then he drew out his mobile and called his friend Stanley Pao.

"*Ei,*" Stanley answered.

"It's me," Ng Fan said. He listened. Through the phone he could hear the air conditioner going there in Stanley's porcelain room. He could see Stanley sitting there, white hair slicked back, comfortable paunch, face lined in well-lived elegance. "I have a few things for you," Ng said. "Some real stars."

"Mmm." The older man's voice took its time, as always, to consider. Then he said: "I'll come over."

MICHAEL DOYLE HAD slipped a note under her door with the address of a teahouse on Dizhimen and the time, seven o'clock, and when she got there she found him waiting, talking to a Chinese man in his forties with a gray ponytail. They waved her to their table.

"Lia Frank," Doyle said with a brief gesture, "meet An Xing." The American man gleamed with delight. He sat upright, pulled in around his center, hands on the table.

"Fan Luo Na," Lia said, indicating herself. "Pleased." She and An exchanged cards.

"Ah, you are a real specialist," An said, looking at her card.

She laughed, pushing this away as she glanced at his. "You work at Chongwen Hospital too?"

"You speak," he said. "Very good. Yes. We work in the same research."

"Right. The lead project."

"Yes. You know, Tong Madou"—Michael's Chinese name— "has told me you are very good at spotting fakes."

"Well," she said, "I hope so. It's my job."

An snapped open a black faux-lizard attaché case. "Take a look at these."

She started. Inside were dozens of pairs of sunglasses in neat rows, all expensive designer models. "Whoa, some collection."

"Thank you. Miss Fan, I hope it is some fun we can have. It's like this. These are the real lines, the current imported designer glasses. Look closely. Then we'll go out in the street, where they are selling them; we'll look for fakes."

"Okay . . ." She looked again at the glasses, not connecting with the reason for this. Of course they'd find fakes. Fakes were everywhere in China. There was a huge demand for products, especially name brands. Everybody wanted to be a player, and if real props weren't available, fakes would do. So fakes abounded. "But why?" she said.

Doyle leaned his upper body forward a few inches. "There's a law in Beijing," he said in English. "If you catch someone selling you a fake, they have to return you double your money. Double!"

"*That's* interesting."

"Theoretically at least, the consumer does have a few rights. But making it happen"—he grinned across the table—"that takes a man like An."

"Yes," the Chinese man said. "And it's true that right now I specialize in sunglasses. But I do whatever interests me at the moment." He held up a pair of Lauren frames. "These are nice."

She picked up the soft cable of her hair and looped it back over her shoulder. She could feel the American's eyes on the expert turn of her hand. "They are nice," she agreed.

"I will tell you," An said. "There are more subtle distinctions than you think. This is high academic stuff. Seriously."

The waitress brought their tea. Lia had ordered pine flavor, a tall frozen-slush mix of tea, milk, sugar, and sweet pine essence. They drank and talked, and all the while she studied the contents of the case. Prada and Fendi and Dior, frames gleaming in the open case.

"Okay," she said when everyone had drained their glasses, "I'm ready." They went out and walked down the boulevard, and after a while turned east into Han Leng Hutong. She could see it was a prime spot to look for fakes, a lane crowded with upscale stores. In front of the stores stretched a long bank of stalls selling sweaters and cookware and hairpieces and toys, lots of voices and bantering and people.

"Halfway down on the right," An said. "See that store? You're a foreigner. It's perfect. Go in alone."

"Okay." She walked away from him and Michael. The light cloth of her skirt eddied at her knees. She could feel them watching her from behind.

Here was the shop; she turned and went in. The bell tinkled above the door. It was crisply air-conditioned. All the sunglasses were arrayed on Lucite shelves, plenty of space between them as befitted their price tags. Lia walked slowly around the store, taking the glasses in, snapshot-quick at first and then pausing, combing through the details. Armani had the gilt shadow drop behind the logo. Blass had the oval paper label on the earpiece, electric blue. Prada had a certain tag. And this was Western civilization.

Then she came on a sleek pair of black and silver Fendi wrap-arounds. One glance, nothing. Second glance, she felt the secret righteousness start to rise. Oh yes. This pair was not right.

The tag didn't have the quota import code. It had to, if it had come from Italy.

She looked at it a little more, then pretended to occupy herself with several more pairs. After a minute she left. She walked up the hutong to them. Michael stood with his hands in his pockets, loose button-down shirt tucked in. In contrast to his top half, she saw he had such narrow hips and legs that his khakis fell all but uninterrupted from his belt.

"Hey," she said, a quick, smiling American syllable, and then turned to An in Chinese. "Are you ready? Fendis. Center, a little to the right when you walk in. Black and silver. The quota code is missing from the tag."

"Fan Luo Na!" he said. "You're keen as a knife." He handed the case to Michael and was gone.

"Impressive," Doyle said with a smile.

"Come on." She saw that his eyeteeth pushed out a little. She liked that. He had a round mouth and it might have been too sweet, on a man, but the teeth gave him an air of license, so she noticed anytime he smiled, she wanted to smile too. "How long have you lived here?" she said.

"Eight months. I'm on a two-year fellowship."

"It's a choice."

"It is."

"Why China? Just the work?"

"No," he said. His small brown eyes, deep-set under low brows, glanced away from her. "It's never just the work, is it?"

"Not usually."

He gave a small rumbling laugh that said he was weak, only a man, but at least he forgave himself. "Here's what happened. I had cancer. It was bad. In the end I beat it, at least into remission. Although that's the thing about cancer, it's always there with you. Even if it seems to be gone." He stopped and looked at her. He wanted her to hear him. There was a zing of connection between them, he could feel it, and as he'd learned over time, that meant she could feel it too. But he was a poor risk for any placement of affections. She was nice, he didn't want to hurt her. He thought of himself as honorable. He was the big-shouldered, well-meaning one who was always kind to women, took care not to use them, was not above taking pleasure just for pleasure but was careful where he took it. He pushed the fine, straight hair off his forehead. "And so you can never really be sure about things. Anyway, then, at least, I got better. And after that my wife and I split up. So." He pushed his hands deep down in his pockets. "Good time to move."

"I guess so. My God."

"Life," he said.

"Life. I'm glad you're okay, though. Really. I am."

"Well." He rolled his eyes, the who-knows roll.

She was looking at him carefully. "I understand something about your room now," she said. "I saw it. It's very plain. It's not like the other rooms in the court, is it? It's more like someone's way station. At the time, I couldn't understand it. And now you tell me this, and I do."

He was a few beats back. "You saw my room?"

"Yes. I was walking through the guesthouse. This was before we met. I just walked back there without thinking. You turned on the light. I stood there for a minute and watched you through the window."

"Ah."

"Just for a minute. And then I left." She paused. "I hoped I'd meet you."

"And you did." He liked looking at her, straight across. She was tall. He'd always felt so much bigger than the women he was with. "And what about you?" he said. "What's your reason for being here?"

"But I'm only here a short time. I live in New York."

"In your mind," he clarified. "Work."

"Oh. Right, that way I'm always here. But not the modern here! I mean"—she raised a long hand to the pounding, honking, chattering street around them where they stood, waiting for An—"this is all strange to me. I'm back in the history of China, the art."

"You still haven't told me the reason. I mean, you and China."

"Oh, I think I knew as soon as I was born that it was time to move someplace else."

"Did you," he said, and she thought he was looking at her ears, but actually he was looking beyond her shoulder. "Here he comes."

"*Ei,*" said An, walking up. "Success."

"What'd you get?" Michael said, his broad face public again, his grin social.

"Two pairs! I had the man confirm that they were real, on the receipt, before I said anything."

"Excellent," Doyle said.

"Oh yes. Beyond excellent. And now fourteen hundred has become twenty-eight hundred *ren min bi.*"

Lia raised a hand to protest. "That's a lot of money for him to pay you."

"There is a law!" An replied. "If a man sells a fake, he refunds you double! If the law is not enforced, nothing will ever change."

"Rule of law," Michael said. "Consistent, systemic rule of law is the road to change in China. My man's got a point."

"Okay. Overruled."

"You see." He leaned close to her. "An does this as a man of principle."

"Actually I'm the Robin Hood of Beijing," An twinkled in Chinese. "You may think of me that way if you like."

"Oh well," Lia laughed. "Thanks. I'm honored." She was aware of standing close to Michael.

An touched the wad of cash in his pocket. "And now let's go out to dinner. You'll give your choices, yes or no?"

"Jinyang," Michael said at once.

"You always want to go to Jinyang," An said.

"You're right, I do, I'm hopeless. But it should be what our guest wants." Michael turned to Lia. "What do you feel like eating?"

"What's Jinyang?"

"A Shanxi place. They use a brown vinegar on everything."

"Is it good? Is it authentic?"

"Authentic?" said An. "Oh! Very. They are bringing that special vinegar all the way from Shanxi in gourds."

"Well then." She looked around her for a second, at the imported cars, the fast-food chains, the towering Western-style buildings. "Sure."

"Wonderful!" An was giddy from having made so much money so quickly. "Miss Fan. I know you are a master of porcelain."

"A student," she corrected him.

"Don't be polite. I have a pot you must see. It's a Kangxi bowl, damaged, but special. From my family's collection. Will you see it and have tea?"

"With pleasure."

"An Xing," Doyle joked. "Are you pressing my social schedule?"

An turned in a show of surprise. "Did I invite you?" he said. "Did I hear myself? However"—he was so magnanimous—"you may come along if you like. If you're nice to me."

"Enough," Lia said. "Let's go eat."

9

THE NEXT NIGHT AFTER WORK LIA TOOK A taxi downtown and found that when she got out, at the top of Qianmen, she didn't really feel like eating. She walked south instead through the press of Chinese, some shopping, some brisk in suits with cell phones clapped to their ears, some young and louche and provocative in low-slung pants and platforms. Out of an elementary school's iron gates poured a river of parents, clutching purses and briefcases and the hands of their children. But mainly Qianmen was a commercial district, with more stores and restaurants packed in along the sidewalks than she'd have thought possible. Their jutting vertical signs made a barrage of overhead characters. She read them easily, without thinking or silently translating, just scanning as she walked.

This was the one thing she was good at in Chinese, reading. Her spoken Chinese suffered not just from insufficient use but from her imperfect hearing. Pronouncing the tones never felt natural, and as a result she tried too hard, she always tried to fill in when she didn't feel sure by letting the sound of the language slide a little. It was sloppy, especially for her. She didn't like it. On the other hand, she was not on the Mainland very often.

Just then she caught a glimpse of herself in a shop window and for an unfortunate second looked older and harder than her thirty-two years. Her body was too long, with too many angles. And she seemed to be missing some pliant, feminine element of invitation. Other women had it. In the glass she saw Chinese women passing behind her. They had it. They were softer-faced, more quietly built; their arms were rounded and their eyes gentle.

She turned right into a venerable alley called Dashanlan, or *Dazhalar,* as the word was locally pronounced. It meant "great wicker barrier" street, and the name came from the screen that had once been there to shield its entertainments of the night from the eyes of the respectable passersby on Qianmen. Lia smiled at the memory. It was still a stretch stuffed with thronging commerce, the gray overhanging buildings dark with age and looped with phone and electrical wires. She stopped in front of a window displaying bolts of iridescent silk-satin, electric blue, scarlet, jade. She could never wear anything like that. She reached around and took her long plume of loose hair and brought it around to the front, smoothed it with her hands. It was dark copper, long, like her face. She had her palette. She looked again at the brilliant row of silks. Well, something in here might suit me, she thought, and she pushed open the door and went in.

"I'm thinking of having a dress made," she said to the salesgirl.

"*Hao-de,*" the girl said crisply, and gave her a clipboard of styles from which to choose.

Lia flipped through the pages. All the models were Chinese, and the lines and shapes of the dresses were those that flattered the Asian body.

It must have shown in her face. "*Ni kan qipao zenmoyang?*" the clerk said, What about the *qipao?*

Lia looked at the old-fashioned high-necked garment, slit up the leg. It was a cliché. She'd never wear it. "Too Chinese for me," she said.

"But change to a square-cut neckline," the woman said, tracing what she meant with her finger. "No cross-button."

Lia looked at it.

"Side slit. Good for long legs."

Lia did have long legs; this was one reason she wore clinging, close-cut skirts and pants. "Shorter length," she said, pointing to a spot a few inches above her knee. "No slit."

The woman raised her eyebrows at first, then stepped back and eyed Lia critically. "Not *qipao* anymore, no relationship, but you're right." Her expression had migrated to one of interest. She went down the row and picked a sage-green silk, soft, not shiny, with a design of falling leaves in gold and russet.

Lia was amazed at the vitality that suffused her face when she held the fabric up against her. Things might be possible in this dress. "I love it," she said, surprised at herself.

In the fitting room the girl reached out and plucked the cling-ing vest away from Lia's body. "Shirt off," she said. "Skirt off."

Lia stood up in her underwear while the Chinese woman pinned muslin pieces expertly against her. The clerk's hands were forthright, professional, remote. "What's your name?" Lia asked the clerk.

"Xieli." The word was slid around a mouthful of pins. "You?"

"Luo Na."

"Pleasure's mine," the woman said, and the politeness was jangled by the pins, which made them both laugh. "Enough!" Xieli said, and slapped Lia's leg lightly. "Stand still."

She found she liked the feeling of the muslin soft as air on her. This dress would make her lighter and kinder, more female. That was how she wanted to be.

Xieli finished around the hem at the bottom. She took a long look under the fitting-room light, then picked up a charcoal pencil and drew a clean line on the muslin across Lia's chest. "Where do you think?" she said. "Here?" She drew another line lower down. "Or here?"

Lia looked. The second was about as low as her comfort level went. But she had seen the American man looking at her. "This one," she said, and touched it with her finger.

They finished the fitting and Lia paid a deposit. "Wednesday," the woman said. "Don't worry. I think he will love it."

Lia let out a surprised laugh. "Thanks," she said.

And Xieli waved her away.

JACK YUAN AWOKE to the sounds of movement in the bathroom, to the rush of water, to Anna stepping into the shower and the muffled clank of its glass door closing behind her. He knew what she looked like. He could see her in his mind's eye, her black hair plastered flat to her head, her skin streaming. He had seen her like that so many times.

Jack knew what day it was. He had known it deep in his cells before he even opened his eyes. He turned to the left, to the bedside table gleaming in Balinese teak beside him. There it was, the flat white stick. They had a deal, he and Anna. She left it here, on these days. She brought it out of the bathroom and put it here and did not return to look at it. He took care of it. If he had anything to tell her, he would tell her. They both knew that. It seemed better this way than always to hope, to discuss. If nothing came of it he would tuck it into the garbage can and say nothing. That was what he did every month. She was a little irregular and, always, she hoped for the possibilities.

After a while he heard the water go off. It had to be gone when she came out. She would come out naked, or maybe with a towel; the damp heat would make tendrils of hair cling around her nape and the intelligent dome of her forehead. She would look, only once, at the bedside table to see that it was gone, then walk into her dressing room. He would watch her lucid beauty from behind. She was his ideal. He rolled over and picked up the stick.

Nothing.

He heard the bathroom door opening. He slipped it under the pillow and closed his eyes. Anna came out.

THE NEXT DAY she found another fake. It was a putative pair of Daoguang wine cups, beautifully painted, thin-walled, but with one giveaway—an overly calibrated texture along the base rims. Of course, these were copies of much less valuable originals. If actually from the Daoguang reign, 1821–1850, the real pair would be worth only twenty thousand U.S. dollars. That was a far cry from more expensive pieces like the chicken cup, worth millions. But its very modesty set off alarm bells of its own. There was a certain class of fakes that seemed to pass muster by appearing more common, inviting less scrutiny. The forger counted on the appraiser to look at such a piece quickly.

She packed them up and moved on. Every additional fake was a greater disturbance in the pattern. She didn't like it. The game board wasn't supposed to shift.

But she had to go ahead. She went on to the next piece, which was real, and the next one after that, and a string of others. No more fakes that day. But the fear didn't leave her. This was different. This was a pattern of fakes. When the car dropped her off in the evening at the guesthouse, she didn't even go out to eat. She went right inside and set her computer up and returned to work, scrolling back over the inventory.

Because if she'd found two fakes, there had to be more.

AT THE SAME time, while Michael Doyle was preparing to leave work for the night, the lab results came back on Xiaoli's tooth. He didn't read Chinese, but he knew the characters for her name, and the layout of the lab report was a thing with which he was intimate. He scanned it until he found the number he was looking for, the lead level in the child's tooth, in parts per million. At birth, Xiaoli's cord-blood levels had been eight micrograms per deciliter—an entirely different measurement, apples and oranges; lead concentrations in solid tissue were much smaller and reflected prolonged exposure. Now her solid-tissue reading was twenty parts per million. Not good news. This was a very bad lead level for a seven-year-old child. And lead poisoning was so endemic here that only the sickest kids got chelation therapy.

So record it, he thought, and he made his mind a blank as he had learned to do. He pulled up the forms on screen, entered the data, recorded this little girl's current reading. Click, enter, send. It was done.

He went out and took the subway up to Andingmen and

walked to Jiaodaokou Nan, then turned on Houyuan'ensi Hutong. The noise of the city fell away. Down the lane he was grateful to see, small and far ahead, the green sign of the guesthouse. One reason was her. He had caught himself wondering where she was, what she was doing. Thinking about her. So when he stepped through the gate, he walked into the courtyard where she was staying instead of the one on the other side where he lived.

He could see she was there. The light was on. Pausing by the door, looking through the thin cotton curtains, he could see her cross-legged on the bed. She was curved over her computer, concentrating. Her legs were bare, just her long shirt.

There was a pressure on his chest, he was afraid to breathe, afraid even the sound of air filling his lungs might alert her to the fact that he was there, looking at her. On the desk by the window he saw her hearing aids, delicate little bumps of plastic. Her attention was on the screen. He stepped back, and this made a small scritch on the stones. He stiffened, waited; still she didn't look up. She couldn't hear.

He turned and walked quickly out again, to the lane. She had not eaten; that much he knew. He could tell by looking at her. He knew that manic, overworked look. The mania that hides fear. The fear that hides aloneness. The aloneness that leads to more work.

So he went down the hutong, west, curving south. Down this way there was a big food intersection. He would buy something to take back to her. It was dinner, he told himself. That was all. He was taking her dinner.

He found the food bazaar vibrant with people, bright with lights strung around the overhanging branches. Cooks called out to him from behind sizzling griddles. People hurried with stacked steamer tins to take home. Young girls cruised in tube tops, skin-tight pants, high heels. Older men sat on the steps, at their leisure, in undershirts; cotton trousers rolled up to their knees and legs planted wide apart.

Doyle moved past the griddle-masters to the little enclave of people who made soup dumplings and noodles. They were big-voiced and dramatic with their frothing tureens and their board-loads of noodles, fresh-pulled, soft and clunky. This was what he wanted.

He picked out a square-shaped man with receding hair and big square hands and asked for a broth with dumplings. The man brought the broth to an instant and furious boil, ladled in steaming square-folded dumplings with skins like see-through pearls, and then filled the container to the brim with hot soup. *"Man man chi,"* the man said politely, Take your time in eating, and Michael paid him and walked back.

By the time he got to the guesthouse, to her room, the thin cardboard soup container felt like it had burned all the skin off his fingers, and he'd long since wrapped the bottom of his T-shirt around it. He knocked gently. She didn't respond. He could see her on the bed with her computer, still working. He knocked again, hard enough to make the wooden door vibrate. This time she looked up in a start. He waved, then stepped back and turned away to let her get into her clothes and her hearing aids. A few seconds later she yanked open the door. "Hi!" she said, surprised.

"Hi." He held out the soup in both hands. "I brought you something."

She shook her head in disbelief, a smile spreading across her face.

"Take it, it's hot."

"Sorry!" She took it. "You are so *kind*. I can't believe you did this. Please." She reached down and scooped a pile of papers off the desk chair, wiped the bare wood with her hand. She smiled back up at him. "Come in."

He took the chair. "You're working too hard," he said.

"You're right. I am. I'm over the edge. But—my God, Michael. I can't believe you brought me this."

He liked the softness in her eyes. "It's nothing," he said. "I was happy to do it."

"No. You don't know what it means to me. It's just one of those things for me, you know? Chicken soup." She smelled it and her smile welled up again.

"*Man man chi,*" he said in Chinese, just as the man who'd sold it to him had said, and laughed.

She sat back on the bed, the only place left. She took a spoonful. "Oh," she said, "it's wonderful. Thank you."

"Enough," he said. "Eat."

"Okay."

He watched her approvingly. "Your Chinese seems very good," he said after a minute.

"Somewhat. My spoken Chinese is okay. I never use it. I don't live in that—you know—that vernacular world, which is basically only here on the Mainland when it comes to Mandarin, here and Taipei. Most of my work is in Hong Kong, New York, and London. I mean, there are always Mandarin-speaking clients, but . . ." She shrugged. Clients were by their nature rich, cultured, globalized people. The final language of all the biggest transactions tended to be English. "With Chinese I read and write. I have to for my job." She bit into a dumpling and got a spill of hot savory ground pork. "Do you speak Chinese?"

"I'm trying. I've learned a little. I took six months of classes before coming here. Basically I'm pathetic."

"I doubt that."

"And don't give me that casual 'I read and write' stuff," he said. "I know how much it takes to read and write Chinese."

"But that's what I majored in."

He was watching her. "Your hair is down," he said.

It was true, her hair was loose from the nape of her neck. She had twisted it back out of her way while eating. "I can't braid it up all the time. I have to take it down and let it rest."

"It's nice."

She let go of a laugh and touched her mouth with the back of her hand. "It's not a fashion statement."

"I like it." Watching her, the clarity of her skin, her fingers, he reminded himself to apply the brakes. "What is it you're working on?" he asked.

"I'm logging some of the things I saw today."

"Don't you do that as you go along?"

"I create an inventory for the job, sure. But at night I make sure I'll remember the pots. That I've committed them to memory."

He leaned his body forward, balancing himself on his elbows against his knees. "You want to remember them?"

"It's a thing of mine, memory. A sort of world. I put all the pots I see in their places and that way I'll always have them."

"Personally, I try to forget as much as possible."

"That's like most people." She smiled, and went back to eating.

He watched her, watched her mouth, a wide thin mouth. He liked how it changed when she smiled. "How'd you come up with this? The memory thing."

"It's nothing new. People did it for thousands of years, up to the advent of the printing press. Before that it was a big part of intellectual life. And I still do it the way people did then."

He let her eat for a moment. "And what way is that, exactly?" he said.

"I use an imagined structure." She put down the spoon and shaped a square, fingers jointed like the bare tips of trees. "In my case I use the old imperial examination grounds—do you know the ones I mean? They had all these brick cubicles."

"Oh yes, they were over by Chaoyang. Thousands of cubicles! And what, you put what you're remembering in the cubicles?"

She looked up in faint surprise. "That's right."

"Amazing." He stood up and stretched and, with just a few steps and a soft feline thud, came to stand over her. He was looking down at her computer. "And this is one of the things you're memorizing?"

The image of the chicken cup was up on the screen. "Yes. Isn't it lovely?"

"It's beautiful," he said, surprising himself. He had never really looked at porcelain. Yet this cup was so perfect that just glancing at it, on a computer screen, gave him a jolt. "Is it valuable?"

She smiled. "It would be, if it was real. It's a fake."

"Really?"

"Really. Totally fake." She grinned in delight. "But it's gorgeous. Isn't it? Isn't it gorgeous?"

"I admit it. It is."

"Do you know what it would be worth if it were real?"

"No." He smiled down at her, waiting.

"Four million dollars."

"What! For this little thing?"

"Some people will pay anything for the perfection that will never come again. This was from the emperor's collection. It was the greatest art collection on earth." He watched her delicate shoulders shift, her arms, her fingers move over the keyboard. "Look at this view." The cup turned on the screen.

"And it's a fake?"

"Yes."

"How many people are there on earth who can tell the difference?" he asked her. "Besides you."

She saw where he was going and laughed. "Four," she said. "Five."

"Well?" He lifted his hands.

She picked up the soup again and scraped out the last spoonful. "Michael," she said again, "I really needed this. You are wonderful."

"Don't mention it," he said. She had her face turned up to him. She looked happy. He could just drop his hands right now and rest them on her shoulders. He could do it, gather her to him. Or he could hold back. But the thought had arisen and was now lodged in his mind. He stood looking down at her shoulders. "What?" she asked, sensing something.

"Nothing." She was so serious. "I ought to go. You have a lot of work to do."

She sprang up. "Thank you. You brought me such a perfect dinner."

"It's nothing." He looked at the screen. "And it's a great cup too," he said, "by the way." He brushed his legs, somewhere in his loose pants. "Okay then."

"Okay. Thanks again. Really. Thanks." She stood and held the door while he left. They still had not so much as shaken hands.

THE AH CHAN stepped out of a taxi on Stanley Street in Central, into the honking line of cars that bumped down the narrow road between the lunchtime streams of walking, hurrying Hong Kongers, a few light-haired Europeans riding along above the black heads.

Stanley was an older street. The buildings that lined it were only four and five stories high, their stone fronts stained with the gray of decades, their upper-story crank metal-case windows open to the hot, damp air. Stanley was a step up the hill from Des Voeux Road and Queen's Road, where flowed the magnificent skyscrapers. There were no glittering towers on Stanley. This was the start of the ur-city, the Chinese jangle that coiled away from the main business district and climbed the hill.

Bai ran up three marble steps into the Luk Yu, its doors framed in the understated dark wood of one hundred years earlier. The foyer paved in marble gave way to a large main dining room floored in old-fashioned tile. The ceilings were dizzyingly high, and even with the clusters of tasseled silk lanterns the room was an open hangar of sliding, deafening Cantonese.

Bai and his friends preferred the second floor, the northeast corner. This spot commanded a superb view of the stairs and of everyone coming or going. As he topped the steps and approached the table, he saw that his friend Shen had ordered *baat-tow* abalone, which was indecently expensive. Shen must have had a great run. This was the celebration, the customary squaring of accounts after harvest. He smiled, walking toward the table covered with abalone, fresh slabs of it brought up alive by divers. He could smell it with its deep bottom notes, perfectly braised, hanging shamelessly over the sides of the plates.

Today was Shen's turn to spread his feathers of success. Waiter Kwan was off to the side, smiling broadly at them, leaning ever so slightly forward in his white tunic, his swollen hands clasped. Bai was smiling too. Soon he'd be the one celebrating. He'd get in here with Gao Yideng's shipment. He'd receive half a million *ren min bi*. That would definitely earn him a new name. Emperor Bai. Success was stirring in him, he could feel it.

"*Ei!* Bai!" The voices rippled up in Mandarin, the language they all shared. The table groaned under platters of slippery rice noodle with scallions and soy, steamed chicken feet in five-spice, emerald-crisp Chinese broccoli, and whole steamed fish from a mountain river in Guangdong Province.

He raised a joyful hand in response to them. "*Ei*, congratulations, Shen!" He grinned his greetings at his friend. "You'll live the rich life now! Light fur and well-fed horses!" He picked up one of the full, thimble-size wineglasses. It was brimming with *xian jiu*, immortal wine, made from rooster testicles. This was a favorite of rough men in Jingdezhen and brought in specially for this occasion. It would be the first thing he swallowed this morning. "Isn't it so?" he called, raising the glass high, and all his friends gathered up their glasses in response.

"Long life for all of us, present and absent! Long life!" Bai held the glass high with a smile that was as broad and full of promise as the midday outside, then tipped it back and drank the foul, clear liquor.

Everyone followed, everyone drank, but there was a tremor of uncertainty. Bai felt it instantly. Then he saw the glasses replaced on the table, half full. "What?" Bai said.

"Bai." He looked down. It was one of the younger men he knew from Ningbo.

"Hu and Sun were caught," the man said.

"Caught?" Bai said dumbly.

"Arrested," the man said.

In a terrible instant Bai raked his glance around the table, but no one contradicted, no one said it was not so. The men looked down at their plates, their teacups, their smoldering cigarettes. Someone's cell went off. The man reached into his pocket and silenced it. Everyone knew what would happen to Hu and Sun now.

Nevertheless, Shen, their host, raised his glass. "Drink to their safety," he urged, and this time everyone drained their glasses.

10

"**WOULD YOU LIKE TO SEE MY DUCKS?**" GAO Yideng asked when she answered her cell phone.

Her comprehension was fairly good, but she wondered if she'd heard him right. "Mr. Gao? Your ducks?"

"My ducks," he repeated. "I keep ducks and chickens and pigs on a place out in the country, not far from the city's edge at all. It is my *dacha*," he joked, using the sinicized version of the Russian word. "Right now I will take a short ride there. If you like, I can pick you up."

He made it sound entirely incidental, a casual excursion, when in fact he was an enormously busy man and she had left word that she wished to talk to him. He was so seamless. "Of course," she said. "When?"

"Trouble you to come out to the gate, facing the lake. In fifteen minutes I will be there."

So they drove out through Beijing's southwestern suburbs until wooded valleys unfurled between jagged green hills. She marveled again at the personal, very private treatment she was getting from this mogul. Obviously the collection mattered to him. She looked at the light from the sunroof gleaming on his bare head, his imported sunglasses. Prada. She smiled. Real, not fake.

They drove up beside a little stone house with a low-walled animal yard; ducks and chickens, pigs. A garden on the south flank of the house teemed with vegetables.

"This place is always kept for me." He unlocked the door, opened several of the windows to the June air. "That's better. Let us drink some tea." He went into the small kitchen to prepare it. She asked if she could help, but no, he would do it. She watched him at the simple stone counter. That was all there was. A sink, a half refrigerator, and a single wok-ring. It was crazy, she thought; it was theater. It was a fake *dacha*, but the rustic kitchen and the plants pushing up were real, the ducks genuinely clamorous. He poured boiling water into the teapot. Back at the table he let it rest a few minutes and then filled two plain cups with it, frothy, astringent green. He raised his cup to her and they both drank. "Now tell me how you progress with the collection," he said.

"It's magnificent. Overall. I have found more copies, though."

"Really. What?"

"A so-called pair of Daoguang wine cups. Tiny, delicate, quite lovely. But fake. This tea is excellent."

"It's just what happened to be here."

"As forgeries the cups are of no consequence. The pieces that they impersonate are not terribly valuable." She shrugged as if it were perfectly normal for them to come all the way out here to discuss such a trifle. "Rather it is a matter of . . . accumulation." She had found the chicken cup, the Daoguang wine cups, and earlier today two more fakes. It was then she decided to leave him a message. She smiled at him. "Now I've seen several more. I thought you'd want to know."

He looked at her with a faint, constructed touch of a smile. "I am grateful that a collection like this should even pass through my hands, no matter what its flaws."

"I understand," she said.

"Both sides depend on you to look at it most carefully."

"I will. But, Mr. Gao, I think it would really be best if I had one of my colleagues come to Beijing and look everything over with me. In view of the situation."

"As you wish," he said.

"Not that I'm not confident," she said. "I am." She drew the plain gray fabric of her tunic loosely away from her body. "But forgeries have been found. A second person should go through it."

"Miss Fan." Gao was already looking at his watch. *"Women gai zou-le,"* I think we should go.

MICHAEL TOOK HER to An Xing's place the next night to see the bowl. The Chinese man came to the door in shiny athletic warm-ups and led them in to a couple of rooms, commodious but cramped. "Welcome to my ancestral home," he joked.

"I love it," said Lia. She saw that one wall of this main room was all books; the others were hung with Asian minority textiles. There were a few shelves of well-chosen contemporary lacquerware and one especially charming row of ceramic goldfish pots in motley sizes.

"I'm a bad host!" An said delightedly. "Ah, you are looking at my things. There isn't much."

"I like it."

"It really was my ancestral home, for three hundred years."

"Is that so?" So they had let him stay, she thought, or come back, and now he was down to what was basically a small corner of the place.

"I still have a few things. Books. Family papers. Old records."

"Records?" Her eyes lit. "What kind of records?"

"Family holdings. Financials. Genealogies."

"Art collections?"

"Yes."

"Inventories?"

"Yes."

"Porcelain?"

"Yes."

"May I see?"

"Of course!" He pulled out a chair for her at the small table and turned his back to scan the floor-to-ceiling bookshelves. He touched his ponytail absently, looking, then after a minute he reached up with a jubilant cry and pulled out a crumbly stack-paged book. It was open-bound in old Chinese style. She and An bent over it. Doyle stood behind. It had a hand-brushed character title. *An Family Porcelain Holdings, from the Ivory Fan Study.*

"How wonderful that you've kept this," she said.

"It's come down to me, that's all," An said. "I'm not the only descendant, but there are no others in China. Just me. Look. Here are the lists of their art collections." He opened the first page for Lia.

She scanned through it. "Oh, it's marvelous."

She could feel Michael's eyes on the back of her head and smell him, a spiky brown-eyed smell, softened by his fair hair, individuated by the turns of his life. How old was he? Past forty, by the look of him. But he'd been very sick. He might have been younger.

"Do you want to memorize it?" she heard him say behind her. "Because An and I can go in the other room."

She smiled back up at him. "That's nice of you." Ordinarily she might say yes, please, go away and let me work. There was never enough for the memory world. Never enough histories, gazetteers, catalogs, auction descriptions, records, inventories. But she didn't want to do it now, in front of him. She'd rather talk to him. "An Xing, thank you for showing me, thank you. Another time perhaps I'll read it line by line."

"These are only some old lists, hardly worth an hour of your attention."

"*Nali,*" she said, Nonsense. "There have been great collectors in your family."

"But speaking of porcelains! We are forgetting the bowl I have to show you."

A ringing sound bleated out. An's cell phone. He took it from his clip, excusing himself with his eyes. "*Wei?*" He listened. "*Ei. Dui, dui. Deng yixia.*" He turned to Michael. "You show her," he whispered, covering the mouthpiece.

Michael opened a door. "In here," he said, and slipped ahead of her into a small anteroom lined with shelves, a bathroom at the far end. He switched on a lamp, took down a plain indigo box, unhooked the bit, and opened it. There was the ruby ground Kangxi bowl. He reached in.

"No," she said. "Let me." He pulled back. Her long fingers made a net under the bowl and she lifted it out. "Do you mind?"

"Not at all."

"It's so beautiful," she said. "Really *hoi moon.*"

"*Hoi moon?*"

"That's Cantonese. *Hoi moon geen san.* The Mandarin would be *kai men jian shan.* Let the door open on a view of mountains. The dealers in Hong Kong, the runners who bring the pots out of China—they all say this. They love to say it."

"And it means?"

"It means, it's beautiful. It's right. It means, look at it! That's when it's said admiringly. When it's said in exasperation it means damn you, don't you see, don't you get it? Of course it's right. You idiot! It's gorgeous."

"What does it mean when you say it?"

"When I say it right now, about this piece? My God. It's lovely." She looked at him. "Don't you think so?"

"I do," he said. "I think so." He did like the bowl. He had seen it before. But right now he was watching her.

She held it closer to the light and he caught the soft pink of her hearing aid.

She felt his eyes there. That's me, she thought; take a good look. I wear them to hear, to be like everybody else. She could still hear her mother's voice: "Don't ever take them out! Don't do it! Ever! You're to leave them in at all times!" But I'm all right in here, she would think. And in time she learned to just take them out when she could, when she was alone. "Do you see the enameling?" she said to Michael. "The painting, the Jesuit style. Very fine. This bowl was fired in the biscuit in Jingdezhen, then brought to the Palace to be painted."

"Where's Jingdezhen?"

"In the south, in Jiangxi Province. The emperor's porcelain was made there for almost a thousand years. It's still the center of pots culture. The best artists are there. Ah, it's too bad about these cracks. That's what An meant when he said it was damaged. Remember?" She ran the soft pad of her finger along one, coming down from the rim. The crack itself was a rift as wide as the ocean under her skin, a wilderness canyon, tragic. She felt a stab of such empathy. Would that she could heal it. "Do you know this bowl would be valued at one or two million dollars if it wasn't damaged? Even as it is, it could fetch twenty thousand U.S."

"I don't think he'd ever sell it."

"No. He shouldn't." To possess something of this order was to possess the past, but she sensed she didn't need to say it. He knew; she could tell by the way he looked at the piece. She could feel the warmth of him. "Look," she said. "Look with me when I turn it over. It will have a four-character reign mark in puce. So rare, the puce. Usually the reign mark was cobalt. Ready?" She upended it. "See?"

He looked. She was right. Four characters in puce on a white background. And rarer still, a collector's seal was applied to the base in tiny spaced droplets of sealing wax. Not quite connecting, impressionistic, a tiny masterpiece of dripped-wax calligraphy, they suggested the characters for *Ivory Fan Study*, the family collection name.

"Watching you, I see . . . you use your hands with pots, don't you?"

"Yes," she said. "You're right. In some way I know how it's supposed to feel." She fitted the bowl back into its box and hooked the lid down, put it in his hands.

He pushed it back on the shelf, all the way against the wall. He could hear An talking on the phone in the outer room. He turned to her, right next to him, her eyes on a level with his, and to his faint surprise he saw the web of exhaustion around her eyes, the shadows on her face. "You're tired," he said. "You look tired."

She met his eyes gratefully. "I am. I haven't been sleeping. Not enough anyway. My pots are so incredible. And there are so many of them."

"You have to sleep."

"I know."

"Come on, I'll take you back," he said, and he reached to touch her shoulder in an easy American way. Then An Xing was in the doorway. "Well," he said, *"zenmoyang?"* What do you think?

"It's fantastic," she said to An, "completely lovely. Thank you. And thank you," she said to Michael in English, with an inflection she was sure he would understand, because in the nicest possible way she felt shepherded by him and she wanted him to know she got it, she felt it, and she liked the way it felt.

BACK IN HER room she settled down in her favorite spot on the bed. She had really enjoyed herself with him. She felt the link with him. She wished she didn't live on the other side of the world. She wished she weren't leaving soon. But she did and she was.

So she worked. After calling Dr. Zheng and leaving a message asking him to send Phillip, she found herself pulled back to the chicken cup. She brought the image up again on her screen. The form and shape were sublime. The pots of the Chenghua reign had low, ideally balanced bodies, with a graceful emphasis on the horizontal. Relaxed yet precise. This little cup nailed it.

She rotated the image. There was something quirky about one of the chickens, something that pulled at her. That chicken's tail. The way its proud feathers rose bristling into the air. What did she remember? The exact flip of that tail—

She knew something about this. She had heard David talk about this. He had seen it.

David. Dr. Zheng had told her explicitly not to talk to David.

But she could e-mail him, she reasoned. Just this one question. Hospital or home, David checked his e-mail.

For she sensed this might be a forger whose work David had followed. David called him the Master of the Ruffled Feather. The Master gave a signature curl to his chickens' tails. She herself had never seen it.

She clipped the image from six angles and attached it to the message. Atop she wrote: *Is this the Master of the Ruffled Feather?* She pressed SEND.

He must have been sitting at the screen, because a few minutes later his reply came. *Don't tell me. You found one.* And then, underneath that: *If he's alive he's in Jingdezhen.*

That's right, she thought, when she read it. That's where he had to be. While she was staring at the message she heard her cell phone going off in her purse. She didn't answer it. She was thinking about Jingdezhen. There were answers there. Could she do it? Could she leave for a few days?

She took out her phone and dialed in to the voice mail. Dr. Zheng. "Lia, I got your message. I think you're right. Second pair of eyes, just at the end. I'm arranging for Phillip's flights back from England, and then to China. It will take about two and a half days. Gao will have him met and brought to you. Call me." She felt herself relax for a moment, the ground a little firmer.

She could go to Jingdezhen and be back by the time Phillip arrived. And there, in that smoke-pluming town in the south, she might find the card her hand was missing.

IN JINGDEZHEN IT had been raining. When Bai got back from Hong Kong the place was cleaning up after summer torrents that had swelled the Chang River as high as a house. The lowest parts had been flooded. The waters had just receded the night before. Up here where he was walking on Fengjing Road everything looked scrubbed, soft, newly vital. Tender June leaves unfurled in the trees. The birds had come back and they trilled and chattered.

He walked along the river, with mattresses and clothing spread out to dry all along its banks. People squatted among their possessions, scrubbing off mud and drying their pots and their baskets and their books one by one.

After a while he raised his hand for a clattery little aluminum-can taxi and rode northwest, away from the center of town, toward Yu's place. The awnings and poor storefronts fell away. Dark leaves crowded along the base of the old stone and concrete walls, lowering and settling, closing around little houses and courtyards that spread out and relaxed into larger, more rambling spaces as the puttering taxi left the downtown behind.

Many of these dwellings were also studios, or small family factories. Ninety-five percent of the people who made pots here in Jingdezhen worked at home. Yes, some of the big factories were still running, turning out dishware, pouring black smoke up to heaven. They supplied the world with what was everywhere called "china." But the factories employed only a fraction of Jingdezhen's porcelain people, and the less skilled ones at that. The best artists worked alone.

He had the driver take him out to where the road turned to hard-packed dirt, now wet and rutted. He got out of the taxi when they came to the opening of Yu's alley, barely a meter and a half wide. He could touch the old houses on either side. Here was the gate. He called out softly, pushed it open, and stepped in.

The long, narrow yard was a repeating trestlework of wooden trays and poles, rows of pots in all phases of production. Three worktables were squeezed in, and Potter Yu sat at one. He was incising something with a fine-pronged tool. At other tables his two assistants bent over their wheels. One was a middle-aged man, maybe his son. The other was a teenage girl. His granddaughter?

"*Ei,*" said Bai.

"*Ei,*" answered Yu without looking up.

"These smoke-dried fish are beneath notice," Bai said, and deposited a package on the bench behind the worktable.

"They're appreciated," Yu answered without ever breaking the rhythm of the delicate little tooth scraping in the clay. Bai saw that he was using a stencil. Of course, most people did these days, when putting in a precise background pattern, scrolling or curling leaves, for example. But Yu's studio was known for its rare freehand work. Maybe the old man was just taking a break. Bai watched him work.

He was relaxed, the rhythm of his hands companionable with the passage of time. "How have you been?" he asked Bai.

"Well. And well traveled. You?"

"Well enough. How about business?"

"I stand a moment in fortune's favor. That's one bit of a beautiful cup." He nodded at the piece under Yu's hand.

"After the Ming prototype," Yu said. "There's a reason why the sweet-white ware from the Yongle reign remains all but unsurpassable. It's not easy to reproduce! Truly. Everything depends on the materials used."

"It is inappropriate for me to even say, for I'm a rank beginner," Bai said, "but is it not so that in the body of the sweet-white, the level of alumina should be high?" He glanced at Yu to see if he was right.

The older man dipped his metal point into a saucer of water, swirled it. He patted it dry on a towel and looked up expectantly at Bai. "And?" he said.

Bai sang inside, for that meant he was right. "Yongle pots had higher kaolin content. They needed higher firing temperatures. So the body was stronger and could be as thin as eggshells, thin as a spectrum of light."

"And are you on equally intimate terms with the sweet-white glaze?"

"I am a poor student," Bai said gleefully, blessing all the nights he'd spent, elbows on the table, forehead in his hands, bent over the books in his room. "In the glaze there was less lime and more potash. This means there was more feldspar, and that change, combined with the lowered lime levels, evaporated away the blue tint of a lime-ash glaze. And that is what made the sweet-white color."

"Good!" Potter Yu laughed. "How did you know?"

"That one! I admit, Old Ma over at the Ming excavations told me."

"Ah! Is it so? Old Ma!" Yu knew the man very well. Old Ma had been minding the kiln site for more than fifty years. Over the yawning hole in the ground he'd built a little brick structure, with wire-mesh windows high up in its walls. Old Ma himself had dug the great pit a spoonful at a time, had exposed the centuries-old stones of the firing chambers, the work area, the all-important shard pile. Here, in the northeast corner of the excavation, he had unearthed thousands of pounds of broken china.

And these pieces were the true prizes. They were some of the tens of thousands, hundreds of thousands of pots smashed because they were not perfect.

Through shards, every compositional detail of the best imperial porcelains could be dissected. If a man knew exactly how kaolin and petuntse were combined in a given reign, what minerals, what levels, that man, if otherwise an artist, could make a pot that had the ineffably correct look.

Yes, Old Ma was the place to learn, Yu thought. And if this ah chan was smart enough to listen to the old man, he might succeed. His tortoise-frame glasses slipped a little as he moved to his feet, untied his blue apron, and laid it over the chair. "Come inside, Bai. I have something to show you."

Bai followed him down the long aisle—on one side, finished works of majestic scale: garden stools, great oversize standing urns, enormous goldfish pots, all painted in a riot of styles from Ming to new China kitsch. On the left, the horizontal racks of narrow rough-hewn boards held marching lines of unfired pots: bowls, cups, plates, ewers, vases, jars. Dozens of each type.

Yu pushed back a swinging door and they were in the room where he kept his finished wares. There were two facing couches and a commodious, low felt-lined table for looking at pots and drinking tea, but otherwise the room was all shelves. Shelves of porcelain were interrupted only by a few crank windows in their metal frames, kept more or less permanently open to the sultry hillside air. The room was well lit with thoughtfully placed spots. Yu knew what his wares were worth.

Bai circled appreciatively, drinking in Xuande bowls and Yongle stem cups and Chenghua wine cups and Yuan platters and Hongwu vases. Yu had chosen to work in *fang gu*, the reproduction of past masterpieces. All the best potters made *fang gu*, but for some it was an occasional thing. There were only a few like Yu, who placed it above all other pursuits.

Bai admired an ingot-shaped covered box of the late Ming, the Longqing reign—blue and white with swimming dragons, it was scoop-waisted, like a dumbbell, and its upper half was a fitted lid. The Longqing emperor had reigned from 1567–1572; a short reign, but one that had left its own stamp on porcelain's evolution, with covered boxes, wine pots with overhead handles, and other objects of art intended to suggest use. Not that these pieces were actually used. The whiff of use, the patina, was enough. They were far too perfect to use. Their utilitarian aspect was purely metaphorical.

"Beautiful," Bai said. It was so pitiable about Hu and Sun, he thought suddenly, so terrible. To have been caught. For lightning to have struck.

But he was still here. The bolt wouldn't strike again, not so soon. He would make it through and he would be rich and everybody would call him Emperor. He needed something magical, some symbol of power, some connection to the gods to carry with him. "Potter Yu," he said. "I'd like you to make me a chicken cup. If you can get it right, make it truly fine, I'll pay double. Really! This is a thing I want for myself. I want a cup that is exactly like the ones made for the Chenghua emperor right over there—" Bai cocked his glance north in the direction of the Ming kiln, with its pit of shards. "I will rely on you. Truly. I want a piece that from every angle, on every facet, is as fine as the cup of the Chenghua emperor himself."

"NO, NOT NANCHANG. I want to fly straight to Jingdezhen. What do you mean?" Lia pressed the phone to her ear, crossed out what she had written and started again. "One flight a week? Are you serious?"

She listened. "And when's the next flight there? And when returning?" She closed her eyes. She would have to leave the following evening, right after work. She could finish the rough inventory by then. When she returned, she and Phillip could go over it.

Unfortunately she'd have to fly to Nanchang, and from there take a four-hour train to Jingdezhen. Then a day in Jingdezhen could follow, and she could catch the weekly flight from Jingdezhen to Beijing. It made her tired just to think about it. "Book it," she told the phone agent.

It was worth it. The history of pots was impressed into the very texture of Jingdezhen, like ingrained kiln dust. The town was the art, and the art, the town. She knew a few people there. Through one she would meet another; it always happened that way. She might even find the Master of the Ruffled Feather.

She stepped out into the night air. It was fresh, cooler, with a half-moon rising over the roofs. Standing in her court she could feel a pull, a well of life, from his court on the other side. It's amazing, she thought, the observational side of herself off to the side, marveling; as if feeling can actually change physical laws. Specify the bend of light. Make me want to go to him, right now, and tell him I'm leaving Beijing.

But she saw through the gates his courtyard was dark. She couldn't tell him. He was out somewhere. Of course, she thought, why shouldn't he be? It was strange, the way she felt. Nothing had been said and yet here she was wanting to go and tell him she was leaving town. She had the uncomfortable sense that her feelings had gone out of line with the situation. Abruptly, she turned around and walked out and away down the lane.

MICHAEL HAD SLIPPED out earlier and caught a taxi on Jiaodao-kou. First he spent an hour at a Hunanese restaurant next to the entrance to the Yonghegong Temple, complete with altar to Mao— surely the twentieth century's most famous native of Hunan—the altar draped in red velvet and decked with candles, incense, cakes, fruits, and brimming miniature glasses of high-octane white liquor. He squeezed into a booth at the end of the room. He couldn't read Chinese, he didn't even bother looking at the menu, but he had memorized the names of certain dishes and he ordered food to sear the soul, pungent with whole cloves of garlic, cured pork, tiny smoked fish, and peppers. He wanted it to burn everything out of him, fry him, make his nose run and his eyes water. It did, but when he was through with eating and back on the street the past was there again, still too much with him. He stood shifting from side to side, clearing his mind, thinking about where to go and what to do. Then a taxi was coming along with its light on, and his hand went up in the air. This was a daily wonder of Beijing: Even though the traffic was awful, taxis were ubiquitous and cheap. He would go find some music. He opened the door and clambered into the back.

Where? He closed his eyes. Definitely not Sanlitun. The bar district was dense with loud, light-flashing clubs. There was Japanese techno, Thai grunge, Malagasy trance, reggae, and hip-hop, and Chinese punk bands with names like Anarchy Jerks and Scream Frame and Body Fluid. There were raves almost every night, but they moved around, first one venue, then another, easily found by the hordes of young, hungry avant-garders in face paint, outlandish garb, and two-foot-high hairstyles frosted with glitter. They were on their own group radar. When he went to Sanlitun he would see droves of them, milling, laughing, and hammering in Mandarin, and scattered among them foreigners and all manner of other young Chinese. There were bands from Mongolia, from Qinghai, from all over China. He liked to go sometimes. It felt good to walk through pounding low-register rhythms from the open doors.

But not tonight. He didn't want a long, curving bar and hordes of laconic, heavily made-up young people. He wanted someplace quiet. *"Sen di ka fei,"* he told the driver, naming a jazz club called CD Café in English.

When he got there he took a small table upstairs on the balcony. The club was dark, generic, softly lit with yellow arcs of light. He had a light rickety chair at a tiny round table, a brimming beer. He looked down at the small stage. The piano player was Italian, the drummer and stand-up-bass player Chinese—sober clothes. Long hair. They flexed their fingers and shoulders in the manner of reserved jazz players, preparing to play. Then they turned the pages of their music and all held together for a single, counting breath.

The piano player set up an insistent stride of a rhythm, and the bass and drums accented in behind. Doyle felt himself pulled in with them, a river stumbling, sailing, pouring over the rocks. He had come in here to forget, but instead he was remembering.

He remembered the day he had moved out into his own apartment. Daphne had come over to bring some books he'd left behind. She'd come and given him the books and chatted nicely about his apartment—and this had been painful, of course, watching his wife talk to him like he was a stranger. But then she had capped it by asking for his key.

"What do you mean?" He didn't get it.

"I want you to give me your key back."

"To our house?"

She flinched. "Yes. I'd be more comfortable."

They had already separated. He had moved out. Even now, sitting here in China, more than a year later, he didn't know why this simple request of hers had put him into such an agony of severance, but it did. And one last time he tried, to his misery and regret, to get her back.

"I really want the key," she had said gently but insistently. Her face was neutral. She looked soft but she was all steel.

He took his key ring out. "We don't have to do this," he said.

"It's just a key."

"I mean separate."

"Michael."

She sounded impatient and sad. There was no conflict in her voice. He could almost feel himself being extinguished. Meanwhile she was waiting. He worked the key off the ring. "Daphne." He wanted her attention, her real attention. He held up the key and took another key off his ring. "Take it. Take my key too. Come back anytime, any hour you're ready. I know you have things to work out. That's okay. Take the key. I want you. I don't want anyone else. I'll wait." He extended both keys.

She took only one key, her own, and slid it in her pocket. "That's very sweet," she said. Her eyes filled. "I'm touched. I'll always remember that you said that." And then she had turned and left.

He remembered the feeling of being sliced, of an ice pick through the center of him. That was the best she could do? Cry a little as she said it? Even now he still felt the sharp blade of hurt here in this bar, the piano marching around him over the slapping of the bass, the drum with its light, dividing accent beats. Evaporate, he told his memory. Go away. It crinkled to nothing. It would be back, he knew, but not tonight. He tuned in to the music, eyes closed, tapping his fingers softly in his own layer of syncopation, behind and all around the tempo from the stage below.

11

LIA'S TRAIN SHOT THROUGH THE DENSE SUB-
tropical hills, a rattling stream of mercury against
the red earth with its rippling shades of green.
It felt good to be alone. Most of the way from
Nanchang she'd sat with a family bringing their
aged father back from the big city after an opera-
tion. They were loud, friendly, all doting on the
old patriarch. They insisted she share their elaborate breakfast, stacked up on the little train table
in tin containers.

They talked about their lives, about the
scenery, and finally at the last town the family had
got off after much exchange of addresses and ex-
hortations to come and visit them in China, to
bring her own family, her husband; yes, she'd said,
of course, she would. She didn't bother telling
them she had no husband, no children. No need

to make it real. They did not actually expect to hear from her again. Still, they were all over her in the fullness of Chinese social grace. "Good-bye," she said again and again, all warmth and smiles, "good-bye."

And then it was only one more hour to Jingdezhen, an hour to herself. At first all she thought about was Michael. It was like he was there inside her, waiting for a private moment so he could well up and fill her mind again. If they kept seeing each other . . . but she pushed this warm-flooding premonition away. Maybe it was not real. Even if it was, she was still going to have to leave in a few days.

Then there was the job. She still had some questions to answer. As the train rocked along the rails she turned over and over what she had gotten from Gao, and what she'd dug out on her own. If the collection had not been moved out of the Forbidden City in 1913 for J. P. Morgan, if it had still been inside the Palace as of the 1924 inventory, then it was separated later.

She still thought this most likely happened during the collection's flight across China, through the war against the Japanese and then the civil war, 1931 to 1947—when the emperor's art made it to Taiwan. *That* was a long, arduous struggle in trucks, trains, and boats, often barely hours ahead of the bombs and artillery of advancing armies. It was the Nationalists, the Guomindang, who had the shipment. They moved it by night, sometimes by whatever rough hands could be assembled. How could some of it *not* have disappeared? The curators of the National Palace Museum in Taiwan, where the collection found its home, always took pride in saying that every one of the six hundred forty thousand pieces moved out of the Forbidden City arrived intact. Oh sure, Lia had always thought. Right.

Of course there were the twenty-one hundred crates that were well known to have been left behind in Nanjing—twenty-one hundred crates with some twenty-six thousand pieces of imperial porcelain. As everyone knew, they remained in deep storage in Nanjing while still, to this day, museum officials from Nanjing and Beijing feuded over who would get them. No one had ever seen them, except for a few curators who weren't talking. Aside from those crates, she had never heard a definitive story about any part of the collection being lost or separated along the way.

The art had started out on trains. Five trains, thirty-nine sealed cars each. The Japanese occupation of Manchuria had reached all the way down to Liaoning Province, perilously close to Peking. They could sweep in at any time. And so in a single night, in the fall of 1931, all the art was carried out of the Forbidden City and taken away.

She went inside, to her most private door. In deep memory she wanted to see this. She plucked out her hearing aids, rested her head against the train seat, and locked her vision through the glass. Out there were blurring, hurtling banks of green, dissolving. Inside her mind were the gates to the examination yard, great red gates with brass joins. They opened and she walked through.

Liu Weijin, one of the bureaucrats in charge of the Forbidden City in 1931, knew the end was near. They'd been updating inventories and packing boxes for months already, and the advance of the enemy had been as inexorable as lava flow. Now all Manchuria was Japanese.

They couldn't take all the art out to safety. They could only take the best of it. They worked fast: open the padded silk boxes, check the contents, add to the list, prioritize—staying, or going?—stack them to one side or another. The best workers were those who swiped like lightning with their brushes, methodical, unemotional, who could comb the dusty piles *without stopping to gaze at the glory they held in their hands. If they stopped to look, to feel, they could not do it. They could not keep up the pace.*

They wrote: a pale celadon vase, crackleware, ring-handled, mark and period from the Southern Song. A pair of mille-fleur wine cups, Qing, mark and period Qianlong. A hanging scroll painting of men crossing a bridge beneath steep mountains, signed by Tai Chin.

And then the word came. No one had known exactly when it would happen. Now it was here. In an instant, in a single turn of the head, they would have to flee. Today.

Liu Weijin put the phone down and turned to his colleague Tan Hui. "They are at the edge of Liaoning." It was only a few hundred li away. The orders went out like fire over dry grass. Crating and loading sped to a frenzy.

Now Liu needed soldiers. It was two miles from the Forbidden City to the train station. He could not transport the collection without armed guard. He knew the streets were awash in refugees, people trying to get out, walking, spilling on either side of the puttering string of motorized vehicles, stepping around the iron-wheeled rickshas, the bicycle-pumped carts, the mules pulling entire families heaped up with children and servants and possessions. Liu needed men—a lot of them. He dialed General Tong.

"General Tong, sir," he said breathlessly. "It is Liu Weijin—"

"Mr. Liu! You have received our message! Everything must be moved tonight."

"Yes." Liu said a silent prayer. "General. We need troops."

"Impossible," Tong said.

"The art must be guarded."

"The capital must be guarded," the General corrected him. "I cannot spare troops."

Liu swallowed. Most residents, of course, had no choice but to either

flee or go inside, lock their doors, and wait for the inevitable. "Sir," he
said, "please listen."

The General lapsed into reluctant silence.

"No matter what happens, we can get the art out. This is cultural
patrimony. This above all we should protect."

On the crackly phone he heard a long breath. Liu knew his words
had flown home.

"All right." General Tong's words all but collapsed Liu's heart with
relief. "You'll have troops."

So Nationalist soldiers arrived in trucks an hour later and dis-
mounted amid the loading of wheeled carts and the harnessing of mules.
Their rifles swung against their khaki puttees as they stepped in and out
of the decrepit Palace buildings, across courtyards with roots and tufts of
grass heaving up the ancient marble paving stones, listening to the
strange bounce of their voices off the timeless stone walls and the whistle
of wind on marble, trading cigarettes, laughing. Most had never been
inside the Forbidden City before. Most were young. Some seemed like
children.

In front of the soldiers, the laborers swarmed the line. They heaved
the crates into the big iron-wheeled wooden carts, stacked them like tall,
fat coffins, shouting, strapping the cargo down, pulling tight the ropes.

Finally they were ready to move. They had closed the streets running
south from the Forbidden City, and they'd closed Jung Hsien Hutong
east, all the way from the main corner where the Guomindang Party
Headquarters faced the Supreme Court to the station. Thousands of re-
cruits with smart brown straps of leather across their chests lined up
shoulder to shoulder along the entire route. They made a human wall
two li long.

When the first mule creaked and clopped through this uniformed
human tunnel, dragging the first cart, Liu Weijin walked beside it. This
was his cart, his most beloved things, and he meant to stay beside it all

the way and make sure it reached its destination. In here were his trea-sured Chenghua chicken cups, his favorite painting, Fan Kuan's "Travelers by a Mountain Stream," his favorite Qin bronzes and Yuan Dynasty carvings in white jade.

The mules set a slow, steady rhythm with their hooves against the broad flat stones, the spindly metal wheels creaked, and everything else held its breath in unnatural silence. The people had been ordered inside and away; those in the buildings on either side of Jung Hsien had been told to extinguish all lights. The only glow was from the torches carried by the mule drivers.

But the people were there. All the windows, all the cracks and cran-nies and peepholes, all the upper floors with their built-out, ornate porches—these were alive with eyes. Liu could feel the avid faces in the shadows, feel the gasping, riveted human energy. Whole clans pressed against windows to watch the emperor's treasures pass beneath. It was unheard of, it tore heaven and earth apart. Some people unrolled plain white banners from upper floors to signify mourning.

This will be a new Chinese world now, Liu thought. He looked behind him at the caravan of carts stretching away into the darkness pinpointed by the flaming brands, the rolling mule-drawn line he knew would rumble all through the night. Soon they would be Japanese subjects.

In a strange way he felt resignation. When the collection was loaded and had pulled out, he planned to melt away into the city, and from that moment on he'd put everything he had into surviving. He was lucky to have no family. Preservation would be his only goal.

And then they were there, rolling into the dark cavernous hall of P'ing Han Station with its soaring metal struts up under the distant roof, and the soldiers now shouted orders, directing, moving crates on the trains. Five full trains to load. Thirty-nine cars each. And as he watched his cart, his crates, his own personal points of light loaded into the first *car, on the first train, he let himself exhale. And then mute, held up by equal parts grief and wonder, he stood witness through all the hours it took the collection to arrive. Nineteen thousand, five hundred fifty-seven crates. One at a time. All night long.*

And from there, Lia knew, the art began its journey. Somewhere along those sixteen years lay her clue.

Jingdezhen was close. Already outside the train window, rising and receding out of the foaming red earth, she could see the low, sharp-topped green hills around the town. They were familiar to her. Like most porcelain people, she'd been here already. On pilgrimage.

She leaned her head against the glass. Thatched mud and brick homes of villagers raced by. Far ahead, down the track, she could see the charcoal haze that hung like a pall over the town, as it had for a thousand years. It was the smoke of pots cooking, an indescribably exciting scent.

The train squealed to a stop. Jingdezhen was the end of the line. The passengers dragged their bags over the steamy platform, across the tile floor, and through a low-ceilinged concrete terminal. The big glass windows were streaked with dirt of many years and admitted only a vague light. She was the only foreigner in the crowd, and tall too. She stood out as they all spilled onto the sidewalk, blinking in the hot liquid glare of the south China summer. Yet no one looked twice at her. They were used to outside pots people.

First she'd go to the Jingdezhen Hotel to get a room. She could see the flashes of Jiangxi's beauty, even here, walking up Zhushan Lu in the center of town. Banana fronds lined the roadway. Trees rustled over the low concrete buildings. Above the noises of traffic and machinery and the modern world rose the cacophony of birds.

She raised her hand for a taxi and had the driver take her high on Lianhuatang Lu, over a park with a small lake, to the Jingdezhen Hotel. It was a pretty, leafy spot backed up against the hillside, a backwater modern hotel with blank, inexpensive furniture, which always seemed empty. She checked in for a night.

From there she went straight to the Ceramics Research Institute. The best local professors and historians were here. She knew a few of them.

"Professor Lu Bin, is he by any chance in his office today?" she inquired of a thirtyish male clerk at the front desk.

"Professor Lu is here."

"Ah, so excellent." She handed him her card. "Please convey my apologies for visiting unexpectedly. But if he's free . . ."

The clerk picked up the phone, punched a code, and began talking in low and rapid Jiangxi dialect. It was a natural, territory-marking response to her having spoken Mandarin. She waited patiently. "He is free," the clerk told her finally, and she turned for the stairs. They were worn to soft, smooth basins under her feet.

Professor Lu was waiting for her at the top of the stairs. "Fan Luo Na," he said with his charming, rumpled surprise. Lu had over-long gray hairs he combed across the top of his head. Sometimes, like now, these picked up electric charge and lifted ghostlike from his scalp. He pulled off his brown glasses and smiled and blinked her into his office.

"It's been a long time," she said, which was a standard greeting whether it had been one year or ten. "Everything well?"

"Everything's well. Now, sit down! Have tea." He pulled her into his office and busied himself briefly with the things. "Now. Here." He set the cup in front of her. "Ah! But I have something to show you."

He fetched a catalog from a drawer in a side table and came back with it. She recognized its cover before he even sat down. It was the book from the last spring auction of Armstrong's, their principal rival house.

He opened it to a marked page. "Just look at this." He turned it toward her so she could see a tall, narrow-necked vase in iron-red glaze with a dragon design. Late Qing. She glanced at the caption below the photograph. *Reign of Xuantong.* She remembered it. It was a good piece, not a great one, but good. It had sold for about fifty thousand dollars.

"I made it," Lu said, unable to keep the glee from his voice.

"You?"

"I made it!" Lu cried. "I sold it to a businessman for five thousand *ren min bi.*"

That was about six hundred U.S. dollars. "You sold it to an ah chan?"

"A businessman," he repeated.

"You know," she said.

"Yes. I know." He wagged a finger at her. "But maybe I prefer not to know. Anyway. I sell it as *fang gu.* That's why my price is low. After that"—he tilted his head in practiced acquiescence—"I cannot control all that happens, can I? Someone may say it is real. I can't stop them!"

"Professor Lu, I am glad you make such beautiful pieces, and that happens to be the end of my judgment on the matter. But I am curious. Did you tell Armstrong's when you found out?"

He laughed. "No! Why should I? It is a good piece. Let its owner enjoy it."

And she smiled with him. But under her smile there was fear, because fakes slipped through all the time, bringing terror with them. In a flashing domino line of memory, she relived all her beautiful pots in Beijing. Which one had she missed; which would still betray her?

She looked back at the catalog Lu Bin was holding open to her, the glossy professional photo of his own work. His iron-red vase was quite good. The *meiping* form was correct, if a little too thick-bodied and overt. The iron-red glaze was authentic-looking. It was a good piece. Like most of the academics here in Jingdezhen, he was first and forever a potter. "Professor Lu, truly, you surpass yourself," she told him.

His glasses had slipped down his nose and his stray hairs crackled up. "This! This is just an old teacher's hobby."

"Don't be polite." She knew that Lu was a serious artist who held an elite status in that world. He made contemporary pieces too. They were technically accomplished. But that was not what porcelain was for him. In the West, where what was fresh and innovative was always sought and always loved, it was different. Here, the heights were often heights of perfection, not genius. Mastery was greater than genius. It was knowable; it could be held in memory with all of its faces and moods. Never fully understood, perhaps—for there was always more to learn—but held and kept. As she knew. "I love it," she told him. "It's very fine."

"Oh, now you are just passing praise." To accept her compliment would have been inappropriate, but he was pleased and she could tell as much. "When creating *fang gu,* one should seek not to express one's soul, but to subsume it, in the prototype."

"You're so right," she said. "There was the man—ah, what was his name?—Geng, was it not, Geng Jiewu?"

"Geng Jiewu!" said Professor Lu. "He used to make the Persian-style Ming pots after those in the Zhengde reign."

"Yes!" she cried. "And with his false Arabic, he could never resist making it just close enough to real Arabic to be read, and in his Arabic making puns."

"Do you remember when that was discovered in London?" the older man said.

"*Ei*, yes," she answered. "What a thing! And the piece was in a British museum already." They both laughed, glee and horror gloriously intermingled, completely at one in the sharing of arcana. "And there are others." She looked across at him. "Do you know, for example, that artist who always ruffles the tail feathers of the chicken when he paints in the Chenghua style? That one? Do you know the man I mean?"

"Old Yu!" he cried.

"Yes," she said, hardly breathing. "Does he still live?"

"Potter Yu? Of course." The professor looked at her, seeing now why she'd come. It was on her face. But that was all right. They had shared so much good face and *guanxi*, she was entitled to ask. "He lives out on Mian Hua Lu on the north edge of the township—off Mian Hua Lu, actually, up the hill; it's no more than a dirt road. The people out there know his place." He smiled thinly. "Yu likes to live in what you might call the suburbs. He needs room to work."

JACK FELT ANNA stirring next to him. He had been awake for hours, propped up on pillows in the pine-pole bed on the lower level of their beach house. This bed, like the living quarters upstairs, faced a wall of glass and one hundred eighty degrees of rain-churned ocean. She moved closer to him. Her voice was half awake. "What are you thinking about?"

"Porcelain." He felt her quiver with laughter.

"You're obsessed."

He refocused through the window. The light was growing, coming down over the mountains behind them, making the small line dividing the ocean from the sky linger a moment in incandescence. "You know what the breakdown looks like?"

"What?" She gave in and pushed up on the pillow beside him.

"There are masterpieces in it. Out of eight hundred pieces, eighty or so are masterpieces. Stunning. Worth millions of dollars."

"And the rest?"

"Many fine, many important, many just good. But"—he repeated something Dr. Zheng had said—"that is the bedrock of any collection."

"You just want to *have* it," she said.

"Yes," he said. "But don't you see? Everyone who collects wants to have it. The hard thing is *getting* it. Here we have a chance to actually get it, a lot of it, the best, uncontested, just like that."

"Do we get a discount?"

He pushed her gently. He had gone over the sample descriptions until his eyes ached. It was pages and pages of descriptions, of digital photos, of resemblances and relationships to other known works in museums, in catalogs, in collections, and sold at previous auctions—sold "in these rooms" was the way they liked to put it. He began to glimpse the net of connections and references under everything. It was numbing, thrilling. "Prices for this stuff have gone nowhere but up," he said.

"You keep saying that," she said. "I know. People have mostly made money."

"Consistently," he said, going a little too far.

"Consistently *recently*. But you're still talking about . . . china."

"People buy paintings for more."

"Paintings don't break."

"Insurance."

"It just seems—"

"Two million isn't even the top," he told her. "One of the Chenghua chicken cups sold in Hong Kong a few years ago for four million."

"A cup?"

"A cup."

She frowned. "We don't have one of those, do we?"

He couldn't suppress the start of a grin. "No. We don't have one of those. There are only eighteen in the world. We have a copy of one in the collection, though—a forgery. Quite masterful, apparently."

"A copy!" Her voice went up to a squeak.

He laughed. "No, no, the appraiser caught it. It's offered only as a curiosity. At a fractional price. But they say it's gorgeous and quite convincing. Actually, there are several copies. The latest e-mail says she has found nine. A little collection of fakes, inside the collection."

"How convenient. It comes with things we can put on our sideboard."

"And at our beach house." He went earnest. "I actually think we should keep some at our beach house. The real ones." He reached down and pulled a blanket of the Skokomish tribe up over them, settled back with his arm behind her head.

"That's crazy," she said.

"Not crazy," he corrected her. "It's our life. Listen," he said. "We'll have eight hundred pieces. An unparalleled group. We could have a museum with that, just with that, if we wanted. But I think I'd rather keep it private."

She shrugged. It appealed to her, though. A whole Chinese past. "We could look into it," she conceded.

The sun's rim crested the horizon.

"What's his total estimate?" she said.

"Oh," said Jack confidently. "I think we could get it for a hundred and fifty million . . . about the cost of three great Van Goghs."

"HAVE YOU HEARD anything about Hu and Sun?" Bai asked Zhou over the phone. He knew Zhou had just come back from Guangzhou. Somewhere near there, the two men were being held. It was at Guangzhou they had been arrested, for it was there, the most crowded, most anonymous overland point, that most ah chans these days chose to cross the border.

"I've heard nothing," Zhou replied.

On his end, Bai swallowed. They'd already been arrested. Now only two possible outcomes remained. One was that Hu and Sun had bought their way out and were already free. That could only have happened if they had enough cash on their persons to do it quickly, persuasively, unobtrusively. That was one possibility. The other was that they could not bribe their way out and were already scheduled to be stood up against a wall, maybe tomorrow, maybe the next day, and shot.

12

SHE SAW THE OLDER MAN LOOK UP FROM his worktable at her, a foreign woman standing in the gate to his courtyard. She shouldn't have just come here. She should have gotten his number and called.

"*Huanying, huanying,*" he said, standing up, Welcome. "You speak Chinese?"

"I do," she said. "Is it convenient? May I enter your studio?" Her eyes raked behind him, took in the rows of pots, saw a prevailing harmonic balance that was immediately exciting to her. He was good.

"Come in. Please. You're a porcelain person?"

"I am. I study pots and appraise them."

"An artist too?"

"No—just a specialist." In China it was more

commonplace for experts to also make pots themselves. Not her. She dug out her card.

He held up his hand. "Wait."

She looked up. Cards always came first in China.

"A small joke! An amusement! Listen. I'd like your opinion." He gleamed with coconspiracy. "I have in mind to make a *wucai* stem cup after the style of Xuande. I seek among these"—he gestured to the thousands of unfinished pots in straight lines—"the right body, the right set of ratios."

She understood at once and followed him down the path, between the shelves, the rows, tightly packed, everything in the biscuit. "Flared rim?" she said. "Everted sides?"

"Just so!"

"What for decoration?"

"Four floral medallions. Flowers all the way open, reds, yellows, and greens."

"Lovely." They walked a moment in silence, then separated, scanning, sidling up and down the tributary rows by themselves. Both knew the feeling they were looking for.

And then after a time she stopped and stood still. "Pardon me," she said.

He turned.

"What about this one?" She motioned to it with her chin. It truly was the ideal stem cup. It was finely potted, faintly squat. There were four sides for painting and a bamboo-node stem. "Beautiful," she complimented him. "So nicely made." She could see what he would do with it—the iconic flowers, spare, outlined, slightly Islamic, in near-primary colors. The reign mark not enclosed in a shape, as it usually was, but instead free characters, circling the base. Perhaps a single or double blue line around the foot and inside the rim.

Lia looked up from the biscuit cup at the thousands of unfinished pieces aligned around her. He had quite a factory here.

She knew how this game worked. Rich collectors in Hong Kong sought to unearth artists like Yu and then would keep them strictly to themselves. And for a while, one *fang gu* after another would be commissioned, and everyone would be happy. But eventually the buyer would grow unsure as to whether it was actually the master or only his assistants making the commissions. One would inevitably find that the master did the pieces he wanted to do, and no more. In time the relationship would sputter down. And then someone else would discover the artist, and it would begin again. She wondered who his patrons had been. He was very, very good. "Very *hoi moon*," she said.

"*Guojiang,*" he said modestly, Pass praise. But he wore a wide smile when he picked up the cup and carried it to a worktable. Turning back, with some ceremony, he removed a card from a pocket beneath his apron. She had hers ready too. They both used two hands. It was quite a show of manners.

"Yu Weiguo," she read from his card.

"Fan Luo Na." She watched him continue reading and register the name, Hastings. "You must come and see our finished pieces," he said. "Please. You will enjoy them."

"With pleasure!"

"You like *fang gu*?"

"More than you imagine!" At the other end of the work yard they entered a low brick house through double wood doors. Yu snapped on the lights. She stared for a minute and then circled the room, lined with all-glass shelves, the pots loosely organized by dynasty. "Oh, they're beautiful," she said to him. Then she stopped in front of a flat-sided moon flask in underglaze blue-and-white, with a scene of musicians playing against a landscape. So rare, for usually moon flasks were painted with birds on flowering branches. But these were musicians, dancing past each other on the path, mountains behind them layered and leveled by mists. "The reign of Yongle," she said softly. "Am I right?"

"You are right."

Because she could barely let herself believe it, but this one looked real. It looked right and gorgeous and real. Another fiction? Or the truth?

And then, looking closer, she saw the crack and, dialing in further still, the accumulation of centuries of fine dirt in the crack. So the flask was real—and damaged. "A fantastic piece," she told him. "So fine. Too pitiable about it."

He shrugged. "If it was not cracked, how would I be privileged to have it?"

"That's so."

He turned to her. "I have an idea," he said. "Will you allow me . . ."

She shrugged. "Of course."

"Sit." He waved to an armchair upholstered in plastic leather. "Be at ease." And he moved quickly around the room, collecting pieces from one shelf and then another, clustering them on the table. It was an echo of her on-the-spot test with Dr. Zheng, so many years ago. "Have a look at these," he said.

Yu had the table covered with pots of every height and shape and description, an ad hoc diagram of the past exhaling the cold clay scent of age. She looked a long time through narrowed eyes, in silence. Finally she went to one end of the table and started touching each pot in turn, wrapping both hands for a moment around each one.

Yu didn't say anything. He stood and watched her.

When she came to the end she looked at the assemblage for a moment, the whole group, and then with brief economic swipes began shifting the pots' positions. The low Zhengde dish with fish and water weeds she put to the left; the green box with its domed cover, its soft *lingzhi* and classic scroll design typical of Chenghua, to the right.

She did this in silence. Real on the left. Fakes on the right. As she shifted each, she held it again for an extra second before releasing it.

She didn't speak until she was done. "Stunning. So *hoi moon.*" She picked up a dish with a double *vajra* design in underglaze blue and switched to Mandarin. "So *kai men jian shan,*" Let the door open on a view of mountains. "Mr. Yu, this one is the mountain itself." She pointed to the four dragons carrying lotus blooms in their mouths, each flower centered with the Buddhist *vajra* emblem, also suggesting the Chinese character *shi,* or ten.

Then she turned the bottom of the *fang gu* dish to the light, with its six-character reign mark *da ming cheng hua nian zi,* made in the reign of Chenghua, in the great Ming Dynasty. The Chenghua emperor had brought back this design, which had not been prevalent since the Yuan Dynasty. Indeed, the reign mark was perfect, encased in a double blue ring. Oh, brilliant. "Excellent. I truly commend you." She put the *vajra* dish back on the table.

But was he the Master of the Ruffled Feather?

She covered the table with a look. She didn't think so. If she had to guess right now she'd say no. She had seen all kinds of designs here, painted flowers and birds of every type, and nowhere had she seen that exact little fillip of style.

She picked up a globular, narrow-mouthed jar with a lotus-pond decoration. It was painted in bright *doucai* of brick red, yolk yellow, and green. "The Mirgentesse jar!" she exclaimed, naming the current owner of the famous piece this *fang gu* reproduced. "Incredible."

"Your eye's not bad at all. Not in the least!" he said.

"Pass praise." She put back the jar.

"You missed only one!"

She stood still for a second. "What?"

"I mean, you missed one pot. One only. That is excellent."

"I missed one?" She turned to her assembly of pieces.

"Come," he said. "You were marvelous! Who could get every single one correct?"

"I should have."

He lifted a brow.

"I know pots. I can't get one wrong."

"It's of no consequence." He raised his hands.

"It is to me." She couldn't stop her mind, her memory—already she was flipping through the Beijing pots, one by one. "Mr. Yu. Did you ever—pardon me for asking—did you ever make a blue-and-white rectangular flask, Yuan Dynasty? With cranes and peonies?"

"No," he said.

Okay, she thought, that one's safe. But the images continued to parade before her memory. "What about an *an-hua*-decorated white glazed bowl, incised with dragons, reign of Yongle?"

"No."

"And a big broad-shouldered famille-rose jar, painted with chrysanthemums, that one, from the reign of Yongzheng?"

"No again." But now his long lantern face, cut in its folds and crevices, creased up in amusement as a light came into his eyes. "It sounds like you have talked to someone who's seen the Wu

Collection. Is it so? Are we thinking of the same one? More than seven hundred pieces?"

The world seemed to rock a hundred eighty degrees. "Eight hundred," she said before she could stop herself.

"You know! You have seen it?"

"No." She hesitated. "Someone I know told me."

"Ah."

"What about you?" She turned it around. "Have you ever seen it?"

"No. Wouldn't that be the good fortune of three lifetimes! But even just hearing about it's enough to make me so jealous my spittle's three feet long."

"What have you heard?"

"*Ei,* the same thing one always hears, isn't it so? It was hidden in the countryside and forgotten. Then discovered again, and sold. But no one knows who has it now. That's why I was excited when you began to describe it! I admit it! I thought perhaps you had seen it."

"No," she said, growing comfortable with her falsehood. "But I'd like to know more about it. The Wu Collection, you said?"

"Yes, that's how they call it."

"Where did it come from? Did someone have it hidden?"

"I don't know anything about it. I can try to find out, if you like."

"Thank you. I'm grateful."

"Your e-mail's on your card?" He pulled it out and looked at it.

"Yes." E-mail; of course he'd prefer e-mail. She'd seen a satellite dish on top of the little building too. "Thank you for checking into this. Let me know, please."

"All right, then."

"Potter Yu."

"Yes."

"Which one did I get wrong?"

"Ah! Yes! I was too distracted by the stream of words. This one." And he pointed to a miniature celadon vase in the archaic style of a bronze urn but shimmering, pale green. It bore the mark and period of Qianlong. A minor piece. And that was the first thing for which she kicked herself—that once again she'd failed to look as closely as she might have, precisely because it was modest.

She had to remind herself that most of the pieces up in Beijing, some five hundred of the group in fact, were modest pieces, good pieces, no more. Dread cut through, a ripsawing cord in high wind. She ought to go back and check things again. Maybe she wasn't even close to being finished. "You made this?" she said, picking up the celadon and spreading her fingers all around it.

"I made it."

"It's terrific," she breathed. The truth was, modest or not, it had fooled her. Now that she knew, of course, she could feel it; the newness of it, the calculation of composition and glazes, the twenty-first-century science applied to every aspect of it. She had to be more careful. Focus better, go deeper, accept nothing but the real truth.

A knock sounded then and the glass door pushed open. A man with a poor chin, a long, ropelike body, and an upsweep of black hair stepped in. *"Ei,"* he said. "Old Yu."

"Miss Fan," Yu said, "meet Mr. Bai."

"Hello."

"My pleasure," Bai said.

If she had not already known by his slickly provincial style that he was an ah chan, she would have known when he made no move to produce a card. Ah chans used multiple names, changed numbers frequently. They moved among their wives. Business cards were not for them. "My pleasure too," she said.

"What brings you to Jingdezhen?" He was looking at her with undisguised curiosity, but that was normal—she was a foreign woman.

She smiled. "As a porcelain person, I am always needing to learn more about pots."

"My feeling exactly," he smiled, and then he and Yu switched over to Jiangxi dialect. She was able to follow only the faintest outlines. The man Bai was coming to pick something up. He was hoping Potter Yu had it ready for him. Something like that.

Yu left the room and came back with a small box. He presented it to Bai with pleased formality. The younger man lifted the lid and a glow of pure happiness suffused his face.

"Can I see?" she asked.

"Of course." Bai turned the open box toward her.

She looked into it and almost lost her balance.

It was a chicken cup.

Oh, she would kill for this. It was perfect. Ineffably right, perfectly potted, it was executed with the light touch that looked so easy though it was so hard. The best thing was the warm, white glow of the clay, the Chenghua light perfectly reproduced. *Oh, why can't I have it? I want it. I'd be so good to it.* "It's devastating," she said with deep appreciation. "It's wonderfully good."

"Old Yu can really make a pot."

"That he can." She watched Bai stare down at the cup with the slack-mouthed pleasure of love. He might have been looking down at a beautiful woman, arms and legs open. He had scored. Here was a thing that had the power to make him feel whole.

She wondered what he planned to do with it. It seemed unlikely to be a money transaction, the acquisition of something to resell as a forgery. The chicken cup was too rare. No knowledgeable buyer would fall for it, as the whereabouts of those still known to exist could be verified with a few phone calls.

No, this ah chan wanted the cup for himself. He loved it. She could tell.

"*Xingsi rongyi, shensi nan,*" Bai said, To attain physical likeness is easy, to capture the spirit, hard. "That is what distinguishes Potter Yu." He held the cup up to the light. "I have many books, you understand. I study them all the time. Now I have a cup I can study too."

So he was one of the would-be scholars. Among the ah chans, one always met those who were book hounds. They were frantic for learning. They were the ones always pestering you for catalog references and attributions. After any exchange, they were always the ones who stayed around for ten minutes of probing questions. And in return, they'd tell you who was making fakes. "Congratulations, Mr. Bai. It's a wonderful purchase."

"*Nali,*" he said, but acknowledged her compliment with a small laugh as he turned the cup. God, the clay, she thought again, the warm light; it's perfect. And the design. Grasses waved in the summer breeze, baby chicks scuttled, a hen bent over and scratched. Another hen turned and looked at her, her own tail feathers flouncing high in the air—

Lia stopped. She cleared her mind. She looked away for a minute, glanced out through the plate-glass door to the work yard with its tables, its potting wheels, its thousands of pots in the heavy, still light of late afternoon. Had she just seen that? Then back to the cup, carefully. Yes. The tail feather curled. It was the ruffled feather. She pulled a photo image of the collection's chicken cup, its *fang gu* copy, from her memory. The same. The feather had the flip.

"Mr. Yu," she said, turning now to the potter, "I cannot bow low enough."

"No, no," he said appropriately. "Nonsense."

"No, I mean it. It's devastating. But if I may ask. Have you ever made another with this . . . feather?" She motioned lightly with her eyes. She knew he understood. A signature such as this was always perfectly conscious.

"Oh yes. The feather itself? More than a few times, when the chicken motif is used. But this exact style, after the Chenghua prototype—we did another one of these too. If I remember it was the year before last."

"And what became of it?" she asked carefully.

"I sold it to a businessman." His eyes slid to Bai. "One of them."

She nodded. From there, of course, it could have gone any-where. But Potter Yu was the one. He had to be. "Mr. Yu."

"Yes."

"Do you know you are famous among pots people? Do you know what we call you?"

"What?"

"We call you the Master of the Ruffled Feather."

Yu smiled.

"It's true, it's true, we do."

"*Ei!* I confess, here in our studio we curl the feather, that is our style. Isn't it amusing how people say a thing, and it sticks, then oth-ers say it! Well, similar sounds echo each other, isn't it so? *Ei?* But the truth is, the Master of the Ruffled Feather is not I! I don't do the painting anymore. I've not done so for a long time."

"What?" Lia looked at him.

"Really, it's the truth, the Master of the Ruffled Feather is someone else! I haven't the eyesight to paint anymore." He looked at her strangely. "Don't you know this? It's true for many families here. All the generations may work together, but it's the young people whose painting reaches the highest marks. Especially the teenagers. They have the hands and the eyes."

"I didn't know this," Lia admitted, stunned at herself—here she was, led along by her fantasy: Old man equals master. How clichéd. And yet her colleagues thought the same. They often talked about how much they feared any *fang gu* artist who could truly, gorgeously paint—since it was so often the "rightness" of the painting that made a piece real and not fake—and this most respected foe was always imagined as a man, and never a young one. Certainly not a teenager. She gathered her composure. "If I may ask," she said, "these years, who has been the master painter in your family?"

Yu let out a pleased growl of a laugh and used the flat of his hand to push open the glass door. "Yu Ling!" he bawled, sticking his head out. He pulled back in, grinning. "You'll see for yourself," he said, and he and Bai exchanged looks.

The door cracked open and a young girl stepped in sideways, her hair back in two braids, dark soft eyes. She looked like a child, though she could have been fifteen. "*Laoyeh,*" she said in greeting to him.

"My granddaughter," he said. "Yu Ling. Yu Ling, Miss Fan and Mr. Bai."

"Pleased," she said, and bobbed her head to them.

"Are you the painter?" Lia asked.

"Yes." Yu Ling was too shy to look up, and only did so in quick darts. "I paint the pots."

And my God, you're just starting, Lia thought. "Words can barely express my compliments," she told the younger girl in a voice full of warmth. "Your work is very, very fine."

The girl gave one small, satisfied grin and then averted her eyes again. "Thank you," she said.

"You can go," Yu told her.

The girl left and the elder potter turned back to Bai. Lia listened as the two men slipped into Jiangxi dialect. Bai paid for the cup—only five thousand *ren min bi,* she saw. A bargain. A paltry sum. He was a lucky man.

The ah chan was ready to go, and polite good-byes went around. "I congratulate you again, Mr. Bai," she said. "It is a great day for you."

"Yes!" He was grinning. "With greater days on the way. Potter Yu? I thank you. Good business. Good luck. Miss Fan? Good luck."

"*Bici,*" she answered.

Then he was gone, the door clicking and jingling behind him. After a silence she said, "I think I've met him before."

"It's possible. Bai is everywhere."

"Why do they do it?" she said, thinking about men like Bai. "They take so much risk, buying up *zu chuan,*" heirloom holdings, "transporting them out."

Yu gave his low laugh again, and this time tempered it with a sad shake of his head. "For them the money is everything. They think all the time about money. Though they are fools with it! They get it and then they spend it as fast as they can and then they are poor again. Then again they get it. So what should they fear? Death?" He laughed, his eyes almost disappearing behind the lined mask of his face. "Why?" He wiped at his eye. "There's nothing for them to fear! Open the door, do you see it or not? Here is the fact. If they have enough money they can make even the spirits on the other side do whatever they want."

13

SHE WALKED DOWN THE MAIN STREET IN
Jingdezhen, her mind shimmering with excitement. She had part of the story now, at least. Her
pots were the Wu Collection, forgotten, discovered, sold, and the center of local rumors since.
This felt real to her; it clicked with the little she'd
heard from Gao. Not only that, now she knew the
Master of the Ruffled Feather . . . a teenage girl.
She still couldn't get over that one.

Her walk was giddy through the drifting clots
of people on the sidewalks, past the open storefronts with their goods stacked up, mostly pots,
pots of every size, quality, and description. Nothing great, most of it crude and cheap, much of it
fang gu. This alone was enough to awaken the
thrill in her. She scanned the stalls, a predator.

When she saw a row of Chenghua chicken cups, she stopped and bent to look.

Unfortunately they were poor copies. She'd seen much better ones for sale in other places.

"You have good eyes," the proprietor said approvingly from his chair. He touched his thick glasses for emphasis, a cigarette smoldering in his hand.

She looked up at him through the crowded forest of pots on the counter. "Yes, Chenghua chicken cups," she said. "After the Ming prototype."

"Well." He made a small laugh. "They're not Ming, exactly."

"No," she said, and thought, *that's* an understatement. She picked one up and turned it over. It did have a reasonable facsimile of the Chenghua reign mark.

"Still, they're old," he assured her, "just not quite that old."

"Old?" she said, playing along. "Let's see. They're not Kangxi using Chenghua marks—"

"No. They are a little later than Kangxi. You have good eyes!"

"Not Yongzheng—"

"No. But, *xiaojie,* they are nineteenth century. They are copies made in the nineteenth century. Trust me on this, they are."

"Well. I could concede that they might be a few months old. Or maybe just a few weeks."

"Good eyes," he said again. This time they both laughed. She waved and stepped out of his stall and back into the flow of the sidewalk. Her cell phone went off and she flipped it open. "*Wei.*"

"It's me."

"Hi," she said. Michael. The sound of his voice wrapped around her.

"I was wondering whether you were finished with work."

She grinned, weaving through the crowd. "I am finished, actually. For today. But I'm not in Beijing. I had to leave for a few days. I'm down south. In Jiangxi Province."

"Where?"

"A town called Jingdezhen. Near Nanchang. South of the Yangtze."

"Are you on the porcelain trail?"

"I am."

"Why there?"

"Oh, but this is the place." She looked around at the honking, hill-climbing downtown, the cluttered jumble of little concrete buildings, the profusion of pots, all colors, all sizes, piled up, multiplying everywhere. "This is our holy city."

He couldn't hold in a joyful little toot of laughter. "Oh, really? Have you met the Maker?"

"Yes! As a matter of fact I have. And it turns out the real master is his granddaughter, who's fifteen at most. God. She can really paint. One day she'll be my undoing."

"And why is that?" In a flicker his voice had dropped its bantering humor and now put out the warmth of wanting to know.

"Because what she makes looks so real," Lia said.

"And what's real and what isn't could undo you?"

"Oh yes," she said, meaning it. And then she thought, you too could undo me. If I crossed the line with you, and learned it was not real.

"Are you coming back?" he said.

"Yes, late tomorrow. I have more work in Beijing. I'm not done."

"Good news for me," he said.

"And for me. I'd love to see you. But not the minute I get back, if that's okay. I have to go see the collection first. The next day, though—should I call you?"

"Just come find me," he said.

"Okay, then." She could feel that sneaky grin of interest in another person tugging at her face. She felt a rising sense of lightness in her midsection. "I think I know where you are."

THE JINGDEZHEN AIRPORT opened only when there was a flight, and when Lia stepped out of her taxi there the next afternoon it was still locked up. In time, though, workers arrived and unlocked the flimsy glass door. Forty minutes later it could have been any little wood-benched airport, anywhere. Families sprawled, young women bounced babies, businessmen carried boxed porcelains and briefcases.

She sat down and watched a woman opposite her share one set of mini-headphones with a teenager, each with a plug in one ear. They were whispering along with a Cantonese pop tune. There was something sweet about them. They sat with their legs splayed out and their toes tapping. Sisters? Lia thought. Aunt and niece? They were so unconscious of themselves in the middle of the crowd, eyes far off, bonded to each other. She couldn't stop looking at them.

"Miss Fan?" said a voice from her right.

It was the ah chan. "Mr. Bai," she said. "How surprising."

"Not really," he said half ruefully. "There's only one flight a week."

"True," she said. She could guess from his stacked lash-up of brocade boxes what business took him north, to Beijing. He had eight or nine of them in a twine-knotted net, with a handle he'd improvised on top. She wondered if he had the chicken cup.

"You return to Beijing?" he asked.

"Yes. This was just a quick visit for me. And you?"

"Business," he echoed, and smiled.

"Good luck," she said.

On the plane she saw him sitting some rows ahead of her with his friends. They were full of swagger, laughing, enjoying one another.

She slept for a while. When she awoke it was to the sound of the muddy intercom system, the voice speaking Chinese through waves of static. She tuned in to it. They'd be late in landing, and something about the situation on the ground in Beijing.

Now she was awake. Situation?

"What situation?" she asked the man sitting next to her.

"Bu da qingqu," he said, I'm not clear. He had been sleeping too, his mouth open, his head collapsed on his shiny pinstriped shoulder, and had just jerked back to consciousness. He rearranged himself with a series of small, staccato throat-clearings and fumbled in his briefcase.

The ah chan Bai turned from the front of the plane and met her eyes with his, a simple nod of acknowledgment. She nodded back. He probably didn't know anything either.

The plane landed and taxied normally but then stopped a few hundred yards from the terminal. First fifteen minutes, then a half hour, then forty-five minutes, everyone nervous and shifting in their seats. She could feel the fear. These days, anything during air travel that carried even the hint of strangeness plunged people into trembling alarm. Lia listened, eavesdropping on the Mandarin around her, and realized that no one knew what was going on. Whatever it was, it had happened after they left Jingdezhen.

Finally the engines roared up again and they rolled to the gate. Lia spilled out into a cavernous hall with the others, pouring through the crowd, hurrying over the mirror-polished faux-stone floors. All around she heard a rolling, burry wash of Mandarin spotted with pockets of English and other foreign languages, everything bouncing off the gleaming surfaces up to the high metal rafters above. Why were there so many people? In the press of faces she read agitation, fear, anger. She wished she didn't have to hear. She wanted to take her hearing aids out. It was too much.

To the right she saw the sign EXIT AND BAGGAGE CLAIM. When they passed through the security doors they hit an even bigger crowd. The massive hall where people customarily came to meet arrivals was jammed with Chinese. She threaded through them in a thin line of exiting passengers, ducked through the doors, and ran outside.

Taxis were in a snarl. She picked one outside the hive and circled to it. A head taller than everyone else, obstinately Caucasian, she cut through the traffic at a sprint. The driver was too surprised to say no when she yanked open the door to his cab.

"Qu nar?" he said to her, Where are you going?

"Jiaodaokou Nan, Gulou Dong, neige lukou," she said, Corner of Jiaodaokou South and Gulou East. He pulled out. They came to the airport exit, he paid the toll, and she waited until they were flying along the Jichang Expressway to speak again. "What is it, this thing that's happened?" she said. "What's going on?"

He looked at her in the mirror.

"At the airport."

His eyes went back to the road. "A flight coming to Beijing crashed."

"Oh. But that's terrible." She sat back like she'd been pushed. Phillip, she thought. Phillip had been bound for Beijing. "What airline?" she said.

"China International."

"Oh. Awful." To herself she was thinking: China International. A Mainland company. Phillip would never take a Mainland airline unless his flight had been canceled and he had no other options. However. Such things happened. She would call the office right away. "Did it crash on landing?" she asked, because she had seen no indications at the airport, no lights, no blinking chaos of emergency. Just all those people.

"No. It exploded over the ocean."

"Oh. That's very bad," she said quietly, fearing the worst kind of scenario. "What happened?"

"Do I know? How can I know? No one says yet." He pointed to the radio. "But some boats in the area saw a light streaking up. So people are already saying it was shot down."

"Shot down?" She leaned forward in her seat, trying to tick through the possibilities in her mind. Which terrorist organization? A domestic insurgent group? "Who would have shot it down?"

"The U.S., is what people say."

"The U.S.!" That is not remotely possible, she thought. How could it be in the interests of the U.S. to shoot down a passenger jet? Not the U.S. Not deliberately. She was sure of it. She looked up at the man behind the little Plexiglas partition so many of the taxi drivers used in hopes it would protect them from assault and theft. She could tell by the narrowing of his eyes and the tight look he threw into the mirror that he didn't agree.

Well, she thought, he wouldn't; there were deeper tides at work. Whenever U.S.–China relations got rough, the well of China's nationalistic resentment seemed to open up again. It was always there. And even though there were times when the government encouraged such sentiment for its own reasons, the sentiment itself was real, a true net of memory under everything, memories of slights and wars and victimization by foreign governments—

despite the manifest greatness of the civilization. *Despite* that. So galling. Yes, and wasn't this one of the very things she had always so loved about this place: that historical memory was so long, so widely held. It was one of the ways art and culture had endured. Yes. And here was memory's flip side, the chronic remembrance of *guochi,* national humiliation. "Whatever happened, it's terrible," she said.

He was looking at her in the mirror. "Are you American?"

"No," she said.

"What then?"

"Me?" She bristled, covered it. *"Xin Xi Lan ren."* New Zealander.

"Ei."

"It's a tragedy."

"Jiu shi le ma," he answered, Isn't that so.

Talking to him had become uncomfortable and she leaned against the window, staring out at the walls and overpasses and buildings, the construction sites. Probably the crash was an accident. The Chinese government would investigate and they would find out and they would make an announcement saying so. At least that was what she hoped. She looked back at the line of the driver's jaw, the hardness in his eyes.

It had better happen soon, because Phillip was on his way and they had to finish. Phillip. Her mind went back to its whirling. Phillip would never fly China International. Would he? Ten to one he was waiting at the guesthouse.

The driver took her to the mouth of Houyuan'ensi Hutong. She got out there and paid him, walked quickly away from the roaring boulevard and down the lane to the guesthouse.

She stopped at the front desk. "Phillip Gambrill from the U.S.? Has he checked in?"

The clerk's expression told her he had not. "Would you look?"

Lia said, and the woman flipped through the register and confirmed it: No, he had not arrived.

So Lia went to her room, put down her things, and called. She
got Zheng's voice mail. She listened to his beautifully modulated
recorded greeting and then, when she heard the beep, experienced
a moment of panic because she was afraid even to articulate what
it was that she so feared. "Hi, just calling to double-check what airline Phillip was on and when he is due to arrive. I'm back in Beijing.
Call me."

She hung up and sat for a moment, just long enough to catch
her breath. It didn't matter when he was going to arrive, she couldn't
wait. She had to go to the pots. She still had a few good hours left.

SHE TOOK A taxi along the willow-lined edge of Houhai Lake to
the compound. The taxi driver was listening to the radio, a talk
show on which people were pouring out feelings about the plane
crash. People sounded wounded and resentful. "Aggressive acts by
foreign countries should be opposed," one man said. "China should
not permit this. We should take a firm stand."

But how do you know it's a foreign country? she thought. How
do you know it's not an accident?

"Hegemony must be resisted," said another caller.

Hegemony, hegemony, she thought, the powerful nation bul-
lies the weaker; definitely a memory-marker word here. Once it
had seemed like a catchphrase of the Communist era, but it still
had lightning-rod power today.

"The issue is a national one! Eight members of the Chinese
women's Olympic team were on the plane!" said a woman caller.

Oh. Lia started forward. Had she heard that right? That was
very bad.

People continued to cut in over each other, louder.

She wondered how the government was going to contain all this. Public opinion could no longer be ignored in China. That was the magical thing that had slowly happened. It was not like the old days when the government could control most of the flow of information. Now the government had to please its constituencies, now the government *had* constituencies, because people knew more, they had phones and faxes and the Internet and a media of sorts. Public debate was here, whether the government liked it or not. And it didn't sound like the public was happy. They had already decided who was at fault and they wanted action.

"The government shouldn't be so soft on foreign powers!" Now the voices were heated and broken up with static.

She got out at the villa, paid the driver, and ran across the humped bridge, along the stone paths, and into the building, through the rooms and the corridors and across the inner courtyard. She clattered in through the glass doors and snapped on the lights. It was all here. She felt completed just to be back with it.

Her phone rang.

"*Wei,*" she answered.

"Miss Fan." Gao Yideng. "You have returned? Your trip was suitable?" She could hear the wire of consternation in his voice.

"My trip was most interesting, thank you. I found answers to a few questions. As for my return, it was only a little delayed."

"You had no problems?"

"No. I'm with the collection now."

"And you progress well? You are close to finished?"

"Not quite," she said. "Almost."

"Ah. One had hoped—"

"Yes," she said. "But my colleague Phillip Gambrill is due to arrive at any time, and we must look at about fifty pieces together. Then we'll be ready. We'll submit."

"Good. Oh, and in case you have been wondering, Mr. Gambrill is at this moment arriving in Vancouver, British Columbia, to change flights."

"Oh!" she said. She let herself go to a quick fall of relief. "Thank you! I had not heard from him." She counted forward. So he'd be in Beijing in the morning.

"It's nothing. Please. I must not keep you from your work."

Gao hung up and turned to the man standing next to him in his office. It was Bai, the ah chan, hands deep in the pockets of his pleat-front pants. "The schedule is delayed," Gao said. "The load's not ready."

"*Ei,* the appraiser is slow."

"Not so slow."

"But he's a foreigner, right, the appraiser? That's why he's slow." Bai gave a small, self-satisfied laugh.

Irritated, Gao looked sideways at the ah chan. The southerner presumed, he imagined he knew every corner of the situation, when he actually knew nothing. Above all he knew nothing about the American woman. So far she had surpassed what Gao had expected. Not just her knowledge—her will. He was impressed. Each time he had challenged her or placed an untruth in her path she had risen to him, easily, and never without a pleasing cover of courtesy. A worthy opposite. In another life she'd have been an ally or a friend. He'd have liked that.

He still needed Bai, so he gave voice to only a narrow refraction of what he thought. "You are mistaken." He looked down to check his watch. "This art expert is highly knowledgeable."

"Of course," Bai said. He knew at once he'd stepped wrong. "So if not tonight, when do you calculate I shall load and leave?"

"Two days," said Gao. "With luck."

The ah chan showed nothing, but inside he frowned. He did not like the mood in Beijing just now, since the news had come out about the plane. He knew all the things that simmered underneath. *Dao shan huo hai,* hills of knives and seas of fire. Best to be gone from the capital as quickly as possible. "What about the vehicle?" he said hopefully.

"Ah! The vehicle is ready."

"It's so? Where is it?"

"Nearby. Would you like to go and see?" Gao Yideng said.

"Yes, through a thousand *li* of crags, if I had to," he said, and Gao laughed.

They went out into the street, which faced the rear gate of the Forbidden City. The avenue streamed with cars, the ancient moat shone with still water and clumps of lotus, the thick red palace walls rose up. The basement of Gao's little satellite office building held a contemporary art gallery; the top floor, a Thai restaurant.

Bai's heart sang with the well-deserved sense of being at the center of things. He was here. He had arrived. Gao's driver brought up the car. To Bai's pleasure, Gao dismissed the driver, saying he would drive and they would go alone. The two of them climbed in front with a satisfying slam of steel doors.

From behind the wheel, Gao Yideng looked over at his grinning passenger. In the provincial man's soft-lipped smile Gao saw everything: skittering joy, fierce ambition. Good, he thought, satisfied with this ah chan from the south, sure under his skin and in the center of himself that this man would take his eight hundred pots successfully out to Hong Kong.

PHILLIP GAMBRILL PRESSED his body as close as he could to the inadequate alcove of a pay phone in a large, roaring, open-domed atrium at the Vancouver airport. Between the stalls selling Vietnamese noodles and boxed planks of smoked salmon, across from the plazas selling fake native art and polyurethaned totems, he applied himself, straining against the noise, to the receiver. "I said, the flight's canceled."

Dr. Zheng was on the other end of the line. "What time's the next one?"

"There is no next one," Phillip told him. "Not now, anyway. All flights to Beijing are canceled. Shanghai too."

"All flights?" Dr. Zheng repeated.

"All flights." Phillip turned, twisted the cord under his arm, looked into the crowd. People standing, walking, sitting, sleeping. Families making islands with luggage and dozing children. Faces full of fear; it was back again. Something bad had happened. There were the relentless booming announcements, the flight numbers, the static names of other world cities, the white-peaked, evergreen-carpeted postcard prettiness of western Canada.

"Let me talk to our travel people. I'll call you back."

"I'll keep my phone." Phillip knew the Hastings travel people wouldn't tell Zheng any different. Right now no one could get him from anywhere in North America to Beijing. Hanging up, shouldering his bag, he gave up on it and walked back into the crowd.

14

MICHAEL DOYLE BENT OVER THE TABLE IN his room, laying out his Polaroids. These were the kids in his study. He'd taken a shot of each during the first interview, all against the same wall in his office. They were all between five and eight. Their little faces called out to him from childhood.

He liked to put the pictures in the order of their lead levels. At first he'd started with their newborn readings, from cord blood. This was maternal exposure, at birth, no more. When he got a tooth, though, he could see what they'd actually accumulated. This marker was much more solid. With each tooth he made another change, put the pictures in a new order. Today he moved Xiaoli. Twenty parts per million. Bottom row center, for now.

He passed his hands over his thin layer of

hair, half gray now since his illness, and his skull, strong, almost rectangular, widest at his ears and cheekbones. He could follow these children but he couldn't keep them safe. Again he reminded himself.

So he put the pictures in order. It also helped him keep his mind off Lia Frank. Why wasn't she back? And wasn't it amazing that he seemed unwilling to leave this room until he saw her get in? She had stepped across his path and somehow gained his attention, the involuntary drift of his awareness. First he had started to let pleasant thoughts breach his barrier, thoughts about what might happen. Now, admit it, he was worried about her. He was in here with the TV playing low because he was worried. He knew perfectly well she had not been on an international flight. She was coming from Jingdezhen. Still, there had been an air disaster. It was getting late. And no lights had come on in her courtyard.

He picked up the picture of Xiaoli, with her little bowl haircut and her quick, amused eyes. He taped it to the door frame. He liked the idea of those eyes following him as he passed by. He wanted to remember her.

Now something was happening on TV. He touched the volume button. It was a statement by—he squinted at the name and title that flashed on the screen—the Deputy to the U.S. Ambassador. The man stepped in front of the camera, cleared his throat, straightened his notes. "The United States joins China in grieving the crash of China International Flight Sixty-eight. We express the greatest regret and sorrow that this accident occurred. Our nation's prayers go to the families of those Chinese passengers and crew who lost their lives and"—a polished little beat—"also to the families of the six Americans aboard the plane, including four young Luce Scholars bound for fellowships in China. Our thoughts are with you."

Michael stood in the middle of the floor, sensed the invisible shift in dynamics. This would alter opinion. It had to. People couldn't think the U.S. would shoot down a plane with its own citizens on board. Or could they?

And where was Lia? He took a few soundless steps to the window and looked out over the half-curtain. He could see down the length of the courtyard and through the decorative rock gate. He could see the fountain spraying in the entry court, the pools of lamplight. But her court beyond was still dark.

AT THAT MOMENT Lia was sitting in a forest of boxes, hundreds of pots and their stories intersecting before her. She had been through all of them once. Now she'd seen dozens a second time. Tonight she had found yet one more fake, something minor, hardly enough to justify the effort. But this brought the count to ten. So it wasn't as if she could stop. She had to keep going, even though it was too much and it seemed insurmountable.

Her cell phone bleated. She flipped it open. *"Wei."*

"Lia," said Dr. Zheng.

"Hi. I'm glad you called. Phillip's not here. Gao said he was in Vancouver." She wedged the phone into her shoulder and lowered a pot back into its boxed froth of white silk.

"He's held up. It's the plane crash. All the flights are delayed."

"I know, I was delayed too, and that was domestic. How long?" She latched the lid down.

"Indefinite."

She paused, hand on the box. "Don't tell me this is turning into a . . . a situation."

"Well, the crash itself would seem to have been an accident.

These days, who can say? As to what they're reporting, about people seeing lights streaking up, I don't know. But there *was* a naval vessel, the U.S.S. *Roosevelt,* in the area at that time."

"Oh. That's sticky."

"I should think."

"Not good."

"No."

"Has the Chinese government made a statement?"

"Not yet. But air travel's frozen—at this moment, anyway."

"And Phillip . . . ?" She was getting the drift and she didn't like it at all.

"Phillip is not coming to Beijing. He made it as far as Vancouver. Then everything was canceled. If his flight had taken off an hour earlier he'd have made it."

"Well, so—when?"

"I can't say." There was a silence. "Luo Na," Zheng finally said. "You'll have to try to finish this yourself."

How can I? she wanted to scream. Nobody ever rules on anything alone, and these are eight hundred pieces, and already I've found fakes . . . it's beyond what anyone should be expected to stand by, alone. It had always been her fantasy to find a cache like this. Only in her fantasy, she was not alone, she was not uncertain, she was not already chipped away by falsehoods. "What choice do I have?" she said. "If I have to do it, I'll do it."

"The sale will be quick. I'm sure of it. He wants it."

"And the shipping?" she asked. Normally their Hong Kong office would take care of this.

"I've thought of that," Zheng said. "We still want to keep the purchase quiet. The buyer plans to remain anonymous. He doesn't want anyone to know he's acquiring it. I don't see any reason to bring the Hong Kong office in on things now. You can do it, Lia. It's only a few more days."

"I know," she said, feeling her adrenaline spike right up through the middle of her fear. "You're right. The profile should stay low."

"Very. Yes. But don't worry, I'll hire Tower Group. There'll be nothing for you to do except keep an eye on it."

"Good." Tower was the Rolls-Royce, the world-class Hong Kong company that specialized in packing and shipping fragile, incredibly valuable fine artworks. This job would be *wei ru lei luan,* as dangerous as a pile of eggs. But those people were masters. She knew that. "Okay," she agreed. "Let me get to work. I'll go as fast as I can."

GAO YIDENG DROVE the ah chan to the northeastern suburbs of the city, where just a decade ago pigs ran along the narrow raised paths between plots of vegetables and rows of poplars. Now it was a low-lying, semi-industrial outskirt with warehouses and factories, mopeds and carts and stores. The farm plots had receded. The wide streets of packed dirt buzzed with people shopping, carrying packages, going to work.

Gao drove up at the back of a blank white warehouse. He got out of the car and opened a combination lock, rolling up the automatic door just long enough for them to drive inside. Then it closed again.

The sedan whispered to a stop on the white concrete floor. In front of them stood a truck. It shone like a light from heaven. All white, it stood bright as ice, *Lanqian Industries* tastefully painted along one side. In the back the cargo compartment, made to order, was precisely measured. It would hold the crates of porcelain tightly and perfectly packed. Then the false wall, and the freezer compartment, as Bai had specified. This was narrow, not too deep, well insulated from the main cargo bay. Bai and Gao opened the rear doors of the truck into this freezer, swinging back the big plates of steel and shafting light into the mist-frozen compartment. The two men laughed in delight. It was early summer outside, blazingly hot already, and the frigid air blasting from the empty freezer was paradise.

Bai saw they'd done a beautiful job. He could do anything with this truck. He could drive this cargo all the way to Australia.

"Well?"

"It's perfect," Bai said. "You know what I say?" He turned to Gao. *"Tan guan xiang qing."* We might as well go ahead right now and congratulate each other and dust off our official hats.

SHE WAS SCROLLING down her list, her mind racing, dizzy with pressure, scanning for the next one she should get out and recheck. There were no more second opinions now. Everything rode on her instincts. The problem was that she'd never had instincts. Data, yes; data forever. More data than anyone. But not instincts.

Her handphone rang. "Lia?" It was Michael.

"Hi," she said. She sat up on her haunches.

"You're back."

"I am. I got back a few hours ago."

"I must have missed you."

"I was in and out."

"That plane crash."

"Terrible, isn't it? I landed in it—all the chaos, anyway."

"Any problem?"

"No. Just delays. I should be worried about what it means, but now all I can think about is work. God." She looked at her rows all around her. "I have so much to do."

"I think I should make you take a break," he said.

She realized her eyes were dry, almost burning. She closed them and touched the lids with her fingertips. "I can't stop," she said. "I have to finish."

"Really?"

"Really. Although—" She hadn't eaten all day.

"Give me your address. I'll come and get you. Just take a little walk. Have a small something. Then you'll go directly back to work."

She shouldn't. There were all these pots. But she wanted to, and that feeling was warmer and more sweetly suffusing than anything else. "Okay."

"You're on Houhai Lake, right?"

"Yes. East side. The road runs right along the lake. Number 1750. Michael, actually I'd love it if you came over here. I want you to. Please come. It's just that I have to finish."

"Don't even ask me to keep you out. You're going back to work."

"Yes. All right." She was smiling into the phone. "See you." They hung up and she phoned out to the gatehouse to expect him.

Some time later she heard the door open and slam, far away, and heard the footsteps following the route she knew so well, the green damask rooms and the long corridor, the inner courtyard, the three steps up. She opened the door before he could knock on it.

"Hi," he said, half-surprised, as if he had not quite expected to smile so at the sight of her. Then he registered the large room. He went still as an animal, eyes clocking down the rows of crates. "Look at all this. I had no idea there was so much."

"You can't tell anyone." In a blink her voice was serious. "I mean it."

"Who would I tell?"

"I'm sorry. But you must promise."

"Don't worry," he said. His voice was soft. He really didn't want her to worry. "Where'd all this come from?"

She laughed with the delight of the one whisking away the veil. "The front man is a wealthy developer, but it's a government-sanctioned sale. As far as I can tell it's a tiny part of the imperial collection, which was hidden in the countryside and rediscovered much later. Kind of a common story. After that it was either nationalized, or the government's cooperating in the sale."

"And the pots? Are they great?"

"Oh." She closed her eyes in bliss at the thought. "I'm telling you, the stars in this room. There are things in here that would make you cry."

"Show me. Make me cry."

She looked at him and thought: But I don't want to do that. "Let me think." She turned her head, tapped through what she knew was in the crates. She paused in her mind on one she'd especially loved, a clair de lune dish.

"How about this." She crossed to the thirty-fourth crate and dug out a box. She really wanted him to like it. "I don't know if this is the right thing to show you. It's a monochrome. Its rarity lies in qualities not easy to see at first." She lifted out a dish of flower shape with gently raised sides and a faintly lobed, petaled rim, in a moonlight glaze of palest blue, almost white. "Can you see what I mean?" she asked. "Its beauty is different. Very distilled."

He lowered himself in one fold to the floor, and again she was amazed at how lightly he moved around, for his size. And look, he was riveted by the dish. "Do you see it?"

"Yes," he said, "I do."

"This is nice." She laid her hand on the inner flat of the dish as if taking its pulse. Then she drew her finger along the curves between the subtly incised, overlapping flower petals. "Here the glaze accumulates just a bit and darkens to make a suggestion of shadow."

He looked at her hand.

"Do you want to touch it?" she said.

"Can I?"

"Of course."

He looked up at her face.

"Come on." She picked up his hand, which willingly came to hers, and guided it into the dish. She felt his strong fingers wrapping around hers, saying yes. But she disengaged and laid his hand in the dish—cool, soft, pearlized. He arched his palm back and rotated the flat of his hand softly in its bottom. Neither of them moved until he withdrew. "Thank you," he said.

"You feel it?"

"I do."

"Look." She turned the dish over and pointed to the reign mark in underglaze blue. "Made in the Qing Dynasty, reign of Yongzheng."

"When was that?"

"The 1720s."

"It looks so perfect."

"Ah!" She raised a pleased eyebrow. "That's porcelain. It is immortal." She placed the pale, glowing dish back in its silk cloud, in its dark box, and latched the cover down. "Good-bye," he heard her say to the box before she pushed it to the side.

Before she could move to stand up, he leaned forward and kissed her, just her lips, softly. He did not enter her mouth. He stayed still and so did she and their mouths floated against each other until he reached out and gave her lower lip one touch. He pulled away. "I promised you, right back to work," he said. But his smile had something different in it now.

"You did promise," she said.

"Thanks for showing me that."

"You're welcome."

"We going out?"

"Yes." This time she stood and reburied the box in its crate. They left the lights on. She knew she'd be back. Following him out the door, walking in his wake, she felt she might have drifted into one of life's brief and temporary harbors.

WHEN SHE RETURNED—they'd said good-bye in the taxi, talk radio still pounding; she'd apologized again and said she had to finish—she ran back in, barely skimming the ground, and went straight to her pots. So much light. She had never in her life seen anything like it in one place.

And now him. He wasn't like men she'd been drawn to in the past. Most of them had had some kind of high-stakes, power-driven edge. He might have been like that once; if so he'd left it behind. He made her feel that nothing needed to be proven, for some reason. It felt great. And he wanted to touch her more, she could tell. That was probably just a matter of time. She walked over to the thirty-eighth crate.

From this she withdrew a Qianlong bowl in polychrome enamels, *falang cai*, painted with a view of rock-garden palace architecture. The inside of the bowl was an empty field of brilliant white with three centered peonies in famille-rose enamels. She circled her hands around it, over the piled-up pigment that made garden rocks, porches, harmoniously drawn palace buildings; worlds within worlds.

One of the hardest things about working with great art was letting it go. As she would let him go in a few days, she thought—no matter what happened. With one difference. This bowl in her hands was real, a perfect and supremely *hoi moon* object. This she could hold in memory forever, unmarked and unqualified.

She put it back in its box and looked around the room. Normally it was her expectation that an appraisal be perfect, that there be no mistakes. That every call be real. Unimpeachable.

She couldn't guarantee this now. She had done her best and she had to let go of everything else. Let it be, she thought. Stand behind it as it is. And strangely enough, as her hopes and expectations of the ideal fell away from her, fear and all its grating tethers vanished too. She felt oddly strong, almost pure. She was ready. It was time to present to the buyer.

LIA SAT ON the bed, working late. The only light in the room was the silver light from her laptop, which changed and flickered as she ticked through the inventory. Alone with it, not even with the pots themselves but their images, their descriptions, their references to other works in collections and museums—just these echoes—she felt the elation of the deal about to be made. It was a right world that had this much beauty. She was a right woman to live in it. She clicked through the inventory, checking, correcting, polishing. She had been doing this for hours. She tried not to even look at the clock.

The next thing she remembered, she was awakened by the euphonious little bell that meant e-mail. When had she fallen asleep? She was on her side now, one arm under her head.

She pushed herself up. The computer was still on, glowing, in front of her. Maybe she should go to sleep after all. The clock on the bedside table said two thirty-eight. And she did have an e-mail. Who was sending her e-mail?

She touched the icon and brought up the mail program. She looked at the sender's name. *Now* she was awake. Yu Weiguo. The potter. She clicked it open.

The Chinese language template activated and the characters spilled across her screen. She drew her brows together and took it in, character by character.

Yu's message started with a typical set of Chinese disclaimers.

Right now, here, this is the best version of the story I can assemble. Who's to say if it's the right one? The facts—haven't you heard it said?—are as clay in the hands of the potter! I can only give you this sum of what I have heard mixed with my own opinions of the matter.

People seem to think the Wu Collection was buried near here, across the river in Anhui Province, for close to fifty years. And then there is a story told—it is told quietly but enough people have heard of it to keep it alive—it's said that of the tens of thousands of pots known to have left the Forbidden City in the imperial convoy, of course there were the twenty-one hundred cases left behind in Nanjing, the ones now stored at the Nanjing Museum, but people say that also a few more cases were separated up in Anhui, in Jinhua County. This is the seven or eight hundred pots they call the Wu Collection. Some people swear it does not exist. They say it's a legend. Others claim they know someone who has seen it. And then you arrived in my studio from nowhere, from America, nothing but an outsider, and *you* knew something about it! Well. Miraculous. How high the sky and how deep the earth.

Tian gao di hou, Lia thought, How high the sky, how deep the earth.

She saw at once the place from which Yu's story sprang. In her mind, in her memory, she followed back along the flight of the imperial art collection. During the sixteen years of their journey, the works were split into three shipments to enhance their odds of survival. One had gone northwest by the Yellow River, one went through the southwest, and one went through the mountains of central China, snaking through the deep belt of green above and below the Yangtze.

It was this central branch of the convoy he was talking about. But how could so many pots be buried and forgotten?

Because no one survived who remembered they were there, she thought. Because grass and brush grew over them. Because when the wars ended and another branch of the Wu clan came to live on the land, to farm it, to release it to nationalization in the 1950s, and then to have it quietly given back to them in the 1980s, they did not know. She looked back at the mail.

The family only discovered the pots a few years ago. They were plowing and hit one of the crates. The Wu family knew right away they could not keep these porcelains. They made arrangements, which were quiet. They were well paid. But who bought the pots, and where the pots went . . . this is unknown. And one cannot ask the family directly, for they emigrated, as soon as the transfers were completed. They went to your country. People say they live in Detroit.

And there the message ended, abruptly. She closed it and shut down the program, set the computer aside. That was it. Potter Yu had gone to the bottom of the ocean and brought her back a pearl. Pearl of knowing. She could feel the truth locking in around her, and it made her almost numb. She crawled in beneath her covers and let sleep take her.

15

THE NEXT MORNING SHE LAY STILL IN THE
gathering light. When you dreamed of someone,
did he dream of you? She had just dreamed, about
him.

Yet she couldn't remember it. She wanted to
get back into it. No. Then remember it, please;
she felt her body stretch as she reached back. At
least a memory. Nothing. Only the feeling.

Dream memory was different; she knew this
much. It couldn't be commanded and controlled.
It rose on its own, when ready. It was stored and
triggered in the body, in the mystery of bones and
muscles, not in the mental world where she felt
most at home. It was not thought that recovered a
dream. It was the shift of a leg, the slight turn of
the torso. Sometimes when the body resumed the

position in which it had dreamed, the dream came back to the mind.

Nothing was harder for Lia than to release herself within thought instead of driving thought to her will. But she wanted this dream. It was a door and she needed to get through it. She rolled over. There was a flash of the feeling, of him. But it stopped and calcified into conscious memory. Then a noise sounded from somewhere outside the courtyard and the light pressed against her eyelids; day was coming up. That was it. It was over.

So she got up and showered, put on a garnet tunic and pencil-leg knit pants. With a shiver she remembered that her silk dress would be ready soon, the one she had ordered on Dashanlan. She pulled her hair tightly up and braided it. She fixed her hearing aids and put pearls in her ears. Usually she wore hoops, but the shirt was a deep color and the pearls had a pale, otherworldly gleam. She rarely wore them at home. Here she looked different. They brought her to life. She blinked at herself. She tilted her head and looked at her ears; the hearing aids were soft-colored, all but invisible, part of her. The pearls made her feel pure. She rolled on a nut-brown lipstick.

Now the world was alive. Out in the hutong she could hear motorcycles stuttering and backfiring, the distant jackhammers of construction, and closer, in the kitchens in the next courtyard, the clatter of the cooks making breakfast. She poured a cup of tea from the thermos and went out with it.

There was no one in the courtyard. She sat at the stone table and drank her dragon well green. She was close, she knew; almost ready to sign off. There was just that last piece of the story she needed.

Her hands laced together on the cool stone. These pots would have left Beijing in 1931, in the convoy. If buried on Wu land in

Anhui, they were part of that leg of the shipment that passed nearby along the Qingyi River.

The flight of the imperial art collection was well chronicled in one Chinese-language history, though no accounts existed in English. She filed back. She had read it, so she could fix the moment in time at which the shipment passed that stretch, near a town called Yijiangzhen.

She released her hands for a long stinging drink of tea and pulled out her hearing aids. Quiet exploded over the stone table and the garden. In her mind's eye she entered the examination yard and walked through chronological time, back through the years of war. Here in the memory world were the photos, the accounts, the stories heard from old-timers. She had random letters, local news accounts, and municipal records—the notes and oddments left behind by all the people of each village who crouched among the crop rows, peering through the fronds and cattails, down the red clay banks to the river on that day. The whisper went through the grass like fire, as the great boat floated by, that here went two hundred thousand shining stars of the emperor's treasure.

Anhui Province, 1939. Commanding officer Captain Lu Guoping stood still in the snapping wind. His pants whipped around his legs. He was looking down through a gap in the trees at the writhing curve of the river against the spring earth. This river led back to the Yangtze, to Wuhu, and to Nanking, which the Japanese had not yet taken. If he could make it there he could breathe.

He pictured the two other shipments. One was far to the north. The second was nearby. It had left Hankou already and would meet him in Nanking.

On the flat silver snake of water below, he could see the ferry approaching. They had waited hours for this fresh boat. And now the enemy was less than a hundred li *away.*

He strode down a steep cramped-back path, between boxes of sunlight shafting through the trees. Moss-covered rocks and ferns, loam, and gravel slipped under his feet. It was spring, the waxing crescent of the second lunar month, but the cold metal of winter was not yet ready to release its hold.

When he broke through to the river's edge, he saw the thick swarm of people on the wharf. They knew the Japanese were coming.

His heart sank. They all wanted to get on the boat. And every one of them might as well fight to the death to do so.

His cross-strapped soldiers, in a powerful line three men deep, held back the crowd from the stacked crates. He shouldered through the crowd, stepping around the women, the men, the elderly on their piles of bundles. He dodged the boys laughing in their high thin voices, darting through the press of people as if this sharp damp afternoon were only another in a long string of their days growing up. Captain Lu thought of his own family, the children, his hometown, which had been taken eight months before. He had to force himself not to think about it. He had the genius of eleven dynasties to see to safety.

The fresh boat was tying up and lowering its planks. "Load the collection," Lu ordered. The smell rose to him, the tarred, weathered wood of the dock; the living, decaying saltwater smell of the wharf; the pressing crowd.

Children were crying. So many women, babies. "Sorry," he said, and elbowed them out of his way.

A woman stepped in front of him.

He pressed her to the side.

"Sir!" She blocked him with her baby. "You've no room. Take my baby. Just the baby." Before he could even perceive what she was doing,

before he'd even fully understood her rough country words, she'd shoved the baby into his arms.

"No!" he shouted, and pushed it back at her.

A torrent of will twisted her face. She clenched her arms down at her sides as if straitjacketed, then turned and ran, craning, dodging, into the crowd. The mass of pushing people meshed back in around her.

"Come back!" he screamed.

A mewling sound came from the infant. Lu looked down at the clear, shiny eyes. "I order you!" he screamed again. In the silence that bloomed in the afterspace, he heard the creaking sound of the ship, his men, their voices. He turned on his heel and continued shoving his way up front, the baby under one arm. Other mothers now held up their babies to him. He cursed them away in three dialects. The air around them exploded with the pressed-down groaning of the ship's horns.

The baby was crying. He looked at it, anger gathering. Now he needed another woman: there. He pushed the baby into the arms of the closest female. Her mouth opened in a stunned circle. But she took the child.

He stepped up to the line of men. "Almost ready?"

"Sixty left, sir."

"Good." But the soldiers were straining at the line. He watched the crowd shoving.

"Should we fire?" his man whispered.

"No! They're Chinese."

But now screams and shouts rose above the wall of wailing. The crowd pushed and retreated as one, with the suck and release of a wave. His men were surging with it, gripping tight to one another's wrists, holding, holding, shouting, how long could they hold? Lu threw a frantic look behind him. Crates were being run up the ramp one after another, men under them, heaving, sinews bursting.

A shout went up. He scanned quickly to his right. They were break-ing now. They couldn't hold.

He yanked his pistol from his belt and fired into the air. A puff of smoke rose above him. A stunned silence.

"Stop it!" he roared. "Let us finish loading and we'll take you on!"

"Sir," the subordinate hissed. "There's no room."

"Quiet," Lu ordered.

The silence still hung.

Then suddenly a man standing near them in the crowd shouted into the emptiness: "There's no room!"

"No room!"

The crowd started calling out again, shoving, and this time the tide gathered itself, breathed deeply in with a bobbing of heads and a last chance to stay alive, and then pushed forward in a tangle of arms and legs and backs and shoulders, one wedge, no stopping it. They streamed up the ramp and onto the boat.

"Stop!" screamed Captain Lu, but now the wind had whipped up and his voice was snatched out of his throat and tossed away. He saw the people fanning out on the deck of the boat, crowding on board until the deck itself sank, groaning and pitching, almost to the level of the water itself.

"The boat will sink!" he screamed. "Some of you must get off! One in three, get off!" At the same time he looked back at the dock and cursed inwardly. There were still crates waiting.

"One in three!" he called again.

No one moved.

"Now!" he shouted, and raised his handgun high and cocked it, to make clear what he meant.

The boat rocked in the waves. Then a woman, in silence, held up her small child above her head. Another woman raised a baby. A wail came threading up, just the thinnest single voice at first, but soon all the women had babies and toddlers over their heads, wailing, sobbing, pleading for their lives. Where was the baby he had given to the woman? But the baby would be all right. The woman would take care of it.

His man was back. "Sir, we have forty crates yet."

Yes. He saw them. Still on the dock. And all the babies, all the mothers.

He turned to the flank of men who had assembled. "Up anchor. We leave."

Eyes popped. "Sir!"

"Ready the boat. We leave." His voice was crisp and hard. He walked away rapidly, concealing his terror and his shame. He could not put them off to their deaths. He ran down the plank and onto the warped, river-smelling boards. He touched one of the crates, laid his hand on it. What was inside? He glanced at the stenciled characters. Meishu taoci. Ceramics. He offered a silent reverence of apology, then he turned and ran, last man up, jumping onto the ship as the ramp rose. The boat's engines roared and it pulled away, turning in its wide arc down the river. He watched the little stack of crates left behind growing smaller and smaller as the dock floated away into the distance.

So, she thought, raising her eyes again to the red-framed doors. Left behind, then taken off the dock, and buried under Wu land and forgotten. The land belonging to the Wus and then to the state and then back to the Wus again. And it was there all that time.

She put her hearing aids in and the world came back, abruptly amplified. A car engine roared up the hutong, cresting, fading. She finished her tea and walked out across the entry court. She passed the fountain with its spattering flow of sound and walked through the gate of ornamental rock.

She thought he was in his room. It was early morning; he'd be getting ready for work. She knocked.

"I knew it was you," he said when he opened the door.

It seemed to her that he stood over her, but actually they were the same height. "I know you have to go to work," she said.

He drew her in and shut the door. "I do have to go to work. I'm also glad you came."

"I was going to ask if you wanted to walk out and have breakfast in the hutong." Usually she didn't eat in the morning, but today she felt alive, she felt hungry, and with her smile she challenged him. "It's wild. I know."

"I love wild." He looked at his watch. "Even if only on principle. I have time too. I have to get to work, but I have time. Let me get my things."

She watched him move around, collecting papers, making a wedge of his hand and tucking his shirt in, all the way around. She looked at his things. A man's things were always, for her, a glimpse of who he was.

But he didn't have much. A desk, a bed, and an old wooden wardrobe. A TV. The white walls were bare. There was a table with rows of Polaroids on it. "What's this?" she said. All Chinese children.

"Those are the kids in my study," he said.

She saw that each child was posed the same way, in the same spot, yet each was a universe of uniqueness. "You took these?"

"I did. Lia?"

She turned and in that questing instant, her eyes alight and the beginning of a smile on her face, he took her picture. The little motor ground and the print shot out in its tray.

"Here." He tore it off. They leaned closer. First it was a pale, ghostly square, then her face emerged, looking over her shoulder. She looked pretty. He took a loop of tape and stuck it to the door frame, just above another instant photo, of a small Chinese girl. "You can stay there," he said, "with her."

"Honored." She liked it. She liked his room too, in a way. "I admire your room. It's so plain it's aggressive. You said something the other day, that you wanted to forget everything. This is the room for it."

"It's true. Here I like to forget."

"Great thinkers have preceded you. You know that? You're like Themistocles."

He turned around slowly, the smile in his eyes canny, awaiting the joke.

"No," she said, "I mean it. Everybody in his era was doing memory work. It was the thing. Memory feats were much admired."

"But not by Themistocles."

"No. *He* was famous for saying he preferred the science of forgetting to the art of memory." She touched on the plain surroundings with her eyes. "Like you."

"Like me," he said.

"And then these," she said, looking down at the rows of photographs. "They're beautiful in a strange way." She picked one up. "Who is this?"

"Hu Meiru. She lives over in the western district, near the zoo. Seven and a half."

She looked at him. "Does she have lead poisoning?"

"Yes. They all have elevated levels."

"All of them? That's terrible."

"All I've gotten back," he corrected himself. "I haven't collected teeth from all of them yet."

"It's awful." She picked up another one. "Who's this?"

He stepped closer to the table. "Zhang Yeh."

"Him too?"

"Him too."

"And what about you?" she said, because in his eyes she was sure she saw an accumulation of sadness. "You think about it all day long."

"It's different for me." He straightened one of the pictures. She saw his hands were careful, precise.

"You care for what you're doing."

"I can't care for them."

"Look at this." She swept a hand above the table.

"I just record them." He picked up one of the pictures and balanced it in his palm.

She took it from him. "What's his name?"

"That's Little Chen."

She looked at him over the top of the picture. "Special," she said. "He's special to you."

He smiled, caught. "Yes. He's one I've gotten to know. He's been in and out of the hospital, though for other reasons."

She looked down at the picture as if it were animate, as if it had a soul, and to his surprise pressed it to her cheek. Then she handed it back. "This one's good to care about," she said. "I think you're doing the right thing."

He put the picture back in its spot. "I just record them."

"That's right," she said, and he could hear the grin in her voice. "The whole world knows that's all you do."

He pushed the fine sandy-gray hair off his forehead and swallowed a smile of his own. She turned away from him, looking down at the pictures, and there was something about her long back, bent over a table, interested, distracted, that made him see her in other rooms in other places. He could imagine her in a room that belonged to them. It was a strange feeling, indistinct, powerful. An involuntary glimpse. He hardly knew her. Yet it felt real. He walked over next to her, as close as he could. "Ready, Lia?" he said, and now she turned to him, happy, looking the same way she looked in the picture on the wall, and they went out together into the hutong.

They walked on the side to stay out of the way of the cars bouncing and honking down the uneven pavement, the bicyclists and pedestrians separating in a constant tide for them, people going to work, and other people, old people and small children, out for the early air, sauntering, talking, sitting. Along the way people were opening their shops and rattling out their metal awnings.

They walked down the hutong to his favorite vendor, an old lady with a starched white cap behind an iron griddle. "She's very particular," he said. "She only comes in the morning, and just for a few hours." He smiled at the lady. "*Zaoshang hao,*" he said to her, Good morning.

"*Zao,*" she boomed back, and then looked at Lia. "You're now bringing your wife! Very good."

They both ignored this. "Two with egg," he said, and paid.

"Two with egg." She reached into the warmer and pulled out a pair of sesame *bing,* palm-sized disc-shaped flatbreads crusted with seeds. She split them, and little clouds of steam puffed out. Eggs were frying on the griddle. She turned them a few more times, until the yolk was almost set and the whites flecked with brown, and then dropped an egg into each of the pockets. She folded them in twists of paper and passed them across the counter. "*Man man chi,*" she said.

"It's hot," Michael warned Lia, but then immediately took a bite of his anyway.

She took a bite of hers too, and thought it might have been the best thing she'd ever eaten. Just a fried egg, with salt, in split chewy bread, but it made her feel for a minute like she belonged on earth. "Michael," she said. "Can we come here every morning and eat for the rest of our lives?"

He laughed. "I will if you will."

She couldn't believe she had just said that. "I was kidding," she said.

He touched her foot with his. "I know. Let's go sit down." And they took a few steps to a low stone wall and perched, eating. "How's the job?" he said.

"Done, almost done. But I can't quite let go of it."

"Why's that?"

"I've found fakes, you know. I think I'm right about everything. But what if I'm wrong?"

He looked at her, chewing, thinking. When he had swallowed he said, "Let's consider it, then. What if you are?"

"Well—"

"What's the worst that could happen?"

"It could mean a lot of money."

"I guess that would be bad." He dropped in the last piece of *bing* and smiled, his round mouth making an amused bow. "But that's just money. Do we really think it would be all that bad?"

She smiled at his saying "we," at the warm sense that someone stood in the ring with her. It was not real, she knew, just a transient kindness, but it felt good. "I guess not. It's just money. Then there's reputation."

"That's a little harder. But still not a killer."

"It's just we never do these alone."

"Well. Tell you what I'll do."

"What?"

"I'll come and stand beside you and we'll look at them, and I'll tell you you're right. Unless of course I think you're wrong. In which case I'll tell you that too."

She laughed.

"Would that help?" He cocked his head at her.

"No. But thank you."

"You're always thanking me. Now I have to go to work." He stood up.

"I do too."

"So." He stood across from her.

"Good luck today," she said.

"Thanks. See you later?"

"Sure." She brought the flat of her hand up to shield her eyes against the climbing sun. Watching him walk away down the hutong, she wished she knew when later would be and what he wanted to do with her then. When she turned the last corner back to the guesthouse, she saw her driver waiting.

AT THE VILLA she went to her big room, flooded with morning, and looked up and down the rows of crates. There was number nineteen, with the gold-decorated white-glazed dish from the Yuan Dynasty; number thirty-one, with its pair of blue-and-white dragon roundel bowls from the reign of Kangxi. She loved them especially.

She sat in the front, before her pots, and clicked on her laptop. She opened the inventory and scanned through it. Everything was there. It was finished and it was cleaned. She scrolled down through, fast, the digital photo images blinking past her subconscious. She had it, okay, she could believe in it. She thought of him standing beside her, large and comforting, telling her yes, she was right. And sometimes telling her she was wrong. This made her give just the tiniest bubble of a laugh. For a second she let herself imagine them together.

In a careful set of keystrokes she encrypted the long document and then entered Dr. Zheng's most private electronic address. Good-bye to all of you, she thought from her heart to the pots in the room; thank you for having come through my life. And she pressed SEND.

JACK AND ANNA had eaten, steak and asparagus off hundred-year-old Limoges. They liked eating alone. They had personal assistants who prepared their food and served it, but then they preferred for those people to leave. They liked to wash the dishes together by hand, listening to public radio. They didn't want employees in the house overnight. They did not even like having guests. They had always been like that, since they'd been together. It was one of the many small resonances that made them happy as a pair.

It was when they were watching sports, later, that he told her. First he turned down the TV.

"What?" she said.

"I want to buy it. Are you agreed?"

"What?" Although she knew.

"The porcelain."

"How much?"

"Seven hundred ninety pieces. She found ten fakes."

He felt the little snort of laughter lift her shoulders, next to him. "I meant money."

"They are quoting one hundred ninety million dollars. I wouldn't expect to pay that."

"I should hope not."

"No," he said. The real offer would never be made up front.

They didn't expect that and neither did he. The most interesting and climactic part of the deal would begin now, the mutual pushing and posturing and retreating that would bring them eventually to an agreed price.

He would find the negotiation diverting, maybe even obsessive, and with any luck it might sharpen him, polish him a little, but the real match was with his wife. All manner of obstacles in the outside world had proven surmountable, but Anna Sing presented a lifetime of challenge. With her he felt alive. He gave thanks every day for having a woman who was his equal.

At this moment she was giving him the raised eyebrow. "You know what I think. It's fashion, taste, art—fundamentally unstable."

"But it doesn't often lose."

She closed her eyes and smiled privately, into herself. They'd been covering the same ground for days. "It's not worth a hundred ninety million."

"No," he said softly. "Actually it's worth more than that. It's worth two hundred million, three. Ten. It's the past. It's objects adored by an emperor. That is something that will never come again. Ever in the world. Xuanfei," he said, deliberately using her Chinese name and feeling her start, because he never called her that. He dropped his hand down from behind and covered her gently curving abdomen. He was calling on her deeper obligations, and he knew it.

"It's not that day," she said.

"Sure it is," he said, and she laughed, and they slowly moved into a different position on the couch.

"You've seen the inventory?"

"All of it."

"Photos?"

"Everything. Well—I just got it. I have to study it."

"And?"

"It's magnificent. Come on. Let's go look."

"In a minute." She smiled that smile he knew, because he was a connoisseur of the many moods of Anna Sing. This smile meant she wasn't ready to say so, she was going to torture him quite a bit longer and get maximum oppositional points out of it, but eventually she was going to warm to his plan.

"Just wait," he said, catching her legs on either side of him. "In ten years, if the market continues this way, it'll be worth three hundred million."

BAI BROUGHT THE truck to the address on the north shore of Houhai Lake before dawn, as he had been instructed. He pulled up to the gatehouse, cigarette dangling casually from his hand, and called a gruff, complicit greeting to the guard, who stood drinking tea from a jar. The guard waved him ahead. Wide gates at the rear of the court lay open to a long drive rustling with trees. He could see a rambling white house with curving red roofs. Workmen were waiting.

Bai pulled up to them and shut down the engines.

"The cargo goes in the back there?" said the head man.

"Just so, but let me show you." He took the man behind and opened the gleaming double doors. He had turned off the freezer before he set out. Still, it was cold. They climbed in and Bai unlocked and slid open the hidden doors in the back. Bai heard a northern expletive of surprise slip from the other man's mouth.

"The cargo goes in here," Bai said, flipping a switch to light up the main compartment. Then he turned and stepped back onto the shiny-speckled metal floor of the freezer. "And when you are finished, this compartment must be left completely clean! This is a hygienic carrier!"

"Yes, sir," the man said, faintly confused. "You can depend on it. Here." And he gave Bai a stapled, fifty-page document. "The manifest."

Bai had understood all along that this was a big shipment, many pots, but until he saw this forest of typeset entries he had not truly known. "May gods witness," he said softly, rifling through it.

"Just get them there," the man said.

"In this lifetime and the next ten afterward, with ease! Do you think I have ever failed?"

"No. But, younger brother. You'd be well served to move as quickly as your wheels can carry you." He looked meaningfully at the incredible value implied by the numbers running down the manifest's right-hand column.

Not until they close the deal, Bai thought, but he wouldn't say this to this man, whom he did not know and who—he had to assume—knew less than nothing. "Come on." He placed a brief brotherly hand on the guard's back. "Let's load it."

16

ONCE LIA TURNED IN HER APPRAISAL, SHE
had to wait all through that day and night and
until the next morning. Dr. Zheng negotiated.
Apparently no pots questions arose, for her phone
was silent.

The first morning she had gone out to pick
up her dress. It was lovely; it molded to her exactly, and it was a mix of green and russet that
brought her to life. She tried it on in the store and
then she had to put it on all over again the second
she got back to her room. After that she folded it
away. It was a dress for an occasion.

There, in the room, she noticed a change on
the TV. News, a cut-in; something had happened.
She turned it up. Commentators were talking in
hushed whispers while the camera showed an
empty podium. Finally, the subtitle in English and

Chinese: a joint statement by the Chinese Minister of Civil Affairs and the head of the Civil Aviation Administration of China. Two men came out. The Minister started to speak. She leaned closer.

"After careful study," the Minister said, "the Civil Aviation Administration of China has determined that the crash of China International Airlines Flight Sixty-eight was an accident. It was a single-aircraft event with no complications or interferences from any ship, plane, or other conveyance; or any person or outside parties. The exact cause of the accident is still under investigation." He gave a curt nod and then turned away; they both walked off camera. It was over. The screen cut back to the anchors, talking excitedly.

And she stood staring. So that was the official statement. That was the answer: an accident. Was this answer real or fake? And would all the ill feeling on the street now evaporate away? Until next time? She felt her usual stab of guilt at how little she really understood certain things here. There was only one facet of China she could fully and responsibly tackle; that was pots. Pots were celestial and endlessly varied and to do them justice took the full force of her mind.

The second morning she took a taxi up to Houhai Lake—just to be there, just to be near the pots—and sat outside, on a bench facing the lake. She watched pleasure boats on the far shore drift under the shade of overhanging branches. Snatches of conversation rose and fell behind her as people passed on the walkway. It was not until she had let go of waiting for it that her phone finally rang. *"Wei."*

"Lia." It was Dr. Zheng.

"Hey."

"We have a close."

"How much?"

"One hundred and twenty-six million."

"What a deal for him!" she cried. "He's so lucky!"

"Yes. Gao could have got more with multiple buyers. But he wanted it done and over. I don't suppose we can complain."

She returned the twinkle in his voice with her own. "No. I don't suppose we can."

"Lia," he said. "Congratulations." He let the word hang, warm with fondness.

She felt the filial satisfaction of pleasing him, the sense that all the world's geometry was right, and she secure within it. "Thanks," she said.

"No," he said. "Thank you. Did you see the statement?"

"Yes! Yesterday."

"Too late to send Phillip."

"I guess so."

And they both laughed at the same time, her glassy peal and his age-cracked chortle. "Ah, it's well done. But you're not finished. Your flight leaves for Hong Kong tomorrow night. You meet the pots there." He gave her the locator numbers. "Your room's at the Mandarin."

"No problems with the flights, I suppose?"

"No," he said. "All back to normal."

"Okay, then." What else could she say? That was it, she was leaving.

"And Lia?" Zheng said.

"Yes?"

"Good job."

"It was just what I was supposed to do," she said.

They clicked off and she put her phone back in her pocket. It was over. Why didn't she feel any different than before? The water kept moving in front of her under the line of willows, the majestic, wind-ruffled pace of its surface unchanged. She had done it. She had wielded her principal sword—intelligence, memory, knowledge—and the deal had worked. It had come to pass. But pleasure boats still passed, the seasons advanced with every minute, and she was sitting alone on a bench.

After a time she walked back up to the road to get in a taxi. She could go somewhere and celebrate by herself.

BAI SAT ON an overturned metal pail beside his rig, smoking. He was parked in an empty drying barn in the countryside outside Wuhan. The arduous drive had brought him much of the way to Changsha, and here he rested. The arrangement had been made through Huang, one of his crew in Jingdezhen. Five hundred *yuan* for the use of the barn, no questions asked. He sat there with his cell phone on, waiting, smoking. When the deal was done they'd call him. Then he'd go further south.

In the meantime he reviewed every facet of his fiction: the false wall, the frozen chickens, all the documents.

He stubbed out his cigarette and lit another one. He thought about the manifest. There was a chicken cup there, one from the reign of Chenghua. Was destiny not smiling on him, to put one of the world's eighteen cups in this shipment? Had he not just, by purest chance, managed to buy a copy of the Chenghua chicken cup so perfect, so bright in the firmament that only a few people on earth could separate it from one that was real? No one could say he had planned it. This was certainly luck. It was the will of heaven.

He had taken careful note of the cup's location in the shipment. It was number four hundred thirteen, crate twenty-seven. He looked up at the truck speculatively. Should he switch the cups now?

Just then his cell phone rang. *"Wei,"* he said.

It was Gao Yideng. "The deal has closed," he said. "You can leave. *Zou-ba,"* Go.

"Hao," he agreed, and as he closed his phone and put it in his pocket he was already climbing into the back of the truck. Indeed he would go. First he had to take care of one small matter.

LATE THAT AFTERNOON Michael and An walked down the hospital corridor. The day had not been good. The head of their hospital was preparing a summary of the city's public-health issues for the fall meeting of the National People's Congress. The two of them naturally hoped lead poisoning would be included. But a few minutes in his office had suggested this hope was unrealistic. Not only were reports from every researcher and department head piled up on the desk, but the harried director had made a pointed reference to the need to avoid those issues that the leaders had already recognized, on which they had already taken action, however insufficiently, and about which they had made it clear they did not wish to hear more.

"At least he was straight up front about it," Michael said later.

"That was for you," An said morosely. "You're a foreigner. Not expected to get it."

"Wonderful. Insult to injury."

"So let's get something to eat," An said.

"You always say that."

"Exactly right," said An. "What else? What better?"

"Not tonight for me, though, thanks. I've got something on."

"You're going to go see that woman."

Michael smiled. An was right. He so liked it that she had come to his room the day before. He liked the way she just stepped in. He had awakened thinking about her and there she was. "I might call her," he admitted.

"Ah." An was staring at him, fascinated. "Well, good luck."

"*Bici,*" Michael gave him back, Same to you, and they each grinned in good-bye. Their eyes met and exchanged an understanding of what had just happened in the director's office; it was disappointing, but they'd go on working. An continued down the corridor and Michael turned to the elevators.

He pressed the DOWN button. He'd never worked in a hospital before. Always he'd been in institutes and research labs. It had been eight months now and he'd gotten used to the faint chemical smell, the constant disembodied voices, the hard fluorescent light. It felt different from when he was a patient himself. Now, in a dogged and unpleasant way, working here felt good to him. It neutralized his balance sheet a little bit. He'd seen things here; he'd seen children die. Nothing had ever affected him like that. He'd seen that the young ones died quickly. He'd heard the staff talk about it. When they were ready they let go. Not like adults. Adults took a long time. It was as if adults had built such a thick, petrified husk around them that this alone gave them the strength, the form to hold on. And by the transient revival that so often came to the dying, adults seemed to find a last little puff of life before the end. They had a term for it here at the hospital—*hui guang fan zhao,* the reflected rays of the setting sun. Children were lacking in this. They went quickly. He watched as the DOWN light came on and the elevator door slid open.

He had a fear that his life now was just an interlude of *hui guang fan zhao,* a brief moment before it all came back, worse. And for so long now he had been in this state by himself. He stared up at the digital floor numbers flashing, descending.

He stepped out the big front doors onto a busy boulevard

clogged with traffic. All over him was a pall of thick, brown-tinged air, gritty with particulates whose names he knew by heart. He fitted on his headphones, dialed up Cheb Mami, and walked against the insinuating Algerian rhythm, a sound that first emerged in the port town of Oran in the 1930s and now was electrified into the modern world, pulsing in his mind as he descended into the subway station at Chongwenmen.

BAI STOPPED AT a chicken farm outside of Changsha. It was a place where he had made an arrangement. He pulled into the dirt yard and right away caught the pungent scent of blood and slaughter. He'd picked this place over many others for its low prices.

He pulled up to the guard and handed down his paperwork. "Preorder," he said. "Two thousand pounds."

The guard with a round face and brushy stand-up hair took the lot number down and punched it into the computer. He squinted at the machine. His face was indifferent. "How are you going to pay?"

"Cash." Bai counted out from a wad of bills.

The guard took it. "Gate forty-six," he said.

Bai backed the truck up to the portal. He had already secured the central compartment where the art was stored. Now he opened the freezer in the back and stood to the side while young men, migrant workers, illiterates, faces dark from growing up outdoors, eyes leathered already at twenty, hands swathed in big rough gloves of undyed cotton, numbly packed a ton of frozen chickens into the back of his gleaming, purring, ice-fogging truck. The plucked, stiff carcasses made a stacked wall against the door. Bai watched, his dizzying ambition lifting him high and his cold death fear whispering to him from hell. He smoked to contain himself. When the men were done he tipped them and he drove away.

BY THAT AFTERNOON, Lia had ended up at a bar she knew on Dengshikou, called Counter Culture. It was one of the theme places that had become so common here as proprietors resorted to gimmicks to draw crowds. It had a sixties motif in the U.S. style, with psychedelic posters, a folkie jukebox, and black lights, none of which especially spoke to Lia. But it also had a pinball machine so light and hair-trigger it might have been brand-new, though it was definitely an antique.

She walked over to the corner, behind the tables, and got out her two-*yuan* coins. The machine was called DMZ, and its back panel had comic-book graphics of American soldiers slogging through a Vietnamese jungle. A little hip humor, she thought, not without edge. She dropped in the coins and felt the machine pop with a satisfying bass thunk as it credited the game. She leaned in, pressed the GO button, and slammed the first ball up the chute.

It rocketed up the side and exploded all over the lit-up bumpers flashing at the top. She used just enough shiver to keep the ball moving, high up, pulling it into pockets and then popping it out again to bounce off bumper pins and side flippers. Not thinking. That was what she liked. Keeping it in play.

She felt her cell in her pocket and was aware of how much she wanted it to ring. She got the ball over to the flippers and caught it, belayed it, held it while she took a long look at the board. This thing with him was only a brief meeting. Or maybe he liked her, but not *that* way. She stood rock-still and looked down at the perfect ball she held on her flipper, the color and glimmer of mercury, breathless and ready for the moment she would let it go. She could feel her phone against her leg. She did want him to call her, though; this was her true and *hoi moon* feeling. Maybe it was just a moment, but she felt connected to him. She just wanted to be where he was, and talk to him. She rolled the ball back, snapped the flipper in the middle of the right millisecond, and sent the ball out into its world of finite space.

BAI DROVE STRAIGHT on to his first wife's farm, the next place where he could safely park the truck. He roared into Daoqi Township, shaking with exhaustion, gripping the wheel at the sight of the familiar road at last. Those curves those passes those hillsides, unrolling in front of him, black road in the dissipating light . . . his steering slipped into unconsciousness. He'd lived here as a young man, newly married. The roads were better now, there were more buildings in the village, but it hadn't changed so much. He circled the terraced paddies in full yield. He wound around green-tufted hills. It was almost dark. The world behind fell away in steps. At the bottom, barely visible in the shadows, ran a silver ribbon of river.

He climbed up and up and finally steered into a small valley: fields, gardens, and animals. Yujia lived here with her brother and his family. They worked the farm. He pulled into the driveway and parked under the mat-shed.

As he stepped across the mahogany earth, smelled the honeysuckle and the gardenia and the rustling wet bamboo, and saw the lit doorway across the packed barnyard ahead, he let joy overtake him. He strode forward, thinking of his wife's round arms, her knot of dark hair, and the meal, spiked with fried hot peppers, she would prepare for him later.

His phone went off in his pocket. *"Wei,"* he said, stopping right where he was, his feet sinking in the animal-rich dirt.

"Bai," said his friend's voice. "It's Zhou. Listen."

"I'm listening."

"They're dead."

"Who?" Bai had to say, though of course, he knew.

"Hu and Sun," Zhou answered. "They're dead. Shot."

"When?"

"Today."

A long silence hung between the two men on their palm-size satellite phones. Bai stared at the low, baked-brick, timber-raftered house against the Hunan hillside, the warm yellow lights already burning in its windows. Life was a gift. Never forget. Let the door open on a view of mountains. *Hoi moon.*

And later that night Zhou was to meet him to help him drive on south. He knew that now he had to at least give Zhou an opening, a chance to back out and still keep face if he did so. "Shall I still see you tonight?" Bai asked as if the matter were an offhand one.

"Of course!" Zhou said. "Don't fear. You'll see me. I'll be there."

IN THE END she had to wait until the next morning for Michael to call her. When her phone lit up she was still half asleep. She clicked in her hearing aids. She didn't know who it was. "This is Lia," she said in her best half-awake work voice.

"Where were you?" he said, and he sounded right next to her, right in her ear. "I watched for you to come back last night but you never came."

"Hey," she said, happiness rising in her at the sound of his voice. So here he was. "I was tired, I went right to bed when I came back. I was celebrating. The deal's done!"

"Over?"

"Yes. Sold."

"That's wonderful," he said. "That's great for you. And it worked out?"

"Yes," she said, "I guess it did." Whether she'd missed something or not, it was over.

There was a long breath.

"I wanted to see you," he said.

"Last night?" she said.

"Yes. And now. Could I come over there now?"

The sentence was simple, but his words had a kind of gravity that made everything exactly clear. She was silent a second.

He waited with her.

The words hung on her tongue, balanced, a long moment before she could say them. "All right." But still a hesitation hung in the air.

"What is it?" he asked.

"It's just . . . I got a deal."

"I know. I'm glad for you! It's great."

"But now I have to go to Hong Kong. I'm obligated to see to the shipping. I have to leave."

His turn for silence. Then he said: "When?"

"Tonight."

"Oh," he said. "How many hours?"

A giggle punched through her anxiety and suddenly she was laughing, and then they both were. "That's so terrible," she said.

"Not terrible. Wonderful. How many hours?"

She looked at the clock. "A lot, actually. Plenty."

"Well," he said.

She was aware of herself. Disparate parts of her felt joined for the first time in so long. "I'll be here," she said.

17

IN HUNAN, BAI HAD SLEPT SOME HOURS IN Yujia's husk-filled bed under a cotton quilt bright with pink peonies. Refreshed, he arose late in the evening, sat down at the table, and ate his first wife's vibrant Hunanese cooking. Then he climbed in his vehicle, brought it sputtering and roaring back to life, and descended the jade-lipped hills to the outskirts of the provincial capital. Zhou had come down from Jingdezhen to meet him.

They'd met on the north side, on Yanjiang Dadao, at the appointed place just above the lapping, iron-gray flanks of the Xiang River. Zhou was there at the Two Friends Café, drinking beer, watching the boats on the river with their lights under the star-strewn sky. For men like them it was the most natural thing in the world to embark on an important, serious adventure late at night, fortified by alcohol. They were always most precise now, lightest, most alert.

And the night driving had been good. There were reasonable roads from here to Hengyang, then Chenxian, Shaoguan, Yingde, and finally Guangzhou. The two men had sailed, with good conversation and laughter. But mainly Zhou drove, and Bai slept, and thought. Everything depended on the next day, when he would run the last lap alone.

Now, in the morning, the city of Guangzhou spread out many miles from its center. Its chalk-colored towers made deep canyons of its central streets and thoroughfares and shimmered in the southern light. The traffic condensed, slowing with every mile. By the time they reached the center of the city, they were rolling at a stop-and-start. Buses, trucks, cars, and taxis jammed the freeway. They got off at Jiefang Lu. Traffic was stopped here too. By sheer power of tonnage, Bai was able to push his way to the side of the road and let Zhou off. The bus hub was just on the other side of this block, and they both knew Zhou could go anywhere from here—back to Jingdezhen, or where he liked.

"Thank you," Bai said, and pushed a small folded wad of *yuan* into Zhou's hand. Zhou protested, but of course took the money.

"Good luck." He climbed out and hopped to the ground, looking up at Bai's thin face, his high hair, and his big, guileless mouth. "Level road."

"To you too," Bai answered from the driver's seat. "Put your heart at rest. I'll get through."

To that Zhou raised a hand and turned and was gone, walking away even as he heard the big chuff of the engine shifting gears and then pulling out and roaring away up Liu Hua Lu.

Zhou walked down the block to a concrete ticket office fronted by potted palms. He used a small part of the money Bai had given him to buy a ticket back to Jingdezhen.

He sat in the waiting area a long time and then much later went out and climbed the three steps up to his waiting bus. He chose a middle row, a window. So much went on in and out of Guangzhou, so much that was illegal, that all the buses had security. Before they left, a uniformed employee got on and stalked up the aisle, videotaping every passenger.

Zhou knew what to do. He knew just how to pull up his collar, lower his eyes to a book, or turn away, interested in something he glimpsed out the window at just that exact right moment. There had never been a discernible likeness of Zhou on any of these tapes. He was very proud of that. He knew the system well.

SHE HAD BARELY had time to wash and get her clothes on when he came and knocked. She felt a jolt of gladness as she opened the door to him, and right after that came the natural flood of fear. Suddenly seeing him inches from her, seeing his white shirt open at the neck and knowing he'd come here for her to unbutton it and take it off, she felt unable to move at all.

"Can I come in?"

"Please. Sorry." She stepped back.

"You okay?" he said. His hand came out to her arm.

She smiled. She felt altogether too shy to speak. "Yes. It's just—you know."

"I know."

"Don't you have to go to work?"

"I'm sick today," he said. But he was smiling.

"I see." She felt his hands exploring the catch at the top of her braid, then sliding down to the end of the rope. He looped it around in front of her. She watched. He pulled off the elastic and started separating the strands.

Then her cell phone went off. She worked it out of her pocket. "*Wei.*"

"*Wei. Fan Xiaojie,*" Miss Fan. It was Gao Yideng.

"Mr. Gao." She looked down at Michael's hands. She could barely breathe. "All is well?" she said into the phone.

"Oh, beyond well, excellent, I should say. You did a fine job! But I must not detain you. I just want to tell you my driver will call for you this evening."

"Your driver?" She looked at Michael. "Thank you, but no. Please don't send the driver."

He was perturbed. "Why?"

"I'll go myself."

"Are you sure?"

"Yes," she said, "I'm sure."

"If you say. But you are my guest! Well, good journey, then, Miss Fan. And thank you."

"Don't be polite," she said. They traded parting wishes and she closed the phone.

His hands were higher. "Everything okay?" he said.

"Yes." She dropped the phone on the table. She felt like everything about her body was standing straight up.

He came to the top of her head and unhooked her hair. It fell loose all around her, and her scalp tingled with the fine ache of unbinding. "That's nice," he said, looking across to her eyes, picking up the strands in front of her and lifting them back behind her shoulders. "Take your shirt off."

IT TOOK BAI a long time to get the truck out of Guangzhou. Freeway traffic rolled at a walk, but that was normal here in the morning. He stopped and started, the brand-new engine hot but humming well, and inched slowly through the ranks of tall buildings, once white, now grimy. It wasn't until he made his way to the ring expressway, which led him quickly south to the city's green suburban hills, that he could drive at a good speed. Here the road flew. Through breaks in the slopes he saw behind him, in his mirror, the forest of white rectangular blocks that was Guangzhou.

He passed the exit signs for Guangcong Road, Guangshan Road. Now there were dull apartment blocks on either side of the road, along with truck yards, factories, little smokestacks belching. And then, just when it seemed to Bai that there was nothing here except trade, business, industry, and the beehives of living, a cleft in the hills would open and he'd see a green spreading valley under syrupy light.

Closer to him, right by the road, brick-earthed banana plantations were scored with marching electrical towers, hauling their power loads away across the hills.

He kept his eyes on the road. Something was happening up ahead. He braked. Flashing lights. Police cars. There was a man lying on the shoulder, an overturned cart near him. Bai could see his short-sleeved plaid shirt against the concrete. Blood spread in a puddle under his head. Someone knelt beside him, holding a towel to his head, shielding his face from the traffic.

There were moments of danger, openings of danger; maws into which any passing man might fall, Bai thought: This was one. It had claimed another man today, not him. An omen. Two hands on the wheel, two eyes on the road. There ahead was his exit lane. He steered, and then he was sailing up and over, across a long steel bridge above the Pearl River.

On the opposite shore he entered groves of lichi, with their fluttering almond-shaped leaves, and then tunneled through the township of Dongguan. Another exit, a turn, and he was entering the demarcation zone that separated Shenzhen, a Special Administrative Region, from the rest of south China. Shenzhen had different tax and banking structures, different accords with foreigners and different industries. Nevertheless, the flood of people and goods in and out of Shenzhen was heavy and unrelenting. Only a simple pass was required to get into Shenzhen, and this pass had been an easy thing for Bai to get. It was getting out of Shenzhen, and into Hong Kong, that was going to be hard.

He pulled into the truck lane and slowed to a stop, to wait for this first checkpoint. He was high, up so high in this seat. He could be calm. This was easy. All he had to do was show the pass. It was a real one, acquired with good money and favors. They had no reason to question him. He'd show the pass, get into Shenzhen. One thing at a time.

His turn at the gate. He nosed the rig forward, and when he stopped, the engine heaved up a big deflating sigh.

"Papers," the man said.

Bai reached in the compartment easily, casually, took out the folded document and handed it down. He watched as the man opened up the triplicate form, flipped through it. Then he tore off the bottom sheet, the blue sheet, and handed the top two sheets back up to Bai.

Bai took them in a daze and set them on the seat next to him. He realized the guard was waving him out. Waving him into Shenzhen. He was in. Quickly he put the truck back in gear and eased out, onto the road, into the hall of mirrors, the crowded neighborhoods, the free-for-all of China's number-one special economic zone.

This part had been easy; it was only the beginning. He followed a long, dreary suburbia through the fertile Pearl River delta to the actual town of Shenzhen, which sat by the border. A generation ago it had been farms; now the road wound through patches of smoking industry, cut with blocks of apartment buildings, windows hung with flapping laundry. He crossed the town quickly, heading for the Border Administration Area.

Here the hills beside the road looked dug out. There were piles of rock and rubble everywhere. It was as if this edge of the city had been forcibly scooped out of rock and planted. And then the road curved around the hip of a green cliff, and there, below Bai and spreading out forever, was the South China Sea, turquoise, brilliant.

And further away, just there down the coast, he could see the hills of Hong Kong—green, carpeted with the white spires of success. His soul rose up in joy. He followed the signs for Huangang, the Immigration and Customs point for vehicles.

Finally he came to the checkpoint. The uniformed man stepped up to the truck, and Bai handed down the packet of papers that he had assembled and for which he had paid so well. His mien was disaffected. It verged on boredom. He was careful not to overplay. He barely glanced at the uniformed man.

But he felt the advancement of every second, every tick, every breath, as if they were random rising knife points. The guard rifled through the papers, checked that the overall package was in order, stopped here and there to study a page, pull his bushy brows down, scrutinize it . . . Bai felt like he was turning to liquid. He noticed his knees were not holding still. He pretended to fiddle with the radio.

"Destination?" the guard said.

"Hong Kong."

"Cargo?"

"Chickens." Bai set the station, turned the volume all the way down, and finally, unbearably, gave the guard his full attention.

"Pull into bay number twelve," the guard said.

Bai nodded. Did his face show anything? No. Calm, a brief nod. But inside him every fiber was screaming.

They were stopping him. They were going to search him.

He threw the truck into gear and lurched forward. As he pulled away from the booth he saw the guard take out his cell phone and speak into it. *Please.* He sent a personal prayer to the god of fire and wind. He thought of the Long Zu Temple back home, all the incense he had lit there, all the fruits and *fang gu* he had left there at the altar. For almost a thousand years the god had protected men who lived for porcelain. *Please.* Slowly he rolled his sighing, huffing truck into bay number twelve.

THEY LAY BACK to front, him behind her, his arms around her and one of his legs between hers. She squeezed gently and he moved in answer. The only sound in the room was their breathing.

She picked up his hand. There in his palm was the human ideogram. He needed love. It was easy to see. It was all over him, in the way he had moved his body, in the protective circle of his arms, in his mouth and the way he had buried himself in her.

What should she keep from today? What to memorize? Already all the things they'd done were blurring. Maybe she could retain the smallest part of his hand, the mound below the thumb. There she saw the lines and creases, his spirit of life, his vitality. The glory that was in him when he chose to let it out.

She would give him a memory room, of course, and a symbol to guard his door. The symbol would have to be a thing she really loved. None less than Thomas Aquinas had written: *It is necessary that a man dwell with solicitude on, and cleave with affection to, the things which he wishes to remember, because what is strongly impressed upon the soul slips less easily away from it.*

Solicitude, affection; it should be something from art, or a line of poetry. She thought about what the Hanlin scholar had written after being sent south to Jingdezhen: *Who knows about me?* Yes, that would do, that could be Michael Doyle's signpost. She pressed her back against the front of him. If only she could just stay here with him forever.

He stirred, his fingers came around her face, and she twisted over like a snake. His broad-boned face was lax with happiness.

"You okay?" she said.

"More than. You?"

"Yes." She smiled. So intimate a while ago, and now so polite.

"Did you?" he asked. She knew he was talking about coming. She could answer yes. She had learned that a lot of men couldn't tell.

"Because I didn't see it," he said.

She pressed to him, her cheek against the reassuring terrain of his chest. It wasn't easy for her, but it was a hard thing to talk about, especially with someone like him, whom she might never see again. Still, he had his arms in such a safe net around her. "It's okay," she said. "Don't worry about it."

"Don't tell me not to worry about it."

"I just don't always."

He pulled her up until her lips were on his, and kissed her with the confident promise of a man who has already been inside. Then he moved to her ear and said, "What makes it easier?"

She touched her hearing aids. "Taking these out."

"And what happens then?"

Instead of answering, she moved against him.

"Really." He was fascinated by her. "That's what you like?" He parted her legs. "Take them out, then."

"If I do I can't hear you. We can't talk."

"Take them out."

Lia lifted them out and put them aside, felt the inflating bliss of belonging. She let herself fall open, looking at him up over her on one elbow, his chest and shoulders, straight falling hair, the rhythm of his arm, the calm acceptance in his eyes. He bent to kiss her ears, in the tender part where her little amplifiers sat. Here, he seemed to say with his mouth, what else can I love about you?

18

AT THE BORDER, BAI WAITED IN THE NUMBER-
twelve inspection bay. He was dying inside. He
would not show it.

Three men walked over out of the gatehouse. *"Xia che,"* one of them barked, Get out.
Bai complied. He snapped open the big shiny
door, lighted on the ground, and held out his
paperwork.

The head man took it, read through it. He
was studying every word. Time fell away from
them, grinding seconds that felt like hours to Bai.

"Destination?" the man said at length, even
though there was only one possible destination
from this checkpoint.

"Hong Kong."

"Cargo?"

"Chickens."

The man folded the paperwork and secreted it in a pocket instead of giving it back to Bai.

Oh, that is *not* good, Bai thought in misery. That is very not good. You should not be keeping my paperwork.

The man turned to the other two. *"Kan kan yixia,"* he instructed sharply, Take a look. He turned to Bai. "You, rest over there a moment."

Bai felt his whole body tingling with fear as he stepped back. Rest, right. But he obeyed and went to stand under the lit-up roof of the guardhouse.

From here he watched the men gather behind the truck. If they found it, would they kill him? He calculated how much money he had stitched into the hem of his shirt. Not enough, maybe, for all of them. Better if he could get the head man alone.

And then if that didn't work . . .

Anguish choked up in him as he watched the men yank open the truck's great rear doors. Dry clouds of smoke billowed from the freezer.

Here was Bai's genius, come to life: two thousand pounds of cleaned, raw, frozen chickens, skins nubbly and rock-hard. He could see the men standing around looking at them, halfheartedly moving a few icy birds to one side or the other. The chicken feet were death talons, extended in clawlike despair, thousands of them. Their heads and sightless eyes were all frozen in mid-scream. Who would want to touch them? The men were talking back and forth. He could hear the elastic pinging of their Cantonese.

Things had changed so much. Just ten years before, most goods were still being moved by sea. China's porous coastline, and the near-infinite range of beaching possibilities in Hong Kong's archipelago, had long made this the main modus of discreet shippers. But then there were the pirates to be dealt with. They were a nest of poison vipers on the sea. They murdered any who crossed them. And one had to pay them outrageously, no matter what.

Modernization had altered the smuggling patterns. Now there were busy roads, and convoys of trucks bearing all manner of goods roaring back and forth, and a big, efficient machine for processing goods and people across this densely populated, heavily traversed border. Bai stood smoking, using his cigarette to control the tremblings in his hand—good, good, now they were arguing with each other. They seemed to be only moving the top layer of chickens around. They had no gloves. It was a job that became uncomfortable quickly, as he knew. As he had calculated.

He drew on his cigarette. Now the voices of the two men had turned sharp. They were arguing. The third man walked back over. For a while he had just been listening. Bai was able to follow Cantonese only sketchily, but it sounded as if the odds were in his favor. He smiled, a small smile but a real smile that came up from inside him. His biggest test, his greatest portal. This took the ultimate in face and wits. To say nothing of power of mind.

The third man opened the packet of papers he'd been holding and read through them again, scanning, checking. Bai held his cigarette tight. In time the third man finished reading and spoke peremptorily. He had a higher rank. Bai strained to follow them.

Finally the man turned. He handed Bai the papers. "You can go," he said in Mandarin. The men were locking the rear freezer doors.

"Good." Bai accepted the papers and folded them into his pocket, as if the matter were casual, insignificant. Silently, he was screaming in jubilation and gratitude. He would make so many offerings and spend many hours on his knees when he got back home.

He waited a few minutes in the entrance lane and then finally pulled onto the expressway, winding down through the new territories. It was suddenly greener, more rural, its grass-and-shrub–covered crags dotted with electric towers. His numb happiness was giving way to excitement. The pointed, emerald hills, the blue sea and dome of sky, all of it fairly pulsated with money. His now, success.

He sailed through a tunnel, a dark hurtling cocoon around his white truck, and then exploded out again into the light. The brilliant light of day. The road unrolled before him. He flew over a massive white suspension bridge with the sea far below. Container ships streamed silent on the blue horizon. Bai felt a part of life at last, here, in Hong Kong. He was at the center of the world.

LIA LAY COMPLETELY at rest. He slept next to her. She felt she was floating outside time and memory, no different than the light on the tile roofs, the lacy pattern of the leaves. She wanted to remember this feeling.

Because soon she would have to get up and go to the airport.

He stirred, opened his eyes, lit up at the sight of her. His hands came down and scooped her up from below, squeezed her. "I feel so good," she said, and wrapped her body around his, hard and tight. He curved around her in return, and they lay, and slept, and woke and talked again.

Finally they got up and climbed in the shower. They were quiet. They washed each other, then stood together under the hot jets of water. Her hair was loose, streaming down. She wanted to stand there forever.

But finally she stepped back from him and moved him under the water until his back was comfortable against the shower wall. She took him in her right hand. He protested, but she touched the middle finger of her other hand to his lips. "Just my hand," she said, taking the soap. "Let me watch you."

She held his gaze the whole time. With a flash of shame she saw herself claiming him, just to show him she could, just to take him—there, she thought, watching his eyes lose their focus under the hot water, that's it. But when he overflowed, her excitement was hot-crossed with the raw wound of her leaving, so that when he doubled over against her she burst into tears—hot, indecently vulnerable tears. And it was he, still gasping, who had to hold her and comfort her as she cried. "It's all right." He wrapped himself around her.

"I don't want to go."

"I know."

She leaned against him, she let herself go, all her weight, and he stood still as a tree and held her until she'd quieted. Then he turned her under the water and rinsed her face of tears.

They went out and dressed and she put her suitcase by the door. The sun was setting. "Lia?" he said. He walked over to her and touched her ears, to see if her hearing aids were in, to see if she'd heard him. They weren't. She hadn't.

He knows me already, she thought. She caught his hand and kissed it and pointed to the little plastic buttons, which still lay on the table. He brought them and pressed them in. "Is that right?"

"Not quite." She twisted them into place. "But thank you."

He smoothed back her damp-braided hair. She smiled at him, but there was something resolute in her now. She was leaving.

They found a cab on Jiaodaokou. "We're early now," Michael said. "We have time. Let's stop at the place on Houhai Lake. You'll see, your pots are gone. You'll feel better." His fingers were twined through hers.

"Thanks," she said softly, and gave directions to the driver.

When they pulled into the outer court, the sight of them brought the guard to his feet, crackling down the pages of his newspaper.

"We just want to go in for a minute," she called to him.

He looked at her, still blinking surprise.

She knew she wasn't supposed to be here anymore. "I just want to look," she said.

He waved them past and went back to his paper.

The two of them ran across the footbridge into the house, through the rooms, and across the back court. Up the steps on the other side, she clicked open the glass-paned doors and flipped on the lights.

The room looked so vast in its emptiness, nothing but scraps, bits of brown paper, wood shavings, and the dust outlines of the crates. This she would also remember. A person could have so much in front of her one moment, and nothing the next.

"Are you ready?" he said.

"Ready." She gave him her hand.

IN HIS APARTMENT over the racecourse in Happy Valley, Stanley Pao took the call on his cell phone. He was sitting in his back room, the door closed against the humid air and his adored Pekingese dogs. In here the air-conditioning was precisely calibrated. Grouped around him, on the floor, covering the shelves and every available surface, were priceless porcelains and reproductions of priceless porcelains—indistinguishable from each other. "*Wei,*" he said calmly, one hand resting on his protuberant midsection.

"Mr. Pao," the voice said. Stanley made an instantaneous shift to full attention. This was not a voice he knew. "A shipment consigned to you has arrived."

"Ah, is that so? And the address?" He reached for a pen and

paper, wrote it down. "I'll be there—" He stopped, looked at his computer monitor on the side table; the racing finals were scrolling down. All today's bets had summed up adequately. "I'll be there in half an hour," he said. "Accepted?"

"Accepted," the man answered.

Pao hung up. He dialed a number he had been given. "*Wei,*" he heard. It was Gao Yideng. This was the tycoon's direct line.

"*Wei,*" Pao answered politely. "Your stray dog has come home."

"Ah, good," he heard the man say softly, and they both hung up.

IN THE BACK of the taxi, they leaned against each other. She felt she had exhausted every possible human feeling with him. All she could do was rest on his shoulder. She would remember it just like this, she thought, the quiet at the end of it. The silence before saying good-bye.

They crossed the north end of Beijing and turned onto the Jichang Expressway, which soared through the high-rise forest to the airport. It wasn't until they were almost to the terminal, right outside the departure gate, that she pulled back and looked at him. His eyes were soft. She had never seen him look so defenseless.

"Okay," she said. She gathered up her bags. He moved to get out but she stopped him. She leaned over everything, her satchel, her suitcase, and her computer, and kissed him one more time, final. "Stay here," she said. "Keep the cab."

He nodded. They both knew it was better. She got out, shouldered her stuff, turned around, and walked in. He watched her. He waited until she was all the way in, then asked the driver to go back to town. They wheeled onto Jichang. Twilight had faded. The expressway unrolled out in front of them. He felt empty and dense, a dark star, as if he could sink right through the seat. His right hand moved to the empty leather where she had been a few minutes ago. After a while he put his head back and closed his eyes. It was hard to believe that a couple of weeks ago he had not even met her.

IN THE AIRPORT, she went straight to the women's rest room. She squeezed into a toilet stall with all her things and threw the latch. Then she leaned her forehead against the painted metal divider and cried as long and as hard as she had ever cried in her life.

When she came out she winced at how awful she looked: Her eyes were puffy, her nose red, her hair undone. Errant strands flew past her waist. She covered her eyes with her big German sunglasses and left everything else. It was all she could do to walk out of there.

She made it first to the Immigration line. But she didn't want to leave the country, that was the problem. She wanted a parallel world in which she would not get on the plane but would turn around and go directly back to his room, and knock, and tell him that she wasn't willing to leave. She wouldn't go. And if he did not care for her he would have to tell her so right to her face. This started tears again. Her turn came and she pushed her sunglasses tight against her nose and walked up to the booth.

The Immigration agent took her passport, entered a few strokes, and then stared at the computer. He hit another key. "Step to the side, please," he said calmly.

What *is* this, she thought, but she did it.

Instantly a uniformed woman was there. "Miss Frank?" she said in good English. "This way please."

Lia, almost a head taller, followed the woman off the concourse and into a small side office. She felt half out of her body. In the office, behind the desk, sat a flat-headed man with a short neck but quick, penetrating eyes. She was seated across from him.

"I'm Curator Li of the First Beijing Antiquities Museum." He slid a card across the wood tabletop toward her. He also looked hard at her. No wonder, she thought, with her face swollen and her hair bedraggled. "Your name came up in the computer. You entered the country to look at art. Correct?"

"Relatively," she said. "Relatively correct."

He looked at her. "You are a high-level porcelain expert."

"Not really—"

"What have you been doing in China?"

"Looking at art." She knew to stick to the script.

"Where?"

Where? she thought. Where? "In museums."

He let his eyes rest speculatively on her, then dropped them to some papers in front of him. "I see you are booked on a flight departing in an hour. I would hate for you to miss it."

"Me too." Inside, time and the world stopped while she screened rapidly for her best card. Gao, of course. She needed a private minute to use her phone.

She pulled her sunglasses off and laid them on the table. Tears still oozed from her eyes.

He started. "Miss Frank, are you all right?"

"No. I received bad news today."

"Oh." He looked uncomfortable. She was really crying now. She didn't say anything, so finally he spoke again. "What sort of news?"

"A family member passed on," she managed.

"Oh." There followed a long, disconcerting silence. He pulled out a handkerchief, which she refused. "Who?" he said.

"My father," she improvised. In fact her father was still alive, as far as she knew.

"Oh," he said. "I'm so sorry."

"Thank you." She crumpled again. "Mr. Li," she said, "may I go wash my face?"

He hesitated only a second. "Of course," he said. He looked over his shoulder. "It's in the hall."

She stepped quickly into the hallway and into the bathroom. She pounded out Gao's private number. *Be there.*

"*Wei,*" he answered.

Yes. "Mr. Gao, it's Lia Frank. I need help."

"Where are you?"

"At the airport. I've been detained by a man named Li, a curator with the First Beijing Antiquities Museum. He knows about me. He wants to know what pots I've been looking at in China. They won't let me through Immigration. I'm—"

"Please say no more," Gao said, concealing his anger almost perfectly. "Do not worry. It will be taken care of at once. Accept my thousand pleas and pardon this gross inconvenience."

"*Mei shi,*" she rebuked his politeness, It's nothing.

"No," he said, rebuking her back, "it's terrible. Just await me for a minute or two."

"Thank you," she said, and they hung up. She thought he was joking, a minute or two, but it had not been very much longer than that when she stepped back into the room and Li asked her if she felt better. She said yes, and then his phone was ringing.

"*Wei,*" he answered shortly, but his annoyance turned quickly to awe. "Vice Minister Pan," he said wonderingly. He had never spoken to anyone of so high a rank. "Who? Oh yes, Vice Minister, I have her here now. I'm asking her some—what's that? Oh yes. Yes, sir. At once, sir." He clicked off his phone.

"You had better go," he said to Lia Frank, just a trace of irritation and lost face breaking through his control. "Your flight will be boarding."

"Thank you." She stood and gathered up her things before he had a chance to change his mind.

"It's too sad about your father."

"Yes, it is. Thank you."

She backed out of the room and ran down the long corridor toward the gates. She felt almost numb. Her phone rang. *"Wei,"* she answered it.

"Miss Fan," said Gao. "Everything's resolved?"

"Yes. A thousand thanks."

"Please! You must not thank me. Again I apologize for the inconvenience."

"That's nothing." She could feel herself smiling.

"No. And again my compliments on your work. It has not been easy. Pure gold proves its worth in a fire, you know."

"That's kind of you," she said, surprised.

"Level road," he said.

"The same." She turned it off and looked up; yes, they were about to board. Now she was really leaving, it was over. Still, everything about her felt different, her skin, her eyes, her cells. She felt tall and beautiful, miserable with love. She pushed the sunglasses up over her red-rimmed eyes. There was the gate to Hong Kong, before her. People were getting on.

19

In Hong Kong that evening, in a warehouse, Bai waited by the forty crates. He had sold the frozen chickens and stored the truck elsewhere. Naturally he didn't want Stanley Pao to see his truck.

He heard the knock and crossed the concrete floor to open the door. There stood the plump, perfectly dressed art dealer, just as he had been described, full white hair, slicked straight back. "Mr. Bai?" the old gentleman said.

"Yes, Mr. Pao. Please." He gestured, and Stanley Pao walked past him, a magnet to iron, straight to the rows of wooden crates.

"May I open one?" His voice was casual over his well-tailored shoulder.

"Of course," Bai answered. He held out the manifest.

But Stanley signaled for him to wait. He didn't want to see it yet. He wanted to gamble on one.

He let his eyes roam. Eventually he settled on a particular crate at the edge of his field of vision. He walked toward it and pulled it open.

Inside, a tight nest of wood shavings. Good packing. The old-fashioned kind. He closed his eyes, arms extended, and then followed his will down into the crate, burrowing with both hands. A box called out to him, settled into his fingers. He pulled it out.

He put it gently on the floor and tipped up its lid. Oh. The light showed in his face, reflected. So *hoi moon*. He lifted it gently out of its silk, just a few inches, never taking it far from safety, just to tip it and turn it, a large *doucai* jardiniere, incandescently painted in emerald, royal blue, and rusty tangerine. Mark and period of Qianlong.

He replaced it securely in its box and reburied it in the wood shavings. He appreciated the chance to have his face turned away for a few seconds—to regain the diffident control of his age and his position. How long since he'd seen something so beautiful? "I'll see that list now," he said, turning to Bai.

He took it and scanned it, flipping the pages. He could feel a smile growing on his face. What a firmament. "The bank is Victoria Shanghai," he said to Bai. He continued reading. Then he removed a card from an inner pocket. "These are your account numbers," he said, handing it to Bai. He never looked up from the page. He half listened as Bai called the bank to verify. He saw the excitement that Bai was quite unable to control upon hearing his own balance.

"All is well?" he inquired when Bai had closed his phone.

"Excellent."

"Thank you for your service."

"To you the same." As soon as the ah chan had politely backed out the door, he stopped to dial up Pok Wen, the manager of the Luk Yu. "Friend Bai!" Pok Wen roared with the crafted gaiety that was his job. "How are you? Does fortune favor you today?"

Bai smiled in the dark linoleum hallway—there it was, the door to the outside. He pushed it open. The soft evening bath of Hong Kong wafted over him. It was the heaviest air in the world. It was pulled down, ripened, rotted just right by the power of cash. "Yes, Manager Pok, I am favored." He laughed. "Start soaking the abalone for me!"

JACK YUAN RECEIVED a call from his import agent as he stood in his lodge room at Crater Lake, Oregon, looking out through a wall of glass at the dark cascading outlines of mountains, the sky blazing with stars. He liked being up this early, in the dark. The edge of the lake was a sheer wall of granite, hurtling down past a silent mirror of black water.

It was the perfect sight to him. He came here to be alone, to drink coffee in the morning in big pine-pole chairs on the deck, to be where no one expected to find him. Sometimes Anna came with him, but this time she had not. And yet still the evening before he had seen someone he knew—a boisterous redheaded gentleman vintner from Santa Rosa, retired from early days in Silicon Valley and consumed with the pursuit of wine. He had been there with a wealthy gaggle of other grape-growers, and they all ate, and drank, and inside himself Jack was thinking: I could never spend my time thinking about wine. I could never pose at living in some country valley. I could never be white. I could never be them.

But he had his own piece of the universe coming, his porcelain. And finally he'd escaped back up here to the silence of his room and the magnificence of the deal he'd just completed, and he had slept.

His phone went off. He flipped it up and glanced at the caller-ID line. Only a few calls were routed to this cell number. This was one. "Yes?"

"Mr. Yuan. Ashok Navra."

"Yes, Ashok."

"Your shipment of Chinese porcelain is in Hong Kong. I've talked to the consignee there, a Stanley Pao. He says the pieces are being repacked for airfreight now." And Jack had felt a daze, talking to him, thanking him, signing off, looking out at the edges of dawn and the lake and the receding forms of glacier-scrubbed rock. The money was transferred. The art would be in his hands in a few days. Before he went downstairs he left a message for the curator he had hired to help him sort things out and make decisions, telling her to be ready to start in four days' time. He wanted to know exactly what he had. And then he wanted to keep this collection very, very private.

THE NEXT DAY Stanley Pao opened the door to Bai, the man who had brought in the shipment. He had been a bit surprised, an hour before, to get the man's phone call. But after speaking with him for a few minutes he had agreed to receive him. This *ah chan* seemed both careful and intelligent. Sometimes the ambitious ones made good allies. But sometimes they were the very ones a man should not trust.

"*Jinlai, jinlai,*" Come in, Stanley said in Mandarin, for Bai knew neither Cantonese nor English. To get ahead he'd have to learn. Stanley led him into his back room, climate-controlled, carpeted and shelved like an English den, crammed with pots of all shapes and sizes. He noted with satisfaction the widening of the man's eyes. "You said you had something tasty for me?"

"Yes," said Bai. He touched the box under his arm, his gaze

roving the room. So many pots, and horse races on the computer monitor. "I have this piece," he said, and extended the box.

Pao eased back the lid with his wrinkled, age-blotched hands. His first reaction was to gasp, for it was a chicken cup, a shockingly good one, and his first impression was all visceral—*It can't be! But it is.* Then he looked closer. Of course it wasn't. But it was almost identical to the chicken cup in today's cargo! Naturally, he'd gone directly to that one the minute he'd seen it on the manifest, as soon as Bai had walked out of the warehouse. He knew it was fake, for there was a small notation at the end of the document referring back to it—*Modern* fang gu, *included at buyer's request*—and yet it was so *hoi moon* he himself had been almost swayed by it. And he was never, never fooled.

This was also a fake, but so very good. He turned it in his hand, held it to the light. Even the color of the clay was correct, the warm off-white of the Chenghua reign, so rare to see it done right. Oh, it was fine. "It's a wonderful piece," he told Bai. "One of the best reproductions I've ever seen. How much do you want for it?"

Bai snapped his head around a little too fast.

Ah! Pao watched him, fascinated. He hadn't known. He'd thought it was real. Interesting. Now Pao saw it. The ah chan had switched one fake for another, thinking he was taking out a real, Ming Dynasty cup and not a *fang gu* at all. "Ask another dealer if you don't believe me. It's a copy. But fine. Very fine."

But the ah chan had believed him. It was as if he had known, underneath, that the cup was too good to be true, too much to expect after all the money he'd made. So he shrugged it off with a gambler's resignation. He accepted a thousand U.S. dollars for the reproduction, protesting that this wasn't his line of work but taking the money, folding it, and putting it in his pocket. "I hope we meet again," he told Pao. "Maybe we can work together."

"Of course, of course," Stanley answered unhurriedly. "Let us keep in touch." Stanley was always polite. But in fact he was too careful to ever do business with this ah chan again.

"So then he came back, and brought me the cup—your *fang gu* from the collection," Stanley Pao said to Lia Frank later that afternoon. She had arrived in Hong Kong the night before. Now they were in his back room, looking at pots, having taken an instant liking to each other. "He'd switched them. I realized it as soon as I saw the one he brought me here, for I had read your most excellent description in the inventory. I switched them back. This is his copy. Yours is in the collection." He peered at her eyes. "Am I right? This is his copy?"

"It is," she said, noting a softer, more translucent quality to the glaze in this cup. No less perfect—only different. This was the one she'd seen Bai purchase from Potter Yu.

So this meant Bai had transported her collection. It was strange, but not unheard of. Ah chans were experts at shipping, after all.

"It's gorgeous, isn't it?" She held it up to the light and felt a full smile form on her lips for the first time since she had left Michael behind in Beijing. *Don't think about that.* She couldn't control the future. *This* was happiness, this cup. "Stanley." Her eyes shone. "Will you sell it to me?"

"Not on your grandmother! How could I let go of this?"

"Oh." She looked down. "So I don't even get to say that I'd double whatever you paid? I understand, though. I do. I'd never let go of it either." And she smiled at him through her hair, which she had decided to leave down today. It felt strange. She had it tucked behind her ears but it kept slipping out.

"What do you say, Lia?" Stanley asked. He gave her a thoughtful look as if he'd been considering the subject for some time. "The repacking will take hours and hours. Shouldn't we go to Central and look at some pots?"

"Absolutely," she said.

Another pair of colleagues would have repaired to a restaurant to enjoy a leisurely meal, but Lia and Stanley went instead to Hollywood Road. They started at the top, where the road twisted most tortuously and where the most discriminating, most exclusive shops held court, and worked their way down to the bottom where the shadows were deeper and the deals more murky.

In most of the galleries the owner would lock up, if they were alone, and take them to some back chamber, through a side door or up some narrow set of stairs. In this world there was always the interior room, the private admittance, the exclusivity shared by friends. There were small sofas grouped around a low table specially designed for handling porcelain—felt-padded, with a low lip shielding its edge all the way around. There were hours of shared enjoyment over the perfections that man, in his finest moments, had made of clay. It was a balm to Lia's heart. It made whole stretches of minutes go by in which she felt the glory of pots, the shared pleasure of connoisseurship, and managed to forget that a part of her felt like it had been torn away.

THAT NIGHT HE called her, not knowing quite what to say to her but not able to go any longer without connecting. He went back to his room after work, where it was quiet, and dialed her cell.

"This is Lia," she said when she picked up.

"It's me."

"Hi." Her voice changed for him, opened, softened.

"How are you?" Already he felt back in her nexus.

"Okay. And you?"

"Not good. I don't like it here without you."

"I know," she said. "I feel the same here in Hong Kong. It'd be better if you were here."

He felt a wave of pleasure inside him when he heard this. "Then come back," he said, simple, quick, straight out.

"But I can't. I have to see the pots off."

"And then?"

"Then I have to go to New York. Immediately. They're all waiting for me. This was a big thing for us, this deal."

"I'm sorry to hear that," he said.

"I know. Me too."

He felt his longing start to skid. While she was in Hong Kong they were still close, or it seemed that way. They could talk and things could shift in a moment; she could turn around. Going back to New York would change things. Then they'd have to go to lengths. Then if they were going to see each other again they'd have to start climbing that long and arduous ladder of intention.

This was what he'd said he wouldn't, couldn't, shouldn't do. But he kept thinking about her. She was always in his mind. "I have to admit I was hoping it would be easy, it would just happen. You'd come back."

"I could," she said. "Not right away, but I could. Michael. What happened meant a lot to me. I would really like to get to know you. I mean that." She was enunciating. He could tell she was speaking from her center. "I really, really would."

"I was hoping that too," he said. "I'm sorry it took so long for things to happen."

"Never mind that now," she said.

He knew it was his turn. It was time for him to say, let's try it. Let's meet again and see. It was up to him.

But he couldn't walk out on the plank just like that. He had to have a little time to think. And so he hesitated. He held the silence.

On her end, she felt hope draining away from her as he said nothing. While she waited, she unlatched the sliding glass door and stepped out on her balcony. The damp, briny air made her feel clearer. "Think about what I told you," she said softly. "Let me know if you feel the same. If you want to see me again, you know, I'll figure something out. Call me. If that's what you want, call me." She was putting the ball firmly in his court. "I'm not leaving for a day and a half."

She closed her eyes. Had she done right, or wrong? She had opened her heart and shown her willingness. She couldn't do any more. She waited.

"You know all about me," he said.

She knew he meant his illness. "I know all about you."

"All right, Lia," he said, with such gentleness in his voice that she felt for a yearning instant everything was going to be okay, "I'll call you."

So he wanted time to think. There was nothing else she could say. She looked out over the harbor, crowded with its descending mass of white towers. Night was falling and the water glowed up from beneath, bathing the sampans and junks and massive cargo vessels in pure aquamarine light. "So, then," she said after a moment. "Even though I don't want to hang up, even though I want to talk to you all night and do a million other things to you, with you, I guess I should say good-bye."

"Okay," he agreed again. He didn't try to hold her. They hung up. The line was dead, a blank space ringing down a cold stone floor in an empty hall. She felt her stomach twist. Now she could only wait. She couldn't let this reduce her. She had work to finish. Some other time, when she had the space and peace, if necessary, she would cry. Not now.

LIA AND STANLEY saw the crates lifted into the underbelly of the jet and then drove back into Central, weak with satisfaction. "What shall we do?" he asked her.

Lia smiled at the white-haired man. She liked being with him. And it helped keep her mind off Michael. *Don't think, don't want. Expect nothing. Let go.* The car was twisting and veering down along the curving, banana-leafed, terraced two-lane road, down toward the heart of Hong Kong. But how could she let go? After what they had done, how could they just forget? In a minute the car came out in Central, just above the business district. "You know what I'd really like to do?" she said. "Let's go back to Hollywood Road."

Pao's face lifted in a gradual grin of agreement. He spoke in Cantonese to the driver, who turned the car around.

WHEN MICHAEL FINISHED that day, he stopped at the ward on three south. His friend Little Chen had recently been readmitted. Chen had come to Michael's attention some months before because his levels of lead were so high. He had a high-risk profile; his family lived on a corner of two of Beijing's busiest streets, and their apartment windows opened on to the intersection with all its exhaust fumes. Little Chen had already been ill from lead poisoning. But then he had also been diagnosed with leukemia. He'd been in for a while, very sick. He'd improved and been discharged. Now, after being home for many weeks, he was back. Michael had stopped and seen him that last day—the day he had met Lia after work. The day they became lovers. The day she left. And now he had to decide whether to risk everything again, or not.

He had hurt her by hesitating on the phone. He didn't want to hurt her—the opposite. He wanted to make a bed for her to lie on. He didn't think he would ever feel that again, but now he did.

He pivoted lightly through the door at three south, his footsteps soft on the tile, and strode past the small beds toward the end where his young friend would be waiting.

Suddenly disoriented, he stopped and rocked his weight from side to side. Here was the door to the bathroom, here the wall against which he'd stood the other day when he talked to the boy. He was sure of it. Yet now there was only a row of empty steel carts. He'd missed it. He turned back.

He walked more slowly and looked into the face of each little child. Little Chen was very distinctive, with a triangular face and a wide, thin mouth. Or was he on the wrong aisle? No, Michael was sure; this was right. This had been his bed. Maybe the staff had moved him.

A female worker polished the bed table. "Where's Little Chen?" he asked her.

She started and turned to look at him, then started again because he was an outsider.

"Little Chen," he said again, and pointed to the bed.

"Gone," she said.

Michael frowned and shot back a different word. "Discharged?" he asked.

Color went out of the woman's face. "No. Gone away."

Gone away. That meant dead, when they said it.

Tears came up out of him and spilled right over from his eyes before he even knew they were coming, before he could think about stopping them. He wrapped his hand around the spindly bed frame.

The woman looked at him with direct Chinese kindness. "It's too pitiable." She handed him a clean square of cloth.

He wiped his face. "Thank you," he said.

"Go home, sir." She patted his arm. "Go home to your wife."

He looked at her.

"Go home to your wife," she said again, as if it were obvious.

"All right," he said, as if he could simply do that, do what she said. He could walk out of here and go to her. Now the hurt he had caused Lia by hesitating, by not stepping over the line right away, tugged at him more than ever. It was almost a physical pain in the center of him. He never wanted to hurt her. *Good-bye,* he thought to Little Chen. And with an effort he walked back out of the ward.

He felt his cell phone in his pocket. He could dial her. Tell her. Make it right. He kept walking, right out of the hospital. But calling her didn't seem like enough, not now.

He should go to Hong Kong.

He took a taxi to the head of his hutong and walked in, under the soft-speaking lindens. There, over his worn limestone lintel, in his tiny room, he clicked on the Internet and looked at airlines. There was nothing available to Hong Kong tonight, not in confirmed seating. But he was adept at navigating margins. Two of tonight's flights had standby potential. He'd go out to the airport and try. He had to leave instantly. And he'd take his cell phone with him. If in the end he couldn't get on a plane, he'd call her.

It felt right to him to go now. It was the correct seed to plant.

Qian yin hou guo, he had heard his friend An say. It's on the basis of what comes before that what follows bears fruit.

AFTER A LONG day of studying bank reports, of weighing the life and viability of various loans, some made by him, some borrowed by him, all part of the frighteningly spit-supported structure that was Chinese banking, Gao Yideng went home to his private study. There he logged on to his personal computer, and through a series of proprietary portals brought up a string of accounts one by one. Even his most trusted advisers did not know everything he had. In the United States, on deposit, he now had one hundred twenty-six million dollars. For a moment, he could enjoy this triumph. He had ninety days to make certain delicate decisions about declarations and taxes. In the meantime he had taken at least one substantial asset and turned it into accessible cash, outside China.

He didn't feel any tugs of remorse over so much treasure leaving the country. In fact he believed it was better. Before he got it, this had been buried in the ground. Let the rest of the world see it. Let it end up preserved and be forever protected from chaos.

A soft knock sounded at his study door. His wife. "Everything's ready," she said, and he knew she meant his two sons, his daughter, their evening meal. They would never know the privations he and Peng had endured. He wondered where Peng was tonight. He was certain the other man was alive, on earth; he had faith that he would know if Peng had passed through the gate and gone away. "*Wo jiu lai-le,*" he told his wife.

And he stood up, turned off his computer, followed his wife down the long wainscoted Shanghainese hallway to the stairs, curving down, and around, to the hallway and the dining room and the eyes of his children waiting under the bright crystal-dripping chandelier. For them, he accumulated. For them he built a future. He met their faces with a smile.

AT THE AIRPORT, Michael was lucky enough to clear standby on a flight that would land in Hong Kong before midnight. That was okay. They'd have some hours together, at least. And they'd go from there.

He kept his cell phone on until they fastened their seat belts on the plane and the order came to turn them off. The crew strapped down, but the plane did not move. They waited, and then they waited some more.

Finally the pilot made a long announcement in Chinese, which was followed by a confusingly brief translation into English. "Because of the crash of China International Flight Sixty-eight, all the flights now are frozen for a new list of safety checks." Michael rearranged the scrambled words in his head. How many safety checks? How long would it take? *All* planes? He sank. The crew got up and moved around. The lights flickered up. The passengers sat belted in, and the jet did not move.

An hour ticked by, every minute digging at him. He tagged a stewardess. "Would I be able to use a cell phone?"

"No!" She looked at him sternly. "No cell phone now."

He had to laugh. Fate always displayed such incredible irony. Belted upright, head back, eyes closed, he laughed silently until his body shook and his seatmate inched away from him.

IN JINGDEZHEN, BAI walked along Jinhua Lu at the bottom of the park with its small, picturesque bridges and gazebos. He passed men hauling back empty carts, old women taking slow, duck-footed steps, clots of children giggling, racing home for the night.

Though it was getting dark, the day was early for him. He had just come from his bed. What was more, he had an obscene amount of money in his pocket.

He was holding himself differently. Was it not obvious? People were looking at him with respect. He was a new man now. He didn't feel like Old Bai anymore.

He covered the winding sidewalk along the bottom of the hill, marked by a stone wall. Up there, somewhere above all that lush foliage, was the Research Institute, where they dispensed with the history of porcelain in a series of desultory cases. Down here, the cars and trucks and buses honked through the street. Exhaust smoked up and joined the kiln grit, in the air for a thousand years. Bai swung his arms with his stride, happy to be walking.

And then he was at the Perfect Garden. He pushed open the double doors and walked into the dim-lit dining room, to his friends, at their usual table. Beer, tea, and food were piled up in front of them. They raised their hands to him. "Emperor Bai!" he heard, *Bai Huangdi*. "Emperor Bai!" And he shook his own hands back to them, and let his smile of triumph light his face like the sun.

THEY HAD SAT on the runway for almost two hours when the pilot finally crackled on and said, with no explanation, that safety checks were complete and that they were tenth in line for takeoff.

Michael sensed a light sweat break out all over him as he looked at his watch. He felt like he could melt in his seat. He could make it.

BY THE TIME Lia was down to the last few hours, her heart was burning. She hadn't heard from him. Apparently he didn't even think he ought to say good-bye. She wanted to kick a hole in the wall, throw something out the window. Instead, she folded all her clothes in tight little squares and stuffed them in her suitcase. She couldn't believe it. She had been so sure he'd call her. But why? Just because she felt something real with him and she wanted to go on with it, at least try, she couldn't expect him to want the same. So he didn't. He had a right to make that choice. That's what memory rooms were for. They had doors that could be closed. Still. She looked at her silent phone and felt everything well up again. It wouldn't have been so very hard to say good-bye with love.

Despite him, outside of him, the irony was . . . she was changed. She felt like a different person, not quite newly minted but restirred. The composition of her cells was altered. She could see it in the mirror. It had been more than two days since she'd been with him, and still she was luminous, perversely so, tragically. Now here was the dress in her hands, the sleeveless, box-necked dress in sage silk.

She dropped her clothes and zipped into it. Made for her, it hugged her all the way down. Oh, she was beautiful in it, with her hair only caught back, and if she wore high-heeled sandals—she looked at herself over her shoulder. She could see the truth and the anguish, the shimmering cloth against her body. Trying to be beautiful was just another form of forgery. The feeling of her and him was a forgery. Admit it. He didn't want it. So I do need my tired old world, she thought, my maze, my rooms; I do. I'll put him there. She took the dress off and told herself, let go of hope. Let it go now. But she felt the same, pulled by wanting. Delirious with it. It overwhelmed even her anger. She folded the dress on top of everything else and closed the suitcase.

Then there was a knock on the door, polite, soft, insistent. First shock wiped every thought from her mind, then a smile formed inside her, deep down. That's why he didn't call, because he came. Hope was a river, bringing back optimism and acceptance and forgiveness. Thought could not begin to contain her. She yanked the dress out again, hurried back into it. The knock sounded again. "Just a minute!"

She pulled the silk down over her hips and opened the door.

Facing her was the concierge. "Miss Frank?"

She thought she might sink all the way to the ocean floor. "Yes," she said.

"A package." He handed her a small box. "From Mr. Stanley Pao."

"Thank you," she said. He was gone.

She went inside and opened it. When she lifted the lid her mouth went soft in surprise. It was Stanley's copy of the chicken cup, the one she had watched Bai buy from Potter Yu. Ah, what genius. She held it up. It gave off a world of grace all its own. *For you,* read the card, *with my regards.* So sweet, she thought, her heart running out to Stanley. So kind. As if somehow the elder man knew.

Because it wasn't him at her door, the American man she couldn't stop thinking about. It was this perfect little object. It was easy, profound, *hoi moon,* just like what she'd had with Michael. Had. Past tense. Let it go, she thought. She balanced the cup on the desk and curled up on the couch looking at it, eye level. It was immortal, whether six hundred years or six days old, the same. A thing perfect and still.

Unlike her. She stood up and pressed her face to the window. The harbor below was a late-night dream of lights, the water glassy and reflective. She had a vision of herself floating down there, alone, safe, spread-eagled on a raft in calm water. Surrounded by lights. It was peaceful and water-silent. She remembered all the good of being alone, the opportunity. She thought of all her fakes back in New York.

And here was the greatest of them all. She picked up her little consolation prize, the cup, her treasure, and packed it safe away in its box. There was kindness in the world after all.

It wasn't so many hours now until her flight. She clicked the room into darkness and crawled into bed, spreading her loose hair over the pillow behind her. She had given the thought of him all of herself that she could—though she left one hearing aid in, just in case the phone still rang. Now she had to try and sleep.

STANLEY PREPARED THE documents. He would send them to San Francisco the next morning, via personal courier. He had a man he could trust. Not an ah chan; an employee. He paged through the documents one last time before putting them in the package. For some reason he stopped to look at the special visa issued by China. He had seen a few of these before. Usually it meant the government was selling off something it owned. Often, as in this case, there was an intermediary.

Yet just as there were famed and noted *fang gu* artists in the world of pots, each of whom turned out his own distinctive style of reproduction, so there were known masters in the world of forged documents. One did not know their names, of course. They were known by the names of their quirks—the same way he had heard Miss Frank call the maker of that marvelous chicken cup the Master of the Ruffled Feather. Just as these document copiers became known by their peculiarities of lettering, shading, and border.

Stanley leaned closer. He knew this artist. He was one of the document masters people talked about. He worked with a flawed inlay machine, and his documents always had a pale patch in the lower left corner.

Stanley looked at the visa. There it was. The pale patch.

A fake.

So this sale wasn't for the government at all. It was inauthentic, a private sale with fake paperwork.

Yet this visa in front of him had only been needed to cross from China to Hong Kong. Stanley smiled to himself. This visa was never presented at that border. It would have been spotted. That meant the pots were not brought through openly. They were smuggled. By the ah chan Bai. And so very many of them. Stanley's esteem for the man, despite everything, increased.

And now the collection was in Hong Kong, legal, unimpeachable. Of course, Stanley thought, with the present tensions between the U.S. and China, if someone on the American side noticed this fake visa, in Customs, say, there might be a problem. More for diplomacy than for legality. Because if the Chinese government found out about this, they would most assuredly strike multiple postures demanding it back. It was just too big, too priceless; and matters between the countries too uneasy.

Well. Stanley Pao slid the visa back into the stack of pages.

He certainly would not be the one to mention it.

HE SLIPPED INTO the lobby of the hotel after two A.M. He felt his chest singing with excitement. He rode the elevator to the fourteenth floor and walked in quick silence down the brilliantly patterned carpet. It was late. Everything was hushed.

He came to her door and knocked. The sound seemed to echo all the way down the wallpapered corridor. He waited. Nothing.

He knocked again.

Inside, Lia sat up in bed. Her hair was down. She got up in the twisted confusion of dreaming. She found the door by its little pinpoint of light that gave out onto the hall. She looked.

Michael. Really? Was it really? His shoulders under his loose white shirt, the sleeves rolled up . . . now she knew she was dreaming. This was false. But his broad face leaned toward her through the peephole, his hand came up and knocked again.

She opened the door. She stood behind it, pale, half lit by the shafting light from the hallway. Three steps and he was in the room, turning, looking for her. *Who knows about me,* she thought. The door clicked shut and they found their way to each other in the dark.

CHINESE DYNASTIES AND REIGN TITLES

Qin Dynasty (221–206 BC)
Han Dynasty (206 BC–AD 220)
Wei, Jin, and Northern and Southern Dynasties (220–581)
Sui Dynasty (581–618)
Tang Dynasty (618–907)
Five Dynasties and Ten Kingdoms (907–960)
Song Dynasty (960–1279)
Yuan Dynasty (1279–1368)

Ming Dynasty (1368–1644)

Hongwu (1368–1398)
Jianwen (1399–1402)
Yongle (1403–1424)
Hongxi (1425)
Xuande (1426–1435)
Zhengtong (1436–1449)
Jingtai (1450–1456)
Tianshun (1457–1464)
Chenghua (1465–1487)
Hongzhi (1488–1505)
Zhengde (1506–1521)
Jianjing (1522–1566)
Longqing (1567–1572)
Wanli (1573–1619)
Taichang (1620)
Tianqi (1621–1627)
Chongzhen (1628–1644)

Qing Dynasty (1644–1911)

Shunzhi (1644–1661)
Kangxi (1662–1722)
Yongzheng (1723–1735)
Qianlong (1736–1795)
Jiaqing (1796–1820)
Daoguang (1821–1850)
Xianfeng (1851–1861)
Tongzhi (1862–1874)
Guangxu (1875–1908)
Xuantong (1909–1911)

ACKNOWLEDGMENTS

Thanks to my editor, Jackie Cantor, a sage and caring guide who somehow, at every turn, made me choose the way myself. Thanks to my agent, Bonnie Nadell, for intelligence, grace and good humor at the helm.

Mee-Seen Loong took me by the hand and led me into her world of porcelain. Her knowledge and love of pots, her adeptness in the intersecting subcultures surrounding them, and her endlessly interesting ideas about them educated and inspired me. My research also owes much to published scholarship, especially the work of Julian Thompson, Regina Krahl, Liu Xinyuan, and Wen C. Fong.

To those in Hong Kong and Jingdezhen who talked to me about ah chans, thank you for your candor and for cracking the door to this underworld, just enough.

I am grateful to the Morgan Library for allowing me to examine the 1913 correspondence between J. P. Morgan's office in New York and F. H. McKnight in Peking, and to James Traub for first writing about this historical episode and then generously answering my questions.

Dr. Joan Rothlein and Dr. Herb Needleman were of great help in researching lead poisoning. In matters related to pediatric hearing loss I am indebted to Beth Cardwell, M.D., and the Audiology department at Oregon Health Sciences University.

For insight, ideas, and information, my gratitude to Fred Hill, Sabrina Ullman Mathews, Richard Herzfelder, Jason Tse, Nicolas Chow, Jon Conte, Marta Aragones, Lucy Metcalf, Jin Mei, Rone Tempest and Laura Richardson, Anthony Kuhn, Kemin Zhang, Chris Perkins, Nancy Beers, and Huang Zhifeng.

A debt of inspiration is due to *The Memory Palace of Matteo Ricci* by Jonathan Spence, "Funes, the Memorious" by Jorge Luis Borges, *The Recognitions* by William Gaddis, and especially *The Art of Memory* by Frances Yates.

Ben and Luke, I could never have written this book without your generosity in releasing me to the task. For everything else, my first and last thanks are for Paul Mones.

ABOUT THE AUTHOR

NICOLE MONES was awarded the Janet Heidinger Kafka Prize for her first novel, *Lost in Translation*, which was also named a *New York Times* Notable Book. She lives with her family in Portland, Oregon.